LOVE AND DEATH
ON SAFARI

Other Books by R. H. Peake

From Papaw to Print: A History of Appalachian Literature
Maplelodge Publication, 1990

Wings Across
Vision Books, 1992

Poems for Terence
Vision Books, 1992

Birds of the Virginia Cumberlands
Maplelodge Publications, 2001

Jack, Be Nimble
iUniverse, 2003

Moon's Black Gold
iUniverse, 2008

Birds and Other Beasts
iUniverse, 2007

Earth and Stars: Poems 2007–2012
Maplelodge Publications, 2012

LOVE AND DEATH
ON SAFARI

R. H. Peake

LOVE AND DEATH ON SAFARI

iUniverse books may be ordered through booksellers or by contacting:

iUniverse
1663 Liberty Drive
Bloomington, IN 47403
www.iuniverse.com
1-800-Authors (1-800-288-4677)

ISBN: 978-1-5320-2446-7 (sc)
ISBN: 978-1-5320-2445-0 (e)

Library of Congress Control Number: 2017912432

Print information available on the last page.

iUniverse rev. date: 08/18/2017

CHAPTER 1

Early morning, as the sun was just rising over the trees, I woke and peered through the light filtering into my tent. I was still tired from my exertions the night before and the early-morning activity in my tent.

It was relatively cool. Listening to the sounds of doves and other forest birds and of Sandy making breakfast, I slipped into my field clothes and crawled out to stretch. I smelled the faint musk of the forest in the air combined with the odor of frying bacon. Surveying the greenery around me, I watched a black-casqued wattled hornbill flying over the campsite. It cheered me up, reminding me of the grotesque yellow-billed hornbills with their red facial skin so common in Kenya, where our tour began. Even though hornbills are relatively common, I never tire of seeing their big bills and huge casques atop their heads—looking like escapees from a horror movie.

After a trip to the latrine, I walked over to Sandy, our cook, took up a cup and tea bag, and offered them to her for hot water. Grunting, she filled my cup. Putting some sweetener in the water, I pulled out a field stool and sat down to savor the tea while enjoying the aroma of a breakfast of eggs and bacon Sandy was preparing. Only then did I notice that no other hungry people were having their morning drinks.

"Where is everybody, Sandy?"

The chef pointed. At a break in the brush on the edge of the cliff, a group had gathered. They were crowded around the edge gawking at something on the ground below. I wondered what attraction could have drawn them from breakfast. Had they spotted a hawk or large cat exciting enough to preempt taking care of their bellies?

"What are they looking at?" I asked, a bit surprised that many of them did not even have their binoculars raised to their eyes.

"Don't know; somebody yelled, and they ran out there. Been too busy cooking to wonder."

I was trying to decide whether to forego immediate breakfast when one of the group disengaged and headed toward camp. He seemed to be in a hurry. It was Cameron MacDonald. I got up and started toward him.

"You aren't going to believe this. Come see for yourself," Cameron blurted out without a good morning. "I wanted to tell you—Jimmy Russo is sprawled out on the ground below the cliff. I've got to get back. I'm the only medical person around."

Gulping the rest of my tea, I followed Cameron. At the cliff, I saw a body, motionless, lying facedown.

"We think it's Jimmy," Cameron said. "It doesn't look good."

"That does look like Jimmy! He had on that outfit yesterday. Remember, Jack?" Iris Fogelman looked at me quizzically and took my hand in hers.

I squeezed. "I think so."

"I'm sure," said Gabe Goforth. "Shucks, he's wearing the same khaki shirt and pants he had on at supper."

"Did he get drunk and wander off the cliff?" I asked.

"I don't remember Jimmy drinking more than a couple of beers," Iris said.

"He's a son of a bitch, but he's not a drunk. I don't think he had much to drink. He holds liquor pretty well," Gabe Goforth said. He pointed at the body below. "Think he's dead?"

"Probably. Who found him?" Cameron asked.

"I did. I was looking for a bat hawk," Gabe said. "Jimmy saw one last evening. Shucks, he bragged about getting another life bird ahead of me."

Cameron sent Gabe to bring Sean and Terence, our leaders out scouting before breakfast. "I won't do anything without our leaders' permission," Cameron said.

When the leaders arrived and saw the body, they expressed their dismay without showing grief for anything other than inconvenient bad luck. Jimmy was not their favorite client. They probably were trying to appear calm despite cursing softly.

Terence Stavens raised his hand. "Quiet, please. Possibly he's alive. He's a troublemaker. Damn the luck."

Sean Selkirk agreed. "Right, Jimmy's a bloke who causes problems."

Stavens shook his head. "Fantastic Flights doesn't need more accidents. Let's get down there and check. Cameron, we'll rely on your medical expertise. Go first."

Accepting his assignment, Cameron led the way down along a narrow path.

Iris and I fell in just behind Cameron. "Do you think he's badly hurt?" I asked.

"From the looks of it, "Cameron said, "I'd say so. Dead, most likely."

Sean and Terence held a quiet, almost whispered conversation as the group descended. I understood why—Fantastic Flights' run of bad luck despite their being extra careful.

I remembered hearing about Phoebe Snetsinger's death by decapitation in Madagascar. Their bus driver fell asleep. The leader grabbed the wheel and kept the bus from going off the cliff. Everybody except Phoebe got off with minor cuts and bruises, but she was asleep on the backseat and smashed through a window. The broken glass severed her neck.

Added to that mishap the near death of the Belgian in Ecuador—a brooding female bushmaster leapt from her nest and stretched halfway across the path to strike his thigh. The coleader had to raft the victim down to a station where he could radio for a plane to take the client to a hospital. They saved his life by cutting off his leg well above the knee.

The mysterious disappearance of the notorious Wandering Willy in Gabon had defied explanation. All they ever found was his hat. Now, a possible death—no wonder our leaders were concerned.

When the group reached Jimmy, Cameron began inspecting a bloody wound on Russo's head, and then he turned the body over, feeling arms and legs for broken bones. After Cameron had worked for about fifteen minutes, he shook his head sadly. "He's dead—no doubt about that."

"Are you sure?" Cameron looked up. He seemed surprised at Iris's being the questioner.

"Yes. There's no doubt at all about that." A murmur went through the hushed group, but few, if any, seemed grief stricken.

"He was a bastard, but I'm going to miss him," Gabe said.

Cameron continued to examine the body, paying particular attention to the head wound and hands while the rest of the group looked on. Only Iris and Gabe seemed genuinely concerned about it. I guess the rest of us were busy worrying about what his death would mean for the tour. I couldn't summon up grief for Jimmy. After all, he had been trying to egg me into a fight for weeks. His jealousy had been growing.

Finishing his examination, Cameron said, "He has broken bones from the fall, but I think he was already dead or dying when he fell or was pushed. Somebody hit him hard on his head with a blunt object before he fell. His skull is gashed. Blunt force trauma—there aren't any rocks where he fell that could have caused this. I'm afraid we're looking at a murder victim. It could have happened very late last night or early this morning. I see no evidence of any animal damage."

Another murmur went through the group. Sean and Terence cursed quietly. They walked aside from the group, probably to avoid being overheard.

"I reckon this will put a crimp in our trip," Gabe Goforth said. He seemed depressed.

"You won't have to worry so much about competition now, Gabe," I said. "You can beat Phoebe Snetsinger's record without Jimmy's badgering you."

"Shucks, that's a really depressing thought," Gabe Goforth said as he stared at his binoculars.

Evidently having made a decision, Terence and Sean came back to the group.

"Cameron," Terence said, "we'll have to notify the local police. Obviously we are all suspects in Jimmy's murder. The police will question us. I'm afraid we'll be doing our birding here in this area longer than we had planned. Somebody needs to tell Jane Russo."

I was surprised when Iris offered that service, but I went with her. I worried about what Jane might say about her recent activity. I considered the situation glumly. We were all suspects, but some of us were more likely candidates than others. But one of us must be a murderer—maybe even planned the murder. Not a pleasant thought.

Terence interrupted. "The group might as well have breakfast while I go to the village to inform the police. You can bird with Sean around the camp until I get back. Be on the lookout for any small birds skulking in the bushes. If you get lucky, you might see a bat hawk before the sun gets really high. Cameron, I'd appreciate your taking care of the body until I return. We don't want any animals having a go at it."

Cameron nodded. "I'll watch Jimmy."

Then Terence started up the trail to camp.

Cameron watched as Iris and I headed back to camp ahead of the rest of the group to look for Jane Russo. I found Iris's lilac scent and the touch of her hand a soothing antidote to the morning's stress. What would happen next?

I thought back to the beginning of our trip.

CHAPTER 2

My quiet life shattered when my wife sued me for divorce. I had given her the ammunition to break apart our lives, but I pleaded for a little understanding—with no success. Susan Burnbridge was determined to end our marriage.

Not that she disliked me. She thought I was handsome. I reminded her of Paul Newman despite my hazel eyes and being barely five feet nine. She was jealous and was of Jimmy Carter's persuasion. She thought lusting in the mind was as bad as putting thoughts into actions. But she convinced herself I acted on my thoughts. I resented her lack of faith.

"Susan," I told her, "it's a well-known fact that college professors are among the most faithful husbands despite their many temptations. Just the other day I read another study saying that."

"Where did you read that, Jack? I'd like to see that study."

"I don't remember. I think it was in the newspaper. They were citing respectable scientists, maybe the *Kinsey Report*."

When our two kids left home, the empty nest syndrome hit with a vengeance. Without the children to worry about, Susan had more time to let her suspicions create a self-fulfilling prophecy. Our sex life might have been a problem. She couldn't believe anybody with my sexual appetite could be satisfied with one woman.

Her accusations became unbearable. Despite my Presbyterian upbringing and its prohibitions against adultery, I finally did have an affair with a married colleague. Susan seemed relieved when she found out, satisfied at last that her suspicions were correct. I felt foolish for taking revenge for her lack of trust. At least the divorce was reasonably amicable, since I gave her everything she asked for.

"Jack," she told me, "I can't live with you anymore. I can't trust you. You've betrayed me. Besides, I think I can find somebody else. Maybe not as handsome as you—-someone who'll be more faithful."

"I finally did what you accused me of for a quarter of a century. That doesn't justify what I did, but that's water over the dam. We might as well forgive and forget—get on with our lives."

So I was left to arrange the rest of my life. I found it was easier to forgive than forget. An emotional wreck, I decided to take a fling at world birding. I had been watching birds and recording my observations for years, ever since boyhood on my family's farm. I'd learned my birds from my dad. He called meadowlarks field larks and accipiters hen hawks, but he taught me all of the birds on our land.

I had kept up my interest throughout my life despite Susan's thinking it a silly activity for a grown man. I even became the president of the local bird club. Susan would have preferred being a golf widow rather than a bird widow, I think. It would have been easier and more acceptable to explain to her friends.

As I had tried to adjust to the depression resulting from enforced bachelorhood, I wrote a great deal of poetry about midlife crisis and published some of it, but that didn't fill enough hours to ease my unhappiness.

So birding tours became a way of life for me in the next three years and a half—-Attu in the Aleutians, Central America, South America, Europe, Asia, and, finally, Africa. I justified my ecotourism as support for the environment.

I took a trip to Gabon in the hope of finding what is known as a rock fowl. I had begun listing bird families, and there are only two species in that avian family—birds in the genus *Picathartes*. I missed the Gabon rock fowl. Now I was contemplating another African trip to remedy this miss. This trip was going to be four weeks—unusually long. I called Susan and the kids to let them know. It was the right thing to do.

After all, our divorce had been fairly peaceful. We used the same lawyer. She shouldn't learn about my trip from one of the kids. I still call them kids, but they're grown-ups now. Their asking for advice has been a welcome surprise. They no longer consider me the complete incompetent their mother taught them to see.

Anyway, I called Susan. She thought my trip a foolish way to see Africa.

"Still acting like a child? Can't you find something better to do than run over the world chasing birds?"

"I thought you ought to know I'll be abroad for over a month. In case anything should happen, you're still the person they'd contact—-unless you'd rather I put down one of the kids as the person to notify." *No need to be a bitch about it.*

"No. It's okay. I hope you have a good trip. Watch out for the snakes."

I was eager to take the trip even though I had misgivings about some of my future companions. I needed this trip. I'd been trying to forget about how I'd screwed up my life—trying to tell myself I'd done the right thing giving Susan the divorce without a fuss. The divorce hadn't worked for me. I still missed married life.

Since the tour would be during summer vacation, I didn't have to make special arrangements other than turning down summer school classes. I usually did that anyway. The younger faculty in my department were overjoyed when those of us higher in the pecking order left the field open to them. They needed the money.

I didn't have to worry about money anymore. Besides my salary, a rather nice inheritance had come to me soon after my divorce. The timing was lucky for me. It hadn't figured in the divorce settlement. It allowed me to travel despite my having to pay alimony. My colleagues thought I was sitting in the proverbial catbird seat. They couldn't imagine my loneliness.

I was highly sought after by the single ladies on the faculty and in town. I did enjoy some tasty meals. People didn't understand how difficult I found single life, yet how fearful I was of another bad experience. But their sympathy for my plight helped to fill many evenings. I enjoyed their company, and even went to bed with some of them, but shied away from a deep relationship. I found it difficult to resist female charm, but I was fearful of another bad outcome. When college was in session, I had plenty to keep me occupied, but breaks brought loneliness and anxiety that literary studies couldn't lessen. Bird tours had become a way to fill the vacuum.

Even before I met others of the Africa group, I worried that something unfortunate might happen. The tour was long—and expensive. But it was a once-in-a-lifetime chance to explore Africa. I shrugged my worries aside before I found out who some of the other nine people on the trip were to be. Jimmy Russo and Gabe Goforth—I remembered them from my Argentina trip.

Still, I was convinced it was too good a chance to see Africa and a rock fowl to pass up. I needed to occupy my mind with something besides loneliness and friendly dinner hostesses.

I decided to go. No point in borrowing trouble, I told myself. I had complete confidence in Fantastic Flights, my avian tour company—certainly one of the more highly respected by people who jet about the world looking for new species of birds. Besides, the two tour leaders were without doubt the most knowledgeable bird experts in Africa. They usually led trips by themselves.

My apprehensions were alleviated by my confidence in Terence Stavens and Sean Selkirk. I'd been on separate trips with each of them already in South America and Asia. These leaders know their birds, and they work tirelessly to see that everyone on their tours has fun.

Even ardent birding enthusiasts don't like to give up creature comforts. So we could ignore the complaints of people new to jet-set birding. Dealt with sympathetically, they would adapt. There would not be many neophytes on this trip. After all, it would be grueling. No other tour company was offering a trip like this.

No, it wasn't the possibility of neophytes that bothered me. Stavens and Selkirk would handle them very diplomatically. I guess my unease stemmed from knowing Gabe Goforth and Jimmy Russo would be on the trip. In Argentina with Fantastic Flights, they showed themselves to be listers of the worst sort, especially Russo. He had grown up in poverty and made a fortune by hard work. Anyone who's read the book or seen the movie *The Big Year* can imagine what an obsessed person I'm describing, an individual driven to do anything necessary within the rules or by stretching them a bit to get ahead of the other guy, like predators in the business world. Russo had transferred his obsessive business practices into his birding contest with Goforth.

Despite my dislike of Jimmy Russo, I was having mixed emotions about seeing Jane Russo again. She and I spent a lot of time together in Argentina while Jimmy and Gabe were out trying to keep ahead of each other. Her charms had proved hard to resist.

Her marriage to Jimmy didn't seem to be fulfilling her needs. I wondered how she could stay with him, but she had insisted she didn't believe in divorce. She and I became very close friends. She was very desirable. Maybe by the end of this trip divorce would seem more agreeable to her.

CHAPTER 3

Trudging through the crowded Atlanta airport, beset by hurried crowds, vehicles, and bright lights, my misgivings receded when I met an elderly but genial man awaiting our flight to Cape Town, the first leg of our trip. He was seated near our departure gate when I arrived. The plastic tag attached to his carry-on showed he was part of the Fantastic Flights expedition.

"Hello, I'm Jackson Burnbridge. I see you're on the African odyssey too."

The man's blue-gray eyes twinkled in a face widened in a boyish grin as he shook my hand without getting up. "Sure am. Name's Cameron Macdonald. Have a seat." I sat down next to him and arranged my carry-on under my seat. We were far enough from the TV to have a conversation.

"Looks like we're the first of the adventurers to arrive. I'm from Texas, from Houston. Where do you hail from?" Cameron asked.

"Virginia, from Norfolk."

"That's a good birding spot too. Have you ever birded the Texas coast?"

"A couple of times—-down the coast and up the valley."

"You're a serious birder, then. Do you belong to the American Birding Association?"

"Sure do. How about you?"

"I was a charter member. It started in Texas, you know. I was one of the last people to see an Eskimo curlew—-that one on Galveston Island back in the sixties. Nobody's seen one alive since."

"I guess you have a pretty good life list, then."

"Well, pretty good for Texas and the US. I haven't done much birding outside North America except for Central America. This trip's a big change for me. What's your list like?"

"I have over three thousand species. I'm hoping this trip will take me close to four thousand."

"Watch out, I may catch up with you," Cameron said, grinning.

By the time others arrived, Cameron and I had established enough rapport so that we could indulge in a running commentary about the new arrivals. Cameron was a retired physician with a wry sense of humor.

A middle-aged couple walked toward us. We could see their Fantastic Flights tags on their carry-ons. No doubt they saw ours also. The man appeared to be in his forties. He was about five-nine, heavyset with dark hair receding down the middle. He reminded me of the pointy-headed boss in the Dilbert cartoons. His swarthiness contrasted with the bleached blonde hair, big earrings, and long pink fingernails of his taller companion. She carried a bit of weight, but she still retained much of her youthful beauty.

Both of them wore upper garments with large floral patterns more appropriate for the beach than the Atlanta airport.

"Judging from the pictures in our field guides, these two look like a pair of huge sunbirds," Cameron said.

"Howdy, I'm Jerry Buck," the man introduced himself. "This beautiful lady is my little woman, Maude. We're from Fairfax, Virginia. I'm a UVA Wahoo to the core. I run a computer service in Fairfax, and I sell optical equipment, especially scopes and binoculars, on the side."

"I'm Jack Burnbridge, and this is Cameron Macdonald."

"Burnbridge, you're from Virginia too, according to the list we got."

"That's right. Cameron's from Texas."

Maude Buck was a bit less exuberant than Jerry, but very friendly. "We belong to the Northern Virginia chapter of the VSO. That's the Virginia Society of Ornithology," she added for Cameron's benefit. "We've been members for four years now. Jerry and I thought a trip to Africa would be a great way to see some birds and big animals."

"Yeah," Jerry added, "I always wanted to see some elephants and giraffes and rhinos outside a zoo. We thought we'd show our support of the environment with some ecotourism."

"You should get your chance to see all those and more on this trip, but birds are what we're after," Cameron observed.

"Sure thing, but Maude's more into the birds than I am. She loves to photograph them."

"Don't believe him. He likes the birds as much as I do, 'praise the Lord,'" Maude said. "He's turned our backyard into a bird sanctuary. We've attracted all sorts of birds to our feeders. Why, we had people from all around to see the varied thrush from out west we had at our feeders last winter. I got some good photos, praise the Lord."

"You seem to be dedicated to nature study," I said.

Maude waved her arm. "We're learning fast, but we're happy to take all the help we can get."

"You'll find Stavens and Sinclair quite helpful," I said.

"Glad to hear it. Well, we're going to find some food. We'll see you later," Jerry said as they turned to leave. "Say, would you mind watching our carry-ons?"

I said I would, and Cameron nodded. Our tour group would be an interesting, though incongruous, group. I like observing people as well as birds.

As Maude and Jerry disappeared, Cameron grinned at me. "Those people are definitely out of their element—-backyard birders who've somehow persuaded themselves that they're ready for the big time. No doubt Maude was overcome by the beautiful photographs in *Birder's World* or some other colorful publication."

"They may be all right. They might moan and groan a bit, but they'll become happy when Terence or Sean shows them awesome birds. A fellow Wahoo can't be all bad."

The airport hummed with activity. An electric cart carrying several people and luggage came by. Behind them straggled a group of four. The men were engaged in heated conversation.

"Cameron, I see Jimmy Russo and Gabe Goforth coming."

A heavyset, dark-haired guy was shaking a fist at a tall blond. Passionate listers—really obsessive—they were undoubtedly arguing about their life lists. In Argentina, I had found Goforth less nasty than the obnoxious Russo. They go around the world to see every species possible to list. They've been engaged in a combative competitive listing for years now—each one trying to stay ahead of the other.

I felt I should warn Cameron. "They're both obsessed with their lists, but Russo's obnoxious."

"But a lot of us take our lists seriously. I remember seeing Goforths and Russos on the list of our tour group."

"That's true, but not all of us are as obsessive as they are. Watch out if one of them misses a bird the rest of us identify well enough to put on our life lists. Goforth will pout for a few minutes, but Russo will make nasty comments for a week. And if one of them sees the bird and the other doesn't, it can be even worse. Sometimes Jimmy comes close to landing blows. I've seen them. Their wives always intervene before blows land. I had my fill of them in Argentina, but their wives are jewels. I've been corresponding with Jane Russo some since then. She's the taller one with blue eyes and auburn hair. Goforth's Alice is the petite lady with dark hair."

"I'm glad you told me about them. I'll try to stay clear of both of them."

Russo and Goforth were competing to see which one would be the first person to break Phoebe Snetsinger's record. She had listed over eighty-seven hundred species of birds. An awful accident ended her birding career. Cameron had not heard how Phoebe died. I filled him in. A guy who was on her trip to Madagascar told me she'd just seen a new life bird and was stretched out on the backseat of the tour van asleep. The driver failed to stay awake, and the van was about to go over a cliff, but the tour guide grabbed the wheel. He saved the bus and everyone but Phoebe. She smashed through a window and was decapitated by the broken glass. No doubt she died happy, dreaming of her last life bird, bleeding to death after escaping recurring cancer for over thirty years.

Their argument over the purity of Gabe and Jimmy's respective lists grew louder as they approached. I heard Gabe's voice accusing Jimmy of counting unacceptable birds.

"My list is perfectly clean. You can't say the same for yours, Jimmy. Shucks, you've counted at least ten exotics that I know weren't accepted by the local authorities," Gabe said, wiping his brow. A displacement action if I've ever seen one. He wanted to hit Jimmy.

"Well, you've been known to count heard birds that nobody but you could hear. Your list has more than ten of those, you nutty environmental piss-ant," Jimmy said, turning away.

"So what? I shouldn't count birds that I can hear just because you can't hear anything? Is it my fault that you have poor hearing?"

"My hearing's okay. It's your imagination that's the problem, you jerk." Russo glowered at Goforth and made an ominous fist.

I had noticed Jane Russo watching her husband with increasing unease. When she saw his hand make a fist, she grabbed his arm. "Jimmy, come on. I see an old friend over there." She waved and called, "Jack, hello!" as she walked over. The Goforths followed, and Jimmy brought up the rear.

"It's good to see you again. It's been a while since Argentina," Jane said as she reached out to shake my hand. Her blue eyes flashed an even warmer greeting.

I introduced Cameron MacDonald. "He's going with us to Africa." Gabe reached out to shake hands. Jimmy shook also—rather reluctantly, I thought.

Pushing her hair back, Jane gave me a smile. "It's going to be a sorta long trip."

"Shucks, that's more time for seeing birds," Gabe said, grinning. "More opportunity for Jimmy and me to close in on Phoebe's record."

Jane's eyes bored into mine, giving me an invitation, I thought.

"How's that going? It's a wonder you guys spend so much time together," I said—*more time for Jane to be left alone.*

Gabe raised his arm and held up a forefinger in a triumphant gesture. "We're way over six thousand species. We hope to reach seven thousand on this trip. That's way more than half the species in the world.

"Collaborating beats trying to find out what the competition is up to. This way we know," Jimmy said. "One of us will win the current competition."

"That's right; keep your friends close and your rivals even closer," Gabe said. "Shucks, it gives me an opportunity to convert him to the idea of sustainable, eco-friendly development. If I can get wind of Jimmy's real estate boondoggles before they're too advanced, I can influence him to damage the environment less."

"Besides, we combine our resources for research about the best places to go to find the birds we need. And Alice and Jane help with that," Jimmy said. "One of us is going to win some money on this trip."

"Help? We do it all. That way we sorta get to find out about where our next trip will be," Jane said.

Cameron lifted his eyebrows. "You ladies go on all of these guys' birding trips?"

"Jane and I don't want to sit at home all the time while these two guys are traveling around the world. We don't mind a little rough going," said Alice. "I grew up in rural Alabama. I know about rough going. Compared to being at home alone, birding trips are pure pleasure."

"I'll bet there aren't many birders who have lists equaling ours, and Alice and I aren't even listers," Jane said, laughing. "Let's get something to eat before the flight."

Alice Goforth chimed in. "That's a great idea. Gabe, I'm not hungry, but let's get a snack to eat on the plane."

Jane looked back and waved at me as they ambled off. Watching them disappear, Cameron and I laughed. "I'm surprised they haven't killed each other when their wives weren't around," I said.

"I wonder if the wives will always stop them even when they are around."

"I'm amazed they're still married. They neglect their women— Russo is really bad. Jane and I talked a lot on that trip to Argentina while Jimmy was out keeping ahead of Goforth. Thing is, though, he tends to be jealous in spite of his neglect of Jane. Alice flirts, but Gabe doesn't seem to mind."

My foreboding about the trip returned. "I'm determined to stay away from those belligerents," I said.

"A wise resolution."

"Yes, but a hard one to keep. Jane's as pleasant as Jimmy is nasty— and a beauty. I don't see how they got together."

Cameron laughed. "It's an old story, Beauty and the Beast. It seems that Gabe and Jimmy find each other agreeable despite cutthroat competition."

A half hour later, the crowd for our flight began to fill the waiting area and form a line. The Goforths and the Russos joined us waiting in line. All of us had booked coach except the Bucks, who were going first class. They jokingly waved us goodbye as they moved to the head of the line and answered the first call for boarding.

We had a direct flight to Cape Town on South African Airways. There we would change for Nairobi, Kenya. It was a smooth, uneventful flight. Being seated with some noncommunicative types, I studied my African bird books, slept a lot, and enjoyed the South African wines and beers the staff served with our meals and between them. I was partial to the Dornier Cabernet Sauvignon and Castle Lager.

Once, walking down the aisle to the restroom, seeing Jimmy asleep, I couldn't help stopping to chat with Jane. She grabbed my arm and said, "Jack. I'm looking forward to another trip with you. We spent some pleasant hours in Argentina."

"I'm looking forward to this trip too. It's going to be a long one with lots of birds," I said.

"Well, if it's anything like the Argentina trip, we'll have plenty of time for chatting while Jimmy's chasing another life bird. Maybe I should have made a different choice then."

"I have great memories of that trip. You were good company. I'm looking forward to more time with you." I couldn't help looking too long into her blue eyes but managed to pull myself away.

Back in my seat, I thought about Jane. Memories of our trysts in Argentina still aroused me. She seemed even prettier than I remembered. She was very friendly. Maybe she would change her mind about divorce.

It was a long flight. Luckily for us, the stewardesses kept us well supplied with drinks, and the onboard movie, *Invictus*, helped me forget my loneliness and my misgivings about the trip.

I lost myself with Springbok rugby skippered by Matt Damon and the story of how Nelson Mandela, played by Morgan Freeman, inspired national unity through sport. Before long, we would be looking at real springboks and other antelopes and counting ostriches and other new birds. After all, competitive birding is a sport too, even if some of the listers don't show good sportsmanship.

CHAPTER 4

At the airport in Nairobi, I endured a long process of going through Kenyan bureaucracy. Getting through customs was like swimming through overly warm bodies in a colorful and aromatic sea of barely organized chaos. Once through the maze, I was relieved when Terence Stavens and Sean Selkirk met our group at the other side with a Fantastic Flights tour sign and men to carry luggage. We followed our luggage to a large white Toyota van.

The only members of the group we hadn't met in Atlanta were a slim, auburn-haired, well-endowed young woman named Iris Fogelman and a balding fellow introduced to us as Algernon Wheatley. He was tall and potbellied with receding hair.

Terence Stavens was head tour leader. A laconic, good-natured blond Yorkshire man almost six feet tall, Stavens wore short khaki pants and a T-shirt under a khaki field vest. A broad-brimmed hat and sturdy hiking boots protected him. He looked very professional, just as I remembered him.

Our second leader, Sean Selkirk, stood nearly a head above Terence. He wore a drab gray outfit. A loud, dark-haired Irishman, Sean quickly introduced himself and Terence to the group. He still seemed to have kissed the same blarney stone I recalled from my trip to Gabon with him.

"You won't find a better leader in all of Africa than Terence," Sean Selkirk said. "I say this despite his being a Brit. Triumphing over that handicap of birth, he married well in Kenya and knows more about African birds than anybody else but me. He holds the Big Day record for Africa.

"I'm Sean Selkirk, as modest a fellow as you'll ever meet, a scientist turned bird tour leader. We hope to show you hordes of mind-boggling scenic views, stupendous birds, and many interesting mammals.

We'll get you settled, and then we'll take advantage of this wonderful weather and show you blokes some local wildlife."

Grinning, Terence assured us that they hoped to make our group as comfortable as possible as well as show us a great many birds. "Possibly there will be places where our facilities will be basic, but be assured they'll be the best available. Now let's get to our hotel and stow your gear. Then we'll go birding."

After we settled in the van, Terence Stavens introduced us to our Kenyan driver, David. "David is a great driver. Besides that, he knows five languages and has a terrific Kenyan bird list. Now, if Sean and I aren't around, just give David your bird question." David grinned, turned, and greeted us, "*Guten Tag*, ladies and gentlemen," he said, continuing in French, Spanish, Swahili, and English. Then he drove the van out of the airport parking lot and onto a busy, colorful Nairobi street where vendors of all kinds plying their trade slowed the traffic.

An uneventful drive brought us to the Midtown Safari Lodge, where Cameron and I found ourselves assigned to be roommates. Struggling with his wife's luggage, Jerry Buck asked impatiently for their room key, and the Bucks dragged off to their room. Next Cameron took our key from Terence, and he and I followed the Bucks down the hall. Inspecting our room, we agreed that our Nairobi hotel was pleasant—separate beds with clean sheets.

Cameron was pleased with our lodgings. "Our room looks like a hotel room back home. This is hardly roughing it. To think that folks back home are really worrying about me."

"Tours always try to provide really pleasant lodgings and good food the first few days of a trip, if it's possible," I said. "To get off well. We may not have many difficult digs. Roughing it doesn't produce clients who rave about their trips to other birders. In fact, only a small number of birders put new birds ahead of comfort. I guess I'm one of those, although that puts me in a class with Goforth and Russo."

"I'll enjoy it while I can," Cameron said. "Let's check the plumbing and lights."

As we proceeded to flush the john and turn on the lights, I asked Cameron what he thought of Wheatley. "Did you notice anything funny about that guy Algernon Wheatley?"

"No. Only that he spends a lot of time writing in his notebook and says, 'Are you sure' all the time. Why?"

"He reminds me of a guy on a Costa Rica tour I took. Left before the tour was over. That balding head, the potbelly, and the notebook remind me of that fellow, but he wasn't using the name Algernon, and he had a mustache and more hair."

All of the plumbing seemed to work. Getting out our cameras and binoculars, we went back to the lobby. I counted over half the group in the lobby when we got there. The others trickled down while Jimmy Russo and Gabe Goforth chafed and paced and expressed their impatience vocally about the thoughtlessness of their fellows.

"You'd think this trip was just another day at the park the way these pissants act," Jimmy said.

"Shucks, what do you expect from a bunch of neophytes?" Gabe asked.

When the last, Jerry Buck, appeared, loaded down with Maude's camera equipment, Sean hustled the group into the van.

Cameron led me to the back of the van while Russo and Goforth grabbed the front window seats, just beating out Jerry Buck, who settled for a second-row window. Pulling rank, Sean assumed a position across from Terence on the front seats as they took the window seats from Jimmy and Gabe. David then drove us to the game park on the edge of Nairobi.

Standing up and turning to the group, Terence gave instructions. "We'll see a great many large mammals, and we'll point them out and stop for a few at waterholes. You can photograph, but remember, our main goal is to *see* as many of these African birds as we can."

Sean added for emphasis, "No photographs until after every one of you blokes has seen the target bird."

A pleasant half-hour's ride followed. Terence and Sean pointed out birds such as several species of doves and starlings we passed. He had David slow down for window views. Though some of the group complained about not stopping to get out, the leaders promised us the group would see many more of these common birds, so we quickly arrived at the park.

Fees paid, we proceeded to drive through sunny parkland. At a water hole, we made our first stop, where zeb-ras (as Terence and Sean termed them in British dialect) competed with elephants and antelopes for a drink while white egrets of several sizes were drinking at the fringes of the water while others were stationed in the water poised to spear unwary fish or frogs.

After noting the difference in size between the great, intermediate, and little egrets, Terence pointed out the difference between the little egret and the snowy egrets we knew from America. "Note the blue lore between the bill and the eyes, not yellow. You Americans get excited when you find a little egret in America. Take a good look at the egrets smaller than the great but larger than little egrets. You don't have anything like those intermediate egrets in the States. Possibly you'll find the oxpeckers riding the backs of several of the zeb-ras more interesting. You have nothing at all like them in the States."

"Which species of oxpecker?" Algernon Wheatley asked, speaking loudly enough for those in front to hear.

"These are the more common oxpeckers, the yellow-billed. Those little birds riding the zebras and other beasts are performing a valuable function—-looking to eat ticks and other insects pestering their hosts," Terence explained. "They don't leave the job to cattle egrets."

"Will we see red-billed oxpeckers?" Wheatley jotted something in a little notebook he carried with him.

"All in good time, Mr. Wheatley," Terence said.

"Are you sure we'll see them," Wheatley said.

I nudged Cameron, speaking in a low voice. "I think Algernon Wheatley *is* the guy that left the other trip. He's got the same balding head, potbelly, and glasses as the fellow I'm thinking of. He had a run-in with one of the other birders. And he constantly asked, 'Are you sure?'"

"What was the disagreement about?"

"The fellow who stayed accused Algernon, or whatever the name was, of being a spy for another tour group, Focus on Flight. They almost came to blows, but the guy like Algernon backed down."

Terence interrupted me. He pointed out a flock of hadeda ibis flying in. "These guys are noisy, and they say their name. Possibly they're so common you may become tired of them."

"Listening to them, I think I'll call them la de das," Cameron said.

After the group's taking a long look at the ibis, I went back to my suspicions of Algernon. "Have you ever been on a trip with Focus on Flight?"

"No, I've seen their ads in magazines. They offer good prices," said Cameron.

"I've been on trips with people who've taken trips with Jake Crumley. He runs Focus on Flight. They complain mightily about him. Some curse. A friend of mine took a trip with him to Japan. Before the trip, the guy hit my friend up for a loan. When Crumley got them to Japan, he borrowed money and credit cards to pay for the hotels and restaurants and their touring van. Some who helped him out never got repaid, they claim."

"Apparently he borrows from one group to get money for setting up another trip somewhere else," Cameron said.

"Look at that huge fellow coming in," Terence said, pointing to a white, very large, ugly wading bird with a huge beak lighting at the water, holding itself as if it was a giant hunchback, a monster from prehistoric swamps scattering the other birds.

"That's a marabou stork, a bird that vies for the title of largest bird in the world capable of flight. They'll eat just about anything. In

Uganda they congregated around the tall building Idi Amin forced his political opponents to jump off of."

While everyone gawked at the repulsive stork, I continued telling Cameron about Jake Crumley. "He didn't speak any Japanese, but he tried pidgin English rather than hiring a local guide who could speak English. He insisted on driving himself rather than hiring a local driver. He constantly got lost. Truly a trip from hell."

"I'll avoid his ads." Cameron said. He chuckled. "Why do people go on his trips?"

"To begin with, they're lured by the seemingly cheap prices. For some inexplicable reason, some sign up for additional trips, thinking things will be different. Evidently he *is* good at identifying birds, if he ever gets his group to where birds can be found."

"How does he learn about what trips to take?" Cameron asked.

"He must look up trips other companies offer. Then he persuades somebody to go on one of these trips to take notes about stops, the birds, and the accommodations."

"So you think Algernon is gathering information for Focus on Flight?"

"If this guy is the one I think he is, yes," I said.

"Do you think we should tell Terence and Sean?"

"Not yet. Let's watch him until we're certain."

Shouts interrupted our conversation. "A hornbill, a hornbill, on the right, a trumpeter hornbill," Sean said, pointing—-so our suspicions about Algernon disappeared in the midst of efforts to see and photograph grotesque but beautiful hornbills.

CHAPTER 5

Staring at these well-tailored black and white hornbills, I marveled at their exotic beauty. They are almost the size of pelicans. I was awed by their heads adorned with huge dark gray bills topped by a large bar of gray horn. I couldn't help noticing the bright red skin surrounding their eyes, giving them a fiendish, sinister look—amazing birds only a science-fiction writer could imagine. Cameron whistled. He was as amazed as I was, I guessed. I was stunned to silence.

"Oh, golly, look Jerry, what unusual birds," said Maude Buck as she shook her dozing Jerry to attention. "They look like freaks."

"I see them, Honey, you don't have to shake me so hard."

Cameron chuckled. I couldn't help myself. I was audibly laughing.

"I can understand her excitement," Cameron said. "I'm a bit excited myself."

I overheard a sound like a tiger's snarl in the front of the van. It was Jimmy Russo complaining that Gabe Goforth was blocking his view of the hornbills.

"Don't be such a horse's ass."

"Don't get your bowels in an uproar, Jimmy. Shucks, I'll sit down so that you can look over me."

"Thanks." Russo's sarcastic response was accompanied by a raised middle finger.

"Has everyone seen these hornbills?" Terence asked after several minutes. Hearing no denials, he waved everyone off the bus. "Let's go outside for better looks and photographs." The odor of animal spoor that met us did not diminish my enjoyment of the hornbills.

"Try to be quiet and don't make sudden movements. But don't wait. They won't be here long," Sean Selkirk said.

Jimmy Russo had his camera out and was jockeying with Maude Buck to get the best shot.

"Get off my back," Jimmy said.

"I have as much right to space as you do," Maude replied. "Besides, I'm here for photographs, praise the Lord. You're just listing. All you really care about is adding a name to your life list. What about their beauty?"

"Well, stay out of my way, you pissant holy woman."

"Stay out of mine too," said Iris Fogelman as she pointed her camcorder at the hornbills. Unlike the other two, she was smiling like a woman in complete control of the situation.

I thought to myself it was going to be a long trip for two of those three, glad that Terence Stavens and Sean Selkirk had already set down the law about photography. The hornbills were making bleating calls reminding me of a herd of sheep as they moved about restlessly in the trees. They stayed just long enough for everyone to get photographs despite the bickering.

After the hornbills moved on, flying from tree to tree away from us, our group returned to the van and continued working through the game park for a couple of hours before returning to our hotel for dinner and bed.

As we prepared for the evening meal, I sat down next to Jane Russo. Cameron sat across from us. Jane had a lavender scent that I found enticing. I was soon aware that she was rubbing her leg against mine.

"Did you see many new birds today, Jack?" Jane asked.

"So many I've lost count," I said. "Did you add any new ones, Jimmy?"

"Six, one less than Gabe."

Iris Fogelman sat next to me on my other side. Sandwiched between two beautiful women who could be twins, I found Iris's lilac scent most attractive. She had let down her auburn hair, which she had had in a bun earlier. On Cameron's recommendation, she tried a Tusker. "Just think of me as one of the guys. After all I'm a Fogelman. Vogel or Fogel means bird in German."

Turning and giving her an appraising look, I almost drowned in her gray eyes. "I don't believe I can think of you as a man," I said.

At what turned out to be an excellent dinner offering both roast beef and fish, Cameron and I downed more Tusker beers. "Tusker's worth the extra money," Cameron told those around us. "This beer is excellent."

I agreed. "It has good body and a tart yet fruity taste."

"You fellows have good taste buds," Iris said. "Tusker's delicious."

I ordered another round for the three of us—Iris, Cameron, and me—to go with our meal of beef, perch, potatoes, and some other cooked vegetables. Aware of the problems with salads in places with poor hygiene, Cameron and I avoided any raw vegetables.

Iris didn't like giving up fresh vegetables. "I miss having a salad, but we've been warned to avoid uncooked vegetables."

It was a tasty meal that went well with the beer, the safest liquid available other than soft drinks. With Jane rubbing my leg, I needed to keep my wits about me to conceal my arousal. Paying attention to the beauty of Iris certainly helped me ignore Jane's leg but didn't calm my libido.

When what was to become the nightly ritual of the list took place, Sean handed us checklists of the birds and mammals expected on the tour. There were lines left for unexpected species.

"We'll try to do the list almost every night. That way, you'll have a convenient means to keep up with your sightings during the trip and a record to take home with you," Terence said. "We'll send you an official, annotated list after the trip." Then he went through the list and noted those birds we had seen or heard that day. When he finished, Sean went through the list of mammals and other interesting animals we'd encountered with special attention to the unusual antelopes like the gnus or wildebeests and the hippos.

"Possibly it surprises you as it does many tourists to learn more people are killed in Africa by hippos than by any other wild animal," Terence said.

He raised his hand. "Let me remind you that Fantastic Flights does not include alcoholic drinks in their fee. Your bar bills are your private expense. We pay for one nonalcoholic drink with meals. Don't forget to pay your bar bill." He grinned. "Possibly this policy will have a beneficial effect, although it may reduce the number of rare birds reported."

Waving his hand at the laughter, he became more serious, "I've been told a leopard has been seen prowling the neighborhood of our hotel at night. Leopards are quite common in Nairobi. Possibly that's why you see so few feral cats and dogs running about. I advise you to get to bed and not walk abroad.

"We leave for the game park early tomorrow morning and leave for the Abedarres from there. We'll pack only for the days ahead in Kenya and will take lunch on the road. Some of you may have to leave part of your gear here."

"What about night birds?" Jimmy Russo asked.

"You'll have plenty of chances for night birds and animals at our lodge in the Abedarres. You'll probably want to stay up late to watch life at the water hole through the big picture window much of the night. Now get to bed and sleep. We're getting off as early as possible tomorrow. Breakfast at six."

Algernon scribbled in his notebook. "Were there any big misses as far as what you expected today?"

"No, nothing I'd call a huge miss. Seeing the hornbills so well was a big plus," Terence said.

Cameron smiled as Jane led her grumbling husband off to their room. "There goes a happy couple," he said.

"I don't see how Jane puts up with such a rotten bastard," I said with a bit too much force. I saw a quizzical look on Cameron's face. I guessed he wondered how far my interest in Jane's happiness extended, but he made no comment as we walked to our room.

Deciding to be more circumspect in discussing Jane with him, I changed the subject. "What do you think of Iris Fogelman?"

"She's not bad-looking. And she seems a genial sort," Cameron said. "I thought I saw her giving you a close look when you weren't noticing. Jane seems to be paying you a lot of attention too. Better watch out with two auburn beauties seeking your attention."

"Thanks for the warning. I think we'll see enough feathered birds for my life list to keep me occupied. Besides, Jane's a married woman tied to a jealous husband, though she's very attractive."

"How many life birds did you add today?"

"I think about thirty. How about you?"

"More like forty. This is fun."

"Did you notice that Algernon Wheatley has single accommodations?" I asked.

"Yes, he's willing to bear extra expense. That could be innocent enough. Iris has a single room too, but from our perspective, his is suspicious. Somebody may be paying all or part of his expenses," Cameron said.

"I'm sure he's spying, probably for Jake Crumley. I'd like to see what he's writing in that notebook. I'll bet it isn't only his bird lists. Did you notice that last question about misses?"

"He's intent on writing down every little detail. I'll see if I can get a look at what's in that notebook," Cameron said.

CHAPTER 6

Next morning, we met for breakfast at six with our bags packed for the afternoon departure. Everybody was there except Maude. It was an English breakfast. The aroma of coffee and bacon enticed us. Cameron and I decided to down our bacon, eggs, tomato, beans, toast, and juice without regard to our diets. After all, this was a holiday.

As we began eating, Maude Buck appeared dragging a trolley with a huge heap of luggage. Terence grimaced and muttered a barely audible, "Shit." He marched over to Maude. We could hear what became rather animated conversation.

"Mrs. Buck, you were told ahead of time you could have only two bags while we're traveling."

"My main reason for coming on this trip was to photograph. I need my equipment."

Rubbing the back of his neck, Terence repeated his demand. "You'll have to get things down to two bags."

"I think that's unreasonable," Maude said, hands on hips.

Terence frowned. "We'll leave the rest here while we're traveling in Kenya. We'll pick those things up on our way back. Get some breakfast and repack as soon as you can," Terence said, turning away.

Maude seemed unhappy but accepted this edict with a sour face and gulped a little breakfast before disappearing. I hoped she was returning to her room to condense her gear and arrange bags to be left behind without revealing their contents to the group.

"You'd think this a photography expedition," Jimmy Russo said as he drank some more coffee.

"Shucks, I noticed you had your camera out at the hornbill stop," Gabe Goforth said, laughing as he downed another helping of eggs.

"You know Jimmy likes to have a record of his birds," Jane said. "He's not so concerned about artistry." This defense did not seem to please her husband, who grunted, loudly. By her crestfallen face, I could tell Jane was hurt by his reaction.

"I never put photography ahead of seeing a bird for the life list," Jimmy said. "It's not that I don't appreciate their beauty."

"Well, I know you missed that Dartford warbler in England the first time because you were photographing a blue tit," Gabe said, grinning.

"Yeah, but I got the bird, pissant."

"To be sure, I hope the lady was not too cold," said Algernon Wheatley. He was laughing, almost choking on his toast.

"At least our mystery client has a sense of humor," I told Cameron, noting Jimmy glowering at Algernon's wit. Everyone else was laughing.

"I think that was an uncouth, sexist remark," Iris Fogelman said. But she was grinning. "I trust you won't make unpleasant remarks about my name. Vogel or Fogel means bird in German, you know."

"I'll promise never to make remarks about your name if you'll agree to invest in some stocks and bonds with me," Jimmy Russo said and smiled at her as he gave her his business card.

Jane appeared upset at his obvious interest in Iris. I couldn't help wondering how he could ignore Jane's charms. She was outfitted in a brief blue outfit that accentuated her curvaceous body and went well with her auburn hair. Iris Fogelman had on an identical blue outfit. They seemed like twins—and both seemed very appealing.

Jane snapped her fingers. "Jimmy, you don't need to do business here," she said.

"Nobody would ever think of you as a man, Iris," Cameron said as he examined her appreciatively.

Iris Fogelman was quite pretty and exceptionally well endowed despite a willowy figure, but I kept silent as I admired her auburn hair and gray eyes. Apparently she was well off financially, also, since she had a single accommodation.

After quiet returned, Maude asked for a photograph of the assembled group. "Photographs can be used to provide a record of people too, praise the Lord," she said. "I'll make copies for everybody." After Maude Buck finished, she and Jerry changed places, and Jerry Buck took another picture of our happy group with Maude in it.

At six-fifty, we climbed aboard the van for another trip to the Nairobi game reserve and the subsequent journey to the Abedarres. David finished loading the van, and by seven we were on the road to the game park. Terence Stavens and Sean Selkirk took the front row window seats again.

Terence Stavens made the leaders' rules clear. "Please understand. Sean and I will always take these front window seats for observation. That way we can stop the bus if we see a bird you need for your lists.

"We'll try to point out as many birds as possible without stopping, unless we see something really rare or hard to find. You'll be expected to rotate seating arrangements clockwise from day to day so that nobody gets an undue advantage in seeing birds and animals," Sean Selkirk said.

Cameron and I retook our places at the back of the van. "I suppose we'll have to move up to fit into the rotation," Cameron said. "If I get close to Algernon, I'm going to find out something about him or make him come up with some interesting lies. You have any ideas?"

Laughing, I cupped my hand at my mouth and whispered a suggestion. "Ask him about Costa Rica."

The morning went splendidly. We saw birds everywhere, so many that some of us paid little attention to the elephants, giraffes, impalas, and other mammals. At the first water hole stop, I saw at the water's edge getting a drink some of the most beautiful birds I had ever seen.

After we left the van, I questioned Terence. "What are those small birds drinking at the water hole?"

"They're called superb starlings. Beauties, sure."

"I can't believe these birds are starlings, Cameron; they're about the same size as those feral birds in the States we call starlings, but these actually cause you to pause and exclaim. They look like they stepped out of a rainbow. They have the color of Jane's and Iris's hair plus other parts of the palette."

Cameron agreed. "They really do justify the name 'superb.'"

Maude was busy taking multiple shots of these birds, bothering Jimmy Russo again as she moved about to find the best light.

"Look where you're going, woman," he growled when she became particularly annoying. "You move like a tank."

"Get your shot for your list and get out of the way," Maude Buck said. "I want a photo to hang on my wall."

Terence intervened. "There's no need to fight about these birds. You'll see them so often you'll tire of them."

I found that hard to believe but appreciated Terence's intervention, because there were other birds to be identified, and the arguing was scaring them off. After getting her fill of still shots, Maude pulled out her camcorder and set to filming.

I noticed that Iris Fogelman had been recording the whole incident with her camcorder.

For some reason known only to her, Maude insisted on complete quiet as she shot her movie, although she included all of our group as well as birds and mammals. Iris evidently was not so squeamish about people's conversation.

Maude assured us she was going to give each of us a copy of her movie.

"I say," Cameron asked the question I suspected all of us were silently posing, "won't it be a bit boring without any sounds?"

"I'll put in whatever sounds I want. I don't want any unpleasantries marring my recording, praise the Lord."

Cameron looked at me and rolled his eyes as I tried to control my urge to laugh. "Well, shut my mouth," he said.

"Watch out, Maude may wash it out with soap," I said.

I looked around. Apparently overhearing us, Iris had turned her camcorder our way. I guessed she had the whole incident on tape.

"Now, boys, you're on candid camera. What do you think about superb starlings?"

Laughing, Cameron said, "I think they're a lot prettier than the starlings we have in Texas. They look like they stole Joseph's coat of many colors."

"I wish we had some like these in Virginia," I said. "I'm glad the Kenyans don't eat them."

Iris smiled a thank-you and turned the camcorder away, waving a casual goodbye, hurrying on to film some yellow-billed hornbills conveniently located in a nearby tree.

"We'll have to be careful, Cameron. Iris is catching all our antics, and she's not leaving out unpleasantries."

"I'll try not to do or say anything illegal."

Sean called the others to see the hornbills and pointed out a red-billed buffalo weaver in another tree, where there were huge nests built of sticks.

Sean sought our opinion. "A better looker than your house sparrows, eh, blokes?"

Soon Terence was calling us to load up the van.

CHAPTER 7

Our second trip through the Nairobi Park turned up a few more new birds, including gray African palm swifts flitting across the sky like cigars with wings, and green and gold little bee-eaters, birds a bit smaller than a mockingbird. Sitting on exposed perches, they darted out to catch insects.

This time the scenery attracted my eyes more than before because I was less overwhelmed by all of these new sights. The sunshine and panoramic scenes of Africa were beginning to become familiar. Palms and acacias breaking the plain were covered in a golden glow. I decided my choice of khaki shorts would be good for what promised to be a long, hot day.

"Cameron, Africa is beginning to grow on me. I think I like the Dark Continent," I said.

Cameron nodded. "It's anything but dark here. Reminds me a lot of the Rio Grande Valley in Texas. Palm trees, brush, and prairie. Kenya isn't as hot as Texas, though."

After a couple of hours, we headed toward the Abedarres, our first major birding headquarters, though we stopped for birds whenever Sean Selkirk or Terence Stavens thought it worthwhile. We were seeing hordes of new birds.

Along the way, I kept wondering about Algernon Wheatley and his prolific writing. At our next stop for birds, after savoring a svelte little blue-gray flycatcher, I spoke to Cameron.

"You said you'd help me find out if Algernon is a Jake Crumley plant for Focus on Flight. Why don't you use this time to have a chat while he's conveniently in the seat in front of you?"

"Okay, I'll see what I can learn."

Back in the van and in his seat, Cameron leaned forward to engage Algernon. I listened as well as I could.

"Algernon, I don't think we've had much chance to talk. How'd you get into birding?"

Algernon yawned before he answered. "Oh, I've been doing it since I was a kid."

"This is my first trip to Africa. Do you go on many of these trips?" Cameron said.

"A few, to be sure." He started turning away from Cameron.

"I'm a retired physician. What do you do for a living?"

"Oh, nothing much now. I'm retired too. I was an accountant." Algernon turned farther away.

"That explains it. You seem to take notes on all our birds, making sure your list is up to date. I guess accountants are like that. Thorough about details."

Tapping his pencil, Algernon leaned back. "Yes, I guess so. I like to be precise."

"You must have done well. These trips are expensive."

"Yes, to be sure they are. I spend most of my extra money this way," Algernon said.

Cameron kept posing questions. "Have you ever been birding in Japan?"

"Yes."

Cameron asked, "What about Costa Rica? That's a place I'd really like to go."

Wheatley's voice took on an edge that hadn't been there before. "Yes ... it's a great place, lots of pretty birds. You should go there sometime."

"Ever been to Carrara? That's a terrific birding spot, I've heard." I thought Algernon visibly winced as he turned away from Cameron again.

"You ask too many questions. I want to update my notes." Algernon bent over his notebook and began writing.

"Sure, Algernon, sorry to have bothered you."

At our next stop, we got out to look at a crowned hornbill. It was just another bird for the list. A drab gray and tan bird, its horny helmet and big bill couldn't compare with that of the trumpeter hornbills we'd seen earlier.

I nudged Cameron. "My suspicions about Algernon are greater now than ever. He really reacted when you brought up Costa Rica. The man I think he really is left the group before we birded Carrara."

"We still don't have any hard evidence," Cameron said.

I crossed my arms. "We have the whole trip to find some," I said.

Cameron and I settled in our seats and began to watch out the window for birds while enjoying the scenery. Our speed was dictated by the condition of the highway, which had very little pavement after we left Nairobi. Most of the way was without macadam once we were about ten miles out, but the track was smooth. We left a cloud of gray dust behind us.

At every settlement where we stopped for gas or drinks, there were throngs of people, mainly women and children, pressing against the van, offering homemade jewelry, soapstone carvings, fruit, and other items for sale.

A few hours on our way to the Abedarres, we were beginning to get hungry. After making numerous side trips to see new birds, we entered a long drive through well-kept grounds. Near the entrance we were greeted by an African man naked except for a loincloth and covered with body paint arrayed in white, red, and black geometric decorations. As we passed him, he brandished his spear and thumped it against his shield. Shortly after the van passed him, we saw a sign: "**Welcome to the Abedarres Club. Please sample our hospitality.**"

Stavens stood up. "All right, folks, you'll be happy to know we're having lunch at the club before we go up to our lodge. Sean will take your food orders to speed the meal. Remember, alcoholic drinks are not covered by the tour. I wouldn't overindulge if I were you, as we have an afternoon full of birding and travel ahead of us," Terence Stavens said. "Possibly you don't want to go to sleep."

We had our choice of several beef, fish, or chicken dishes with a soup or salad and tea or coffee and, if we wished, beer or wine. Despite a menu that reminded us of America, Cameron and I again avoided the salad. We had Tuskers, only one apiece, keeping in mind Terence's admonition about moderation.

We were served on an outdoor veranda. A mild breeze and the many flowering plants exhaling aromas added to the pleasant seating. While eating and savoring the cold cheer of my Tusker, I watched numerous birds eagerly flying about us, looking for morsels dropped from the tables. There were four or five blue waxbills, or cordon-bleaus, as they're called, common but beautiful birds, the males sky blue except for tan caps and backs. Around the flowering shrubs bordering the veranda green and red and yellow eastern double-collared sunbirds feasted on the flowers' nectar, feathered jewels decorating the bushes and lawn in exchange for sweets from the bushes.

"These beauties are the old world's replacement for the New World's hummingbirds," Sean Selkirk told us. "Their sizes don't vary as much as the sizes of hummingbirds, though. Almost all sunbirds are the size of small sparrows."

"It's difficult to adjust to all these beautiful birds. I just itch to get my camera out. But I'm hungry and thirsty," Iris Fogelman said.

"I know the feeling," Maude Buck said.

Her agreement brought a warm grin from Iris, who consulted a mirror. "Maybe we'll lose weight on this trip. We won't have time to eat."

I didn't believe Iris had any cause to worry about weight gain. In her blue outfit, she reminded me of the graceful chic blue-gray flycatcher we'd seen on our drive.

Maude Buck was a different matter. She could stand to drop at least twenty pounds.

Now that we'd seen sunbirds, I decided we had to find a new name for the Bucks, something especially colorful and flamboyant for Maude.

"You ladies have to remember the prime directive. Life birds for all first, then photos," I said. "But I'll try to stay out of your way once you get started."

"Thanks for the support," Iris said. "We know the person we have to watch out for is Jimmy Russo. He's a real SOB."

"I agree. I wish we could get rid of him." Maude glared at Russo at the other end of the table.

I chuckled. "Has he tried to sell you any stock yet? He has tried to do business with Cameron, but he hasn't approached me. I guess because I'm a college professor." I didn't mention that I thought he might be jealous because of my relationship with Jane. "He probably thinks I'm not a good mark. At least his behavior shows he has other interests besides his list of bird species."

Lunch was so pleasant I decided to take a chance on getting sleepy and ordered another Tusker.

"He'd better stay away from me," Maude said. "Jerry doesn't appreciate Jimmy's attitude. If you want some advice about what Russo's offering, just ask Jerry for help getting information online. He doesn't want to bother anybody with a sales pitch while we're on vacation, but he'll be glad to show you what's available and get you some information about stocks, praise the Lord."

"Jimmy's hit on me about stock," Iris said. "I told him I'd think about it, but I've already got a portfolio adviser. I'll run Jimmy's proposal by him."

Lunch finished, the photographers stalked the waxbills and sunbirds while Cameron enjoyed the last of his Tusker. He finished fairly fast and left to look for birds nearer the van.

Lingering behind with me and my second Tusker, Jane Russo walked over and stood by me, smiling. "Could I have a sip of your Tusker," she said, proffering her glass. Her blue blouse and shorts really became her.

"Sure." I poured beer in her glass and handed it to her. She sipped it while rubbing my cheek with lavender-scented hands. Her auburn hair and blue outfit with golden trim reminded me of the blue waxbills.

"That beer was delicious. One good turn deserves another," Jane said. Bending down, she gave me a kiss—on the mouth, not on the cheek. She forced her tongue into my mouth and continued kissing me. Surprised, I responded, greedily returning her kiss while pulling her toward me.

"Let's move over behind those shrubs," Jane said, pulling me in that direction. Out of sight, she hugged me close and kissed me again. Her delightful lavender scent overcame me, and I responded in a way that pleased her.

"I feel your desire." She giggled with delight and placed my hand on her bare breast underneath her bra while she pressed herself against me and rubbed her hips over my thighs as she unzipped my pants.

CHAPTER 8

Separately we made our way to join the group at the van. I was relieved when nobody commented on our tardy arrival—I suppose because Jimmy and Gabe were even later.

"We were chasing a pink-throated twinspot," Gabe offered as an explanation of their tardiness.

"Maybe that was the bird I photographed," Maude said. "It's a beautiful little bird with a brilliant red head and a black breast with white spots."

"Yes, that's the twinspot male we were chasing," Jimmy said. "They're not easy to find—harder yet to photograph."

I detected disgust and envy in his voice. He was glowering with more than his usual malevolence.

My moments with Jane apparently undetected, happily digesting lunch, I boarded the van with the group, and found a seat beside Iris. We headed up into the highlands. The road was rough in places, but the van maneuvered it well. We all became aware that besides having language skills and birding skills, David was also an exceptionally skilled driver.

The road wound through acacia brush and then through deciduous forest as we climbed. We slowed briefly at a bridge over a slow-moving stream but did not get off the bus, although there were a number o herons and egrets visible. We made no additional stops and after several miles arrived at an opening in the woods. In the forest glade, incongruous, a huge lump of civilization rose out of the mountain slope like a hybrid between a New England mansion and a Swiss mountain chalet.

We reached the Abedarres Lodge about two hours and a half before the evening meal would be served. Before we exited the van, Terence and Sean stood and spoke to us about what to expect.

"You should shower and get some rest, because you'll want to stay up late tonight. The lodge has a huge picture window looking out on a water hole and salt lick," Sean said.

"Possibly the feeders stationed all around the grounds have been filled with fruit left over from meals," Terence said. "Birds and small mammals are always to be found there. This evening there'll be large animals at the water hole. Mammals and many night birds will be coming in before dark and during the night. It's a chance of a lifetime to see the Abedarres' nightly animal show."

Sean gave us a warning. "We've moved to a very high elevation, about five thousand feet. It's warm now, but it will get cold tonight."

"Check to make sure you have blankets in your room," Terence said. "You'll need cover before the night's over if you stay up to see tonight's water hole theater."

After finding our room and making sure we had blankets and working plumbing, Cameron and I did a little exploring outside the lodge at the feeders loaded with fruit to attract wildlife. Hoping to approach birds without flushing them, we walked slowly, watching thrushes and ground squirrels and other animals along the walks. We flushed a brilliant orange and tan robin chat and chased a rabbit and a mongoose into the brush.

The first feeding station had large grayish-tan birds feeding on it. They had crests and long tails and were marked with small, delicate, dark spots.

"Look at those blue faces," Cameron said. I consulted my field guide. "Look, this picture fits our birds. They're called speckled mousebirds despite their feathered tails."

"Befitting their name, they look like large rodents covered with feathers, Casanova," Cameron said.

I wondered about his calling me Casanova but didn't ask why. I suspected he might have seen me with Jane after lunch at the club.

Clambering through the vines and bushes to dine on sliced plantains and other fruits, the mousebirds stared at us with bright orange eyes peering from bare blue skin. Their heads reminded me of Halloween masks. Watching birds with such an eerie appearance, I could imagine their inhabiting some prehistoric forest. Joining them were colorful robin-chats with orange breasts. Somber thrushes with heavily spotted chests vied with the mousebirds for food. Sunbirds also visited the fruit but never lingered.

After enjoying this spectacle for half an hour, we walked back to the lodge and our room on the basement floor. Checking for blankets, we headed toward the huge picture window that formed the lodge wall facing the water hole.

Another spectacle appeared there. Just as we arrived, I saw people outside, above us, on a walk, observing the elephants; Maude and Jerry Buck were there. So were Jimmy Russo and Iris Fogelman. Maude and Jimmy were competing for the best place to photograph the elephants arriving to drink and use the salt lick.

Iris appeared to me to be careful to stay away from the crowd and work for different angles. There were a couple of young elephant calves attracting the photographers' rapt attention. Even as the elephant adults maneuvered for water and salt, they protected their calves.

Alice Goforth and Jane Russo were watching the water hole and salt lick through the glass wall. They were sitting on opposite ends of a long sofa.

"I see Jimmy out there. Where's Gabe?" I said.

"He's out birding. Jimmy's photography often gives Gabe an opportunity to get ahead in their competition, but Jimmy always seems to catch up. If there were anything really rare, Jimmy would be out hunting too," Jane said as she moved closer to her end of the sofa.

"Watching this show's pure pleasure. Gabe's staying close so as not to miss night birds coming to the lights of the lodge," said Alice. "He says the birds he needs are best found in the morning."

"Has anybody seen Algernon Wheatley since we arrived?" I asked.

"He hasn't been here," Jane said. "He has single accommodations. Maybe he sorta needs a lot of rest." She spread her blanket out over her and the sofa.

"He doesn't seem very sociable. I've tried to strike conversations with him, but he doesn't talk," said Alice, smiling as she watched Jane. No doubt she recalled our Argentina trip.

"A man of mystery," I said.

"I've dubbed him a secretary bird," Cameron said. "I'm told we'll see the real thing in Samburu, so we can compare him with his namesake. Wheatley takes copious notes. Excuse me, ladies. I think I'll take a shower before our meal. You coming, Jack?"

"I'll stay here until dinner. This window is like a cathedral without stained glass. The animals are preaching the sermon."

Jane lifted an end of her blanket. "Sit here beside me, Jack. I have a great view and a blanket," she said.

"Thanks." I draped the blanket I'd brought over the sofa and sat down beside her in the space she'd left under the blanket between her and the end of the sofa. I intended to watch the wildlife show until dinner. Jane rearranged her blanket to cover me also.

We spent at least a quarter of an hour watching the elephants. The adults moved about to protect their young when hyenas came to the water.

"Oh, look at that baby elephant," Alice said. "Its mother is giving it a bath. The little guy seems to enjoy it. That water is pure pleasure for him."

I felt Jane's hand on my thigh and moving higher. My response indicated this was not good timing. I put Jane's hand in mine and squeezed it, but she moved both hands to my growing privates. I was responding to her movements, but it wasn't pure pleasure for me. I worried about Jimmy seeing us.

"It's close to time for our meal. Maybe I should shower," I said.

Jane continued to fondle me. I could not repress my desire. I stood, trying to hide my arousal. Things were moving a little faster than was wise. I left after giving Cameron time to shower. "I'll see you later," I said, retreating.

"Are you coming back to watch the wildlife after we eat?" Jane asked. "I'd be glad for some company. Jimmy is planning to chase night birds around the grounds."

"I'll keep you company. We'll probably see plenty of night birds from here," I said.

CHAPTER 9

The large dining area continued the high ceiling that we saw in the viewing area, but our floor level was considerably higher. The high beams reduced the need for air conditioning during the day and produced a need for blankets at night when the temperature dropped. African woodcarvings of people and animals of various shapes and sizes decorated the dining area.

Cameron expressed admiration for the art. "I think that some of these figures must have been intended for fertility rituals. They certainly do proclaim the life force."

"They shout procreation," I said. They did nothing to alleviate my quandary of how to deal with Jane's aggressiveness and her obvious willingness to incite phallic demands I found difficult to refuse.

At a buffet table next to a table set for twelve, we found we had a choice of squash or split-pea soup followed by either fish or antelope and Irish potatoes and greens with a dessert platter loaded with a variety of fruit. I was happy to see we were to get some food suggesting we had arrived in Africa instead of an imitation English dinner. I took a plate and helped myself.

Cameron and I sat together. On the other side of the table Iris Fogelman approached with her plate and stood, ready to sit down. I waved her over. She walked over and stood beside me. She had changed for dinner and looked deliciously tucked into a yellow outfit that showed her figure to great advantage. I may have stared a bit too long.

Iris grinned at me and Cameron. "Do you mind having a birdman sitting next to you, Jack?"

"I'm very fond of birdmen and bird women too, especially pretty ones," I said. She was wearing a delicate perfume that reminded me of lilacs. Her beauty added spice to the meal.

She put her food down, pulled out a chair, and sat down.

Cameron laughed. "I'd be glad to make room beside me."

Iris blushed. "I'm comfortable here, Cameron, thanks. Did you see many new birds today, Jack?"

I couldn't help noticing how pretty she was. And how much the scent of lilacs that lingered around her affected me. "I think I'm up to about sixty so far, but I've lost count. Cameron's ahead of me. At the rate we're going, I'll be a cinch to reach four thousand life birds for my list on this trip. What about you?"

"I'm seeing lots of new ones. Almost all of them are new for me," Iris said.

"Me too, Iris," Cameron said. "This antelope steak is really good. I wonder what they marinate it in? It's really tender—almost as tasty as Texas beef."

We were interrupted by loud voices at the end of the table farthest from us. Jimmy and Gabe were arguing about a sighting Gabe was claiming. The argument had become loud enough for us at the other end of the table to hear every word.

"There's no way you could tell a rufous-bellied heron from the van, especially in the light we had this afternoon," Jimmy said. His tone was sarcastic and his face contorted.

"I told you, I saw the rufous belly and the yellow beak with black tip," Gabe said. He spoke in a steady voice.

"In your imagination, Pissant."

"Believe what you want. I'm counting it. There's no other small dark African heron with those field marks."

"Agreed. But did you see them or dream them?" Jimmy said.

"I was wide awake; it was the same size as a nearby striated heron, and there was a great egret for size comparison."

"And you had such a long look. All of a few seconds."

"The van had slowed down for that rickety bridge."

Then I heard Jane and Alice interposing to settle emotions. Jane looked very unhappy, I thought.

I saw her frowning. "Jimmy, don't be such a jackass." I overheard her despite her lowering her voice.

"Gabe likes to be careful with his IDs," Alice said. "I'm sure he didn't keep quiet just to get an advantage in your competition," she added, giving Jimmy s withering stare.

"How amusing the Russos and Goforths are," said Algernon Wheatley, who had sat down across the table from us. "I really find it difficult to believe they spend so much time together."

"You don't seem to need other people, Mr. Wheatley, so perhaps you don't understand that friends can argue," Iris said. "You spend all of your time writing in that notebook of yours."

I wanted to give Iris a pat on the back to indicate a well done but contented myself with supporting her verbally. "Algernon, you remind me of someone I met on another birding tour. He had a notebook that he wrote in all the time too," I said.

"Well, is there a law against writing in a notebook, Mr. Burnbridge? To be sure, I believe in having an accurate list."

"Not many laws I know of exist for just keeping a list up to date. I think that's the purpose of the checklist we use at our nightly ritual." I thought his manner very defensive. I believed he winced a little.

The rest of the meal proceeded quietly. After everyone had finished all but the fruit, Terence Stavens stood up.

"It's time to go over the list," Sean Selkirk announced. Stavens began naming the species on the list, noting the ones we had seen or heard. The procedure went quietly until we reached herons. Terence was about to pass over rufous-bellied heron, when Gabe Goforth announced he had seen one during the drive.

"Where did you see it?" Terence raised his voice. He appeared upset.

"It was in that marsh at the last bridge we crossed," Gabe said.

"Why is this the first we've heard about your sighting?" Stavens asked in a querulous tone. "Surely you knew it's a rare bird. It's marked in bold type on the list. You should have told Sean or me at the time. We would have stopped the van and gotten out."

"I didn't want to say until I checked my field guide," Gabe said. He recounted the field marks he used to identify the heron.

"That sounds plausible. The habitat was right. From now on, when you see a new bird, tell Sean or me. We'll decide whether it warrants special attention. That applies to everyone, not only Gabe. It's better to stop too often for common birds than to miss a rare one. We probably won't have another chance at a rufous-bellied heron."

"He wanted to get a bird up on me," Jimmy said, glowering at Gabe.

"Not true," Gabe said. "I just wanted to be sure. Shucks, I wasn't aware it was rare enough to cause trouble."

"All right," Sean said, "but from now on follow Terence's rule and let us know if you blokes see anything the group hasn't encountered before."

Algernon butted in, "Yes, to be sure, we all want to see rare birds and know where to find them. It doesn't matter if you are sure or not. Our leaders can decide."

Although I agreed with Wheatley's interjection, I nudged Cameron. Using Cameron's nickname for Wheatley, I whispered, "Secretary Bird hasn't seemed this concerned about any other birds as far as I can remember."

The ritual of the list concluded without further controversy, and the group disbanded after Terence Stavens told us not to stay up too late. Breakfast would be at six. We had to choose whether to go outside or down to the show at the picture window on ground level. There was still daylight, so Cameron and I went outside again to look at the feeding stations.

As Cameron and I started down the walk to the feeding stations, a green-and-white bird about eight inches long flew across in front of us.

"Look at that bird. It lit in that tall shrub," I said.

We raised our binoculars and focused on it.

"It has a dark green back," Cameron said.

"Yeah, and a white underside with red stripes down its side. The head looks like a clown's——a green and white mask with a red ring around the eye."

Cameron thumbed through his guide to the birds of East Africa. "Look here, I believe this is it." He pointed to a picture of a diederik cuckoo. "It's handsome."

"That's the bird all right. It's good to identify some on our own. Rack up another life bird for the list."

"Do you know what nests these cuckoos parasitize? They wouldn't lay eggs in nests of very large birds."

"I don't know. We'll have to ask Terence or Sean. It's hard to find fault with a brood parasite that's so beautiful," I said.

"Especially one we've identified on our own," Cameron said, laughing and giving a thumbs-up.

Flushed with triumph, we went to the feeding stations to watch the mousebirds, robin chats, and what we now learned to be a heavily spotted groundscraper thrush. After looking it up in our bird guide, we raised our binoculars and took a good look.

When we returned to the lodge, the sun was about to set. Iris, Maude, and Jimmy were still on the skywalk. Photographing the animals at the water hole, they had put jackets on and were using flash to augment the lights of the lodge. An aroma of elephant dung came to us on the evening breeze.

"I'm not ready to go in yet. It's such a pleasant evening. I'll get a jacket and join the photographers to see what animals at the water hole look like from outside," Cameron said.

"I'm going to get a blanket and watch at the basement window." Our missions accomplished, we went separate ways.

When I got to the viewing window, I found Alice and Jane sitting on the long sofa again. They were watching, apparently entranced by the water hole cinema. They appeared comfortable, covered by dark brown army blankets. So I didn't need the one from my room.

"You ought to look at those warthogs, Jack. Only a mother could love a male warthog. Lord, what an ug-ly crit-tuh," Alice said, emphasizing her Alabama accent. "But his mother gave him that cute curly tail along with his ugly, bristled face and tusks he inherited from his father. It's pure pleasure to look at such ugliness."

"Sit down here by me," Jane said, lifting her blanket and patting the seat between her and the end of the sofa. I did as she asked and was soon engrossed in the evening animal show, especially the male warthog.

This ugly male hog seemed to be staring at us. "That face reminds me of a Japanese kabuki demon's mask," I said. "Look at those tusks. They curve like a new moon."

"But the other end is sorta cute. See how he holds up his little curly tail," Jane said.

"I believe you can find something attractive about any beast," Alice said. "Now I see how you can stay married to Jimmy. It's just pure pleasure, I guess."

"He wasn't always obsessed with that damn list. There was a time when he reveled in avian beauty and interesting behavior. His photography is a holdover from that time. Unfortunately, other features of the old Jimmy are sorta hard to find. I've begun wondering what life without the new Jimmy would be like, if I can't get the old one back."

Jane seemed to be trying hard to defend Jimmy to herself as well as to Alice. She seemed to be wrestling with how much longer she could endure the chase of the Snetsinger record.

"I know. I know," Alice said. "I wish one of them would top Phoebe Snetsinger. I wish one of them would cheat enough to win. Then we could get back to a normal life. Gabe doesn't have much time for me either."

Jane nodded. "No chance of that. I rarely spend time with Jimmy anymore unless it's on birding trips, and you can see he doesn't pay much attention to me then," Jane said. Her voice seemed sad. She smoothed her hair as if she was pushing a bad thought away.

I tried to change the subject. I pointed. "Look at that warthog wallowing in the pool. He's going to look even prettier after a mud bath," I said.

Jane paid my words no attention, but I felt her hand above my knee. "I don't think we can count on one of them cheating. They both swear by the integrity of their lists. They argue all the time about who has the 'cleanest' list. Remember that spat over the heron."

"Look over left," I said. "There's a large male lion coming in. There's a lioness with him." I felt Jane edging closer, her hand on my thigh and creeping higher. "Even the king of beasts has to drink."

"I thought lions lived in prides," Alice said, a bemused smile on her face.

"They do, but when they're mating, the mated pair leaves the pride—a sort of honeymoon," I said, trying to keep my attention on the animals. "I saw a friend's video of the actual act of mating. Talk about wham-bam-thank-you-ma'am. It's over in seconds, but it occurs often, about every fifteen minutes."

"I'm afraid you've sorta destroyed my admiration of the king of beasts," Jane said as she clasped my growing erection.

I couldn't help being aroused by her caresses, but they unnerved me. I was unsure how to deal with them. I had visions of an angry Jimmy Russo descending on me, threatening a fight, or worse. I tried to hold her hand in mine, but she resisted. She used her other hand and directed mine under her loosened shorts and into her panties while she continued to manipulate me.

I began to squirm a little as my moral compunctions caused me to wrestle with choosing between declining to engage Jane in an adulterous affair again, or giving in to my undeniable desire for her. She had refused to leave Jimmy in Argentina. Had she changed her mind?

"Let's go get a cup of coffee or tea, Jack," Jane said. "Can we get you some, Alice?"

"No thanks. I'll get some myself later."

Jane adjusted her shorts, got up, and pulled me up beside her. She led me through the darkened hall to her room.

"I don't think this is such a good idea. What if Jimmy comes back? He might do something drastic," I said. I hung back, reluctant to chance Jimmy's wrath.

Opening the door, she said, "Don't worry. He won't be back for at least an hour." She pulled me into the room.

Once inside, she turned and pressed her tongue deep in my mouth as she unbuttoned her blouse, unfastened her bra, and pressed my face to her breasts with one hand while exploring my manhood with the other. Her lavender fragrance enticed me.

"It's obvious you want me, and I truly yearn for you," she said.

"I do. You're very desirable. But Jimmy would become like a raging beast if he came back and found us here," I said. "You refused to leave him when we were in Argentina. Have you changed your mind?"

She ignored my question. "I told you he'll be away at least another hour," she said. "I want to see if you can outdo that lion." Unbuttoning her shorts and letting them fall, Jane sat on their bed as she unzipped my pants and pulled me to her.

As she continued, my best intentions not to succumb once again deserted me as her lips and my desire overwhelmed them. I found her scent of lavender and her touch stimulating. My fears of a jealous husband disappeared as a wave of lust swept over me.

*   *   *

Alice made no comment but gave us a knowing smile when we finally returned almost an hour later to the viewing window and resumed our places on the couch.

"Has anything spectacular happened while we were gone?" Jane asked.

"A hyena made a pass at a young antelope, but it got away," Alice said. "It was pure pleasure to see that impala escape."

We once again reveled in the animal show. This time I made no effort to remove Jane's hand. I remembered the passage in Dante where Paola and Francesca encounter a suggestive passage in a book and then commit adultery. We're told they read no more that day.

In view of our Argentine experience, I should have been ready for Jane's aggressiveness, but I was still afraid my desire for her might become too great to control. She still refused to leave Jimmy, and I could see no future for us. I wanted more than mere sexual gratification. I needed more.

I was sure that Jimmy would be wild with anger if he ever found out what had happened in their room, but Jane had carefully remade their bed, so the room was as it had been before our visit.

"You seem unusually quiet, Jack," Alice said.

"No, I find the animals entrancing. I'm just trying to create a poem about them in my head."

That was only half true. I was trying to create a poem.

I truly liked Jane and felt sorry for her, but I couldn't help thinking that she was using me to make herself feel appealing. She certainly *is* desirable. I couldn't deny that. Yet I was looking for more than a temporary satisfaction of the senses. But flesh is weak.

I knew she liked me, but I could not believe what she felt for me was love. In Argentina I had offered to marry her if she'd leave Jimmy. She did not want to do that. I did not want the baggage that was likely to come along with an affair between Jane and me. The price for a moment of passion might be too high. The situation kept running through my mind.

I knew Cameron was right. I should try to avoid having an affair with Jane. After all, she was a married woman with a very jealous husband just outside on the walk above the observation window.

She had already refused to leave him. I did not want to be a cuckoo fouling somebody else's nest, no matter how beautiful the tempter or how much it preened my ego to be so sought after. The poem I was creating was prompted by my guilt. Jane would not have liked what I was thinking. So I kept my thoughts to myself.

I was comparing her to Shakespeare's Angelo in *Measure for Measure*—staining his office, committing the acts the viceroy was supposed to guard against. She acted him well, thrust herself in the masculine role with such skill she suited breeches better than a man, her codpiece empty, although it seemed alive and voracious.

Did her performance seduce me? Was it the actor or the acted part that prompted my fall from grace? The epilogue, Shakespearean in its tenor, revealed her Angelo played false by both of us; my codpiece worked too well while hers proved greedily porous, eager to fill its emptiness. I had not stopped like Isabel to consider virtue, and Jane so lustily plied her fiery heat that my weakened better angels could not deny her passion. I argued with myself the rest of the evening and dreamed of my dilemma that night.

CHAPTER 10

Next morning when Jimmy and Jane appeared at breakfast, he looked grim, and her red eyes convinced me she had been crying. I detected some bruises she had tried to cover with cosmetics. I thought I knew why the abuse occurred. Jimmy suspected Jane and me. When he came back from looking at nightjars well after dark, Alice, Jane, and I were still ensconced on the sofa watching the elephants and the lions, plus some hyenas that had wandered in. We also had excellent views of Mozambique nightjars flying in and out of the lights in chase of insects drawn to the lodge's lighting.

Jimmy seemed disappointed when he came in from his hunting night birds.

Jane greeted her husband with a smile, "Jimmy, guess what, we've seen several nightjars flying close, illuminated by the floodlights."

"They flew so close we saw them really well as they banked," Alice added. "It was pure pleasure watching them flit around like huge bats."

I thought I should say something. "Did you hear any owls?"

"No, not a one. I did hear the nightjars. Perhaps you should have been outside listening," Jimmy said.

The sarcasm alerted me to the fact that Jimmy's jealousy might have moved to a new level and that I was now its specific object. I tried not to show any nervousness.

"We've had plenty to keep our attention here. Live African animals offer great entertainment—even the hyenas. But it's late. We'd better get some sleep." I stood up, threw my blanket over my shoulders and left for my room.

Now, the next morning, it seemed obvious to me that Jimmy and Jane had argued after I left. He had cause to be jealous, but he had only himself to blame. He didn't know that Jane and I had been away from the viewing area for a long time. But the knowledge that I had become the specific object of his jealousy caused me to consider my relationship with Jane even more carefully. I didn't want to be the cause of a marital breakup, especially one instigated by obnoxious Jimmy. Having undergone a divorce, I didn't wish that on anyone else. And I was sure a divorce from Jimmy would be much more difficult than mine from Susan had been. After all, if Jane had stuck with Jimmy so many years, she must love something about him, or be afraid of what he might do.

I wasn't the only one who noticed Jane's unhappy face.

Maude Buck noted Jane's sad demeanor. "Honey," she said, "you're looking down in the dumps. Didn't you enjoy the animals at the salt lick last evening? I had a ball photographing them."

"Yes, it was a great show. I guess I just didn't sleep well last night." She seemed to choose her words carefully, looking at Jimmy to see if he approved.

"Why don't you mind your own business," Jimmy butted in. "You were always in the way when I wanted to photograph those baby elephants."

"You think your pictures are the only ones that matter," Jerry Buck said, shaking his fist at Russo. "You conceited bastard. Leave Maude alone."

"Let's all calm down," Alice Goforth said, stepping between Buck and Russo. "None of us got a lot of sleep last night. The animals were too entertaining. We don't want to be late to the van. Sit down and eat breakfast. The food's good. Eating it is pure pleasure."

Grinning, Gabe Goforth bowed and waved his hand to usher the word warriors to the breakfast table.

Avoiding the fray, I found a place beside Iris Fogelman, who greeted me with a pleasant smile.

"Did you get any good photos last evening, Birdman?" I asked.

"Oh yes," Iris said, her gray eyes sparkling. "Some great still shots of the baby elephants and lots of video. Some of it's quite comical. Not just the animals, but the people too. Maude and Jimmy give Laurel and Hardy a run for their money."

"We could see a bit of the photographers' maneuvering from downstairs," I said.

"You were quite comfortable watching through the picture window, I believe," Iris said.

"Yes, comfortable and well-positioned to see lots of animals."

"Cameron told me you were keeping Alice and Jane company," Iris said. "Maybe tonight I could join you—if it wouldn't distract you," she said, smiling.

"That would be *great*," I said, putting on a little more emphasis than I had intended. I was taking Cameron's advice. He had warned me again last night to be careful in my relationship with Jane. So I sat down next to Iris, who was every bit as beautiful as Jane, and her gray eyes seemed to have depths inviting exploration.

I was pleased that Iris was showing so much interest in me, though I was embarrassed. She might be aware of Jane's pursuit of me.

As Cameron came by us with his food, he said he wasn't eating with us. "I plan to continue probing the mysterious Secretary Bird," Cameron said. "He's hiding something."

Cameron sat by Algernon Wheatley down the table from us, next to Jimmy Russo, engaging them in conversation. I guessed Cameron was going to pretend to be interested in Jimmy's stock offer.

An English breakfast of eggs, sausage, tomato, beans, toast, and tea fortified us. After breakfast, I headed for our van, taking a few bananas and other fruit for a snack. I kept close to Iris and managed to sit beside her in the van.

When everyone had boarded the van, Terence announced that we were going to backtrack for a while.

"Sean and I have been discussing Gabe's sighting of a possible rufous-bellied heron. We've decided it possibly will be worthwhile to go back there. It will take us through some territory we'd planned to explore anyway. We will have a chance to see a crowned eagle, one of the world's three monkey-eating eagles. We'll just add on a few miles to look for the heron."

I was jubilant. Even Jimmy seemed to cheer up at the announcement.

"I wonder if our leaders have ever seen this bird," Cameron said to Iris and me.

Iris examined her camera. "It must be truly rare. They seem unusually interested in it. I'm going to be ready for photos," she said as she worked with her photographic equipment.

"Apparently—and a crowned eagle would be even better as far as I'm concerned," I said.

After we started, Iris showed Cameron and me a picture she had taken of a bird earlier in the morning outside the lodge.

"This little bird is a rather drab green above and gray below. But it's cute. Its tail is so small it doesn't appear to have one at first glance. Does either of you have an idea of what it is?"

We looked and laughed. "That's a green crombec. Cameron and I saw one yesterday. They don't have much of a tail. That's a fact," I said.

"That's a tale of no tail," Cameron added, still laughing.

Overhearing, Algernon Wheatley asked for a look at the photograph. "To be sure, it certainly doesn't have much tail. You say you took that just outside the lodge? Are you sure?"

"Yes, early this morning."

The Secretary Bird began writing in his notebook as Cameron and I exchanged knowing glances, and he winked at me.

"Do you mean you haven't seen a crombec yet, Mr. Wheatley?" Cameron asked. "Apparently they're fairly common around the lodge."

"No, I have not. But I expect to see one today. Mr. Selkirk assures me they are quite common."

"I want to see an African paradise flycatcher," Iris said. "Sean told me we're likely to see one this morning. He says they're beauties. Look at it in the field guide. It varies a lot, but it has a willowy look with that long, long tail. The common plumage has a bright auburn back and tail set against a dark, crested head."

"Birds in the field always look better than the ones in the book. An artist can only do so much in catching natural beauty," I said. "Besides, birds have so many plumage variations, and field guides can't show all of them."

The van moved slowly down the track toward the spot where we hoped to see Gabe's rare heron. The sun was climbing, and the heavily wooded landscape on both sides was bathed in sunlight. After several miles, we stopped at an area where forest gave way to grassland mixed with scattered brush on both sides of the road. Outside, Terence ushered us away from the van and drew our attention to a large bird about half again larger than American jays, while Sean fixed a scope on it. As splendid as this crested yellow bird with black and red splotches was in my binoculars, the scope view, when I got to it after waiting patiently in line, was even more dazzling.

"Everybody should try to look at this splendid crested barbet through the scope, so practice scope etiquette. Take a look, and then let someone else have a turn and go to the back of the line if you want a second look," Sean said.

Luckily, the bird remained still, and everyone had at least two scope views, although some people lingered a little longer at the scope than Jimmy liked, and he muttered a bit.

"You pushed to the front to get your view first," Gabe said, "so don't complain."

"It's truly a beautiful bird," Iris said as she attached a big lens to her camera, placed it on a monopod, and pressed off some shots.

We had hardly finished savoring the barbet when Sean called our attention to what he said was a yellow-fronted tinkerbird, a small bird the size of a house sparrow. "Look for the yellow patch on the front of this bird's head. Tinkerbirds are kin to woodpeckers. Look at that heavy beak. They get their name from their repeated metallic *tink* call."

As we watched the white-and-black-striped tinkerbird, another bird flew out from a high bush to catch an insect. Its long-flowing reddish tail stood out in its graceful flight as the flycatcher returned to its perch high in a large flowering bush. "Look. A paradise flycatcher," Iris said.

Urging not needed—it was the first look at this beauty for many of the group. I remembered it from my first trip to Africa. Its auburn back and tail stood out from the green foliage and complemented the red blooms of the bush. I looked at Iris's auburn hair and willowy figure and decided Iris's bird name should be paradise flycatcher.

Loud voices suddenly ripped through, disturbing our delight at watching the flycatcher.

"Get out of my way, you pissant woman," Jimmy said.

"Your way is the road to hell, you self-centered listing nut," Maude Buck said. "You have no appreciation of the beauty surrounding us, praise the Lord."

"How can I appreciate the beauty when you're always putting your sanctimonious ass between me and it?" Jimmy said, his voice rising to a crescendo.

Jerry Buck stepped between Maude and Jimmy. "Get control of yourself and stop calling Maude names, or I'll shut your foul mouth for you," Jerry said.

Carrying what appeared to be a small monkey clasped in its talons, a large hawk that had been silently perched on the edge of the forest close to us rose from its perch, apparently disturbed by the loud noise created by Jimmy and Maude.

Pointing, Sean immediately directed us to the large bird. "Pipe down, you jackasses. Raise your binoculars and watch this hawk. Don't miss this bird! It's a crowned eagle, one of the world's only three monkey-eating hawks. If we're lucky, it will just take its prey away from the noise, and I can put the scope on it, but you blokes try to get a decent binocular view."

CHAPTER 11

We were very lucky. The eagle did not fly much more than a hundred yards before it lit again and returned to eating its prey.

"Oh, let me look first, Sean." Alice rushed to the scope with Jimmy hurrying behind her. "Be nice to an Alabama girl."

Jimmy had to settle for second. "It's a huge adult," he said. "Look at those tremendous claws. I'll bet that monkey didn't know what hit it."

Ignoring Terence's rule, Maude photographed the bloody feast. "Please, a little compassion for the monkey."

Scope views for all followed, and then many cameras were put into action until everyone was satiated with eagle-eating-monkey views and photographs.

"If we find the rufous-bellied heron, it will be an anticlimax," Cameron said.

"You're right," Iris said, "but I for one never tire of seeing beautiful birds, and if I did, I'd still want more photographs, because you never get the perfect picture." She moved her camera to get a better view of the eagle. "Sometimes beauty can be bloody."

"You can see the blood dripping from the monkey," I said. "You are catching nature red in tooth and claw."

"It's time to load up. We've just a few more miles to where the heron was spotted," Terence said when everyone had a fill of eagle photography. "We'll go take a look and then head back to the lodge for lunch."

A jubilant, noisy crew boarded the bus to continue the safari. Wheatley attempted to write in his notebook despite the bumpy ride, while Cameron tried to sneak a look at what was being written. He was sitting up in his seat and using his binoculars. After a few minutes, even though Algernon was hunched over his notebook, Cameron apparently had seen enough. He turned to me, nodding his head.

"I have something to tell you later," he said.

I was looking at some of the photos Iris had taken of the birds we had just seen. "These photos are wonderful," I told her. "You could be a professional photographer. You could sell these."

"It's not my major source of income, but it does help pay for my birding trips. It's just a sideline, a way of making my hobby profitable," Iris said. She seemed pleased with her morning's work. "Now, if I can get a good picture of a rufous-bellied heron, that would crown this morning's photography."

I'll admit that my interest in Iris had been largely spurred by my attraction to her physical beauty and witty conversation, but now I was becoming attracted to her artistry with the camera. Besides being excellent realistic renditions of her subjects, her photographs often had an undeniable artistic flair. She had captured the essence of the flycatcher's gracefulness and the fierceness of the eagle.

"What is your major source of income, then, if photography is just a lucrative hobby?" I couldn't help prying. I wanted to find out as much about her as I could.

"I'll tell you later if you promise not to tell anyone. After supper tonight, if you'd like," Iris whispered to me.

"I promise. I couldn't think of a better nightcap."

She laughed. "Even better than looking at the animal parade?"

I guess I must have blushed or looked a bit foolish. *Lord, to think this beautiful, intelligent, accomplished, vivacious young woman is interested in middle-aged Jack Burnbridge.* It was a heady thought. I felt like I'd just had a shot of tequila.

My world view improved considerably. My weak resistance to the dangerous advances of Jane Russo had put on a new set of armor. I gazed at the magnificent scenery and discussed it with Iris and Cameron. In glowing terms, I described the breath-taking views of the valleys we passed, the shadows playing in the valleys as the clouds played hide and seek with the sun. Buoyed by hope of success in love as well as success in listing, I knew my list now had a rival other than Jane for my attention.

When we finally reached the bridge, Terence told us all to wait while he and Sean scouted the area. If they found the heron, Sean would come back for us and the scope.

Jimmy rebelled. "Why do we need to wait? So you can flush the bird?"

Maude was first to respond. "When did you become the expert on finding African birds?"

Jimmy quieted at the hissing and nasty comments from the rest of us, who were willing to place our trust in Stavens and Selkirk. It was not misplaced. Sean returned in about fifteen minutes. Taking the scope, he told us to follow him slowly and quietly.

"We have found the heron and, if it doesn't flush, everyone will have a scope view, while everyone else waiting will have excellent binocular views. Please don't make any unnecessary noise or movements."

We followed Sean like children following the pied piper, only slowly and quietly. When we reached Terence, he motioned with his hand for us to crouch down behind him. Then Sean set up the scope so that we could kneel and look at the heron. One by one, we crawled to the scope on our hands and knees and took a look. At my turn, I savored the red belly and the yellow bill with the black tip and the size of the bird in comparison to a nearby little egret. *Yeah!* I whispered to myself. After everybody who wanted a second look had taken one, Terence allowed photography.

"Take pictures now," he whispered.

The heron squawked when bothered by a little egret, but it remained in view for us. Only after everyone who wanted pictures had taken them, Terence made upward hand motions for us to stand up. Then he whispered to us to leave quietly, the bird still undisturbed.

A happy group boarded the bus and headed back to the lodge for lunch. Many people were sharing pictures. "These heron pictures should be in great demand," Iris said. I can't remember a photographer's hawking any. This was truly a golden morning of birding."

"I wonder what goodies the afternoon safari will offer us?" I said. "Right now, I'm ready for lunch. I have two bananas left. Would you like one of them, Iris?"

"What about Cameron?"

"I have one of my own, thanks," Cameron said.

"Okay, thanks, I'll take one," Iris said, holding out her hand. I felt like a tern feeding a fish to his lady.

So we munched on our fruit as we rode. Terence did not allow any more stops. I had just time to stow my gear in the room before heading to lunch at one o'clock.

The aromas assaulted my hunger as I reached the dining area. The smell of steak whetted my already considerable appetite. Our table was loaded with platters of antelope steaks and gravy, baked fish, palm hearts, greens, and fruits: pineapple, papaya, and grapes. After everyone had eaten a bit, Terence rose and outlined the plan for the afternoon.

"We'll have a long siesta that you can use for resting, for watching animals at the lick, or for birding around the lodge. At four o'clock we'll go out on the bus again to a different area for a couple of hours, then back in time for a shower before the evening meal. Then you can spend another evening monitoring the salt lick, or however you please."

I wouldn't watch the panorama at the window again unless Iris was with me. Remembering her lilac scent and lyrical voice, I resolved to give my relationship with my paradise flycatcher every chance I could. I would be an insect, eager to be caught.

CHAPTER 12

Cameron waited until we were alone. "I saw Secretary Bird writing something interesting when I was sneaking a look at his notebook. I saw the name Crumley and Focus together. It looks like you were right about our friend Algernon, or whatever his name is."

"I think maybe it's time to tell Terence about our suspicions."

"I agree, but right now I'm taking a nap," Cameron said.

So I hunted for Iris to ask about her secret and to see if she would like to watch the salt lick spectacle with me now. I found her when I saw auburn hair above the couch in front of the big window. She was already watching the animal theater. I made sure it was her and not Jane before I said anything. She was sipping what appeared to be lemonade.

"Would you let me join you? It seems the animal show is still good in the heat of the day."

"Sit down." She patted the sofa beside her. "The show's great, but I could use some company. We seem to be the only ones not taking advantage of the siesta to nap."

I moved to her side, elated to be bathing in the faint aroma of lilac. As I sat down, a small group of impalas edged carefully toward the water, a male and two does with young.

"Those impalas are using the elephants as a shield against predators as they drink," Iris said.

I smiled as I nodded agreement. "If you're at the top of every predator's dining list, you can't be too careful."

Just then, before I could ask Iris about her secret, Algernon Wheatley came to the viewing area and sat on the other end of the couch. Without saying anything, he began writing in his notebook.

"Are you interested in the mammals as well as the birds, Mr. Wheatley?" Iris asked.

"Yes, of course. How could anyone not be awed by this spectacular animal theater. And to be sure it is amazing how easily we see them."

Iris nodded. "It's a window on the private lives of mammals."

Jealous of Algernon's attention to Iris, I showed off. "There are birds too," I said. "Look at those starlings. There are cape glossy starlings as well as more superb starlings. And the doves—there are at least four species of doves and pigeons coming to get a drink, I've counted laughing doves, red-eyed doves, speckled pigeons, and Delegorgue's pigeon," I said. "It's the beauty with the violet body, gray head, and white neck collar. You have my permission to write that in your notebook." Satisfied I had showed enough expertise to impress Iris, I closed my bird guide I had hidden but open by my side.

"Thanks. To be sure, I will." Algernon smiled.

"I use my photos to recall my trips," Iris said. "I guess you have your notes."

"To be sure, they help bring back the moments," Wheatley said.

"Have you ever heard of an outfit named Focus on Flight?" I asked.

"No. Why should I?" He looked surprised. He stopped writing.

"It advertises a lot. Thought you might have heard of it—run by a guy named Jake Crumley. Some friends of mine have taken some tours with him."

Iris turned to watch us instead of the animals, evidently curious about my questions.

"Never heard of the man." Wheatley rose from his seat abruptly and closed his notebook. "I'm still a little hungry. I think I'll go see if I can find something else to eat." He rushed off.

Laughing to myself, I watched him depart. *We've got you now, Algernon*, I thought. Then I became aware of Iris looking at me in a quizzical manner.

"What was that about, Jack? Why are you smiling? Wheatley lit out as if you'd turned a hive of hornets onto him."

"You asked me to keep a secret that I haven't heard yet. Can you promise to keep a secret too?"

"Of course I can. I'll tell you my secret tonight. Then you can tell me yours. Come to my room after dinner." She was looking at me intently. "Can you tear yourself away from the animal show?"

How lyrical her voice seemed. I gazed into the gray eyes of Iris but felt like I was gazing into Aphrodite's.

"I'll be there." My joy made sitting still difficult, so I suggested that we go for a walk outside. I didn't want any more interruptions to my moments basking in the gaze of the goddess.

"Get your camera. Let's see what birds we can find at the feeders for you to photograph," I said.

As we walked to Iris's room, I could hardly contain my enthusiasm. She went in while I waited at the door. Camera in hand, Iris hiked with me to the feeding stations as I described the speckled mousebirds. "They are strange-looking creatures. You'll enjoy their antics, and they'll be good photographic subjects."

Once Iris saw the mousebirds scrambling over the feeders, she agreed. She began snapping shots from many angles.

"You were right. They're so cute. Except for their heads, they don't have much color, but they crawl around as if they're feathered mice. I may not be able to stop photographing them. The other birds aren't bad either, and those ground squirrels are posing. These feeding stations are great for photography."

Iris kept her camera and camcorder active almost until time for the afternoon safari. Best of all, I had her to myself.

"I'm so glad you suggested our afternoon hike," Iris said as we headed back to join the safari. She was radiant, obviously pleased. She put her camera in her bag and took my hand.

The afternoon foray concentrated on smaller birds than we'd seen in the morning—tail-challenged crombecs and other small warbler-like birds that hide in the bushes. What I call small UFOs.

Terence and Sean called the most common small birds cis-ti-co-las and said there are over a hundred species of them in the world, mainly in Africa and Asia. Our leaders pointed out rattling cisticolas and singing cisticolas. Both are little perky brown birds the size of American house wrens.

"These birds aren't much to look at, but they certainly have character," Iris said as she used her camcorder to catch their movements and sounds.

We did see some colorful birds. We had excellent views of a cardinal woodpecker with a red cap and black mustache and a large black-collared barbet, whose red head and huge bill provided Iris some spectacular photographs. Before we returned to the lodge, she showed me her barbet pictures.

"That barbet is one of the strange beauties that cause us to marvel at nature's variety," Iris said. "I'm still thinking about those mousebirds. I'm so glad you suggested our afternoon hike." She smiled at me and threw me a kiss as we parted before supper.

The evening ritual of the list was a happy affair because of the day's successes. It concluded with a tasty fish dinner, a huge local catfish that tasted like trout. Terence ended the meal with instructions.

"Don't spend too late watching the animals at the water hole tonight. We leave tomorrow morning for Samburu, where we'll be in a much dryer environment. We won't be making many stops for birds; our plan is to have lunch at the Samburu lodge."

As we left, I told Cameron about my talk with Algernon. "I guess we should tell Terence, but let's wait until we reach Samburu. No need to break bad news on such a successful day."

"Okay, Casanova, I'm going to watch the animal parade at the window tonight. Are you coming?" Cameron asked.

"No. I've an appointment. I'll see you later." I hurried off. I didn't want anyone, even Cameron, to know I was going to meet Iris. I noticed again that he had begun calling me Casanova. I decided I could live with his humor. After all, I had been called worse, and my interest in Iris was undeniable.

I hurried down to Iris's room and looked around to make sure no one else was around. Nobody appeared, so I knocked.

"Jack?"

"Yes."

"Come in; the door's open." I went in. Iris was lying on her bed clad in a bathrobe, viewing pictures in her SLR camera with lenses detached. A scent of lilacs permeated the room. She looked up and smiled.

CHAPTER 13

Iris's room was bare with metal furniture like mine and Cameron's, but the lilac aroma, the lingerie hanging on the closet door, and the nightgown hanging on the bathroom door gave it a seductive touch.

"Sit down beside me." She patted the bed and pulled my hand as I took my place beside her. Her touch thrilled me. "I'm glad you gave up the animal theater to be with me." Her voice reminded me of violins playing a Mozart sonata.

"I've grown quite fond of you. I've decided you're a paradise flycatcher, and I'm a fly eager to be caught."

"If that's true, then why don't you show it? Kiss me." As she spoke, she pulled me to her and kissed me.

"I think I caught my prey," she said, teasing. "Now, Jack, you first." Her eyes twinkled. "What's your big secret?"

"Cameron and I have been suspicious of Algernon Wheatley. We think he's a spy for a tour group named Focus on Flight run by Jake Crumley. Today Cameron saw the names Crumley and Focus in Wheatley's notebook, yet you heard Algernon say he knew nothing of either one."

"I remember his saying that. He was upset by your questions."

"Now it's your turn. What's your secret?"

"Not as mysterious as yours. I manage a mutual stock fund, a value fund. I don't want anybody else to know, especially Jimmy Russo. He's been hounding me to invest with him. I'm afraid I might have trouble with him if he thought of me as a competitor. He's pushy, and he comes on to me too."

"You don't look old enough to be a fund manager. Your secret's safe with me. You must be a financial whiz to be managing a fund already. I pulled her to me and kissed her long and deep, savoring the taste, yellow delicious apples covered in honey. When I let her go, she was beaming.

"What an amorous fly I've caught. It's great to be rewarded with such enthusiasm. I've been wanting a kiss like that."

"So have I. I've longed to kiss you, though I'm in awe of your beauty and brains. I didn't think you'd find me attractive."

"That's hard to believe with a beauty like Jane panting for you. And I'll bet there are ladies back in your Virginia college town who have set their caps for an eligible guy like you."

"I have been reluctant to form any deep attachments since Susan divorced me. I still have wounds. I want what Shakespeare called a true love without impediments. I won't settle for less."

"You're a romantic. I like that."

"Romantic or not, I find you very desirable."

"I want to encourage those thoughts." She reached over and pulled my face down to hers for another passionate kiss.

"Here, put my camera over on the desk," Iris said as she handed it to me. When I had done that, she told me to sit down beside her again. I was soon next to her. "Now hold me," she said.

"Before I do, I have a question."

"What?"

"You're not married, are you?"

Iris broke out laughing. It was like the sound of tinkling bells. "No. Kiss me again."

I was happy to oblige. I reveled in the sweetness of her taste.

"How old are you, Jack?"

"Forty-two. What about you?"

"Twenty-seven. Age is a relative thing. You seem like you're young at heart. What's your favorite music?"

"I prefer classical music. I'm fairly conservative."

"So am I. I love Vivaldi. I'm especially conservative with other people's money. In college I majored in finance with a minor in English.

After graduation I continued to an MBA and then to Wall Street. I worked my way up to my current position heading a value stock fund."

"You must be a financial genius."

"Maybe, but I wish you'd kiss me again."

It was pleasant fulfilling her wish, so pleasant that I kept doing it a long time.

"I love your fragrance. I think of lilacs when I'm with you," I said. "You must have men lined up trying to date you." I couldn't take my eyes off of her. What I could see was delectable. Catching fleeting views of her allowed by her robe, I imagined the rest of her was equally enchanting.

"I do some casual dating, nothing serious. I didn't want to tie myself to somebody else's star. I was involved in one serious affair, but it turned out badly. I am determined to be more careful from now on. Working hard, I've made it to the top but haven't found many men in finance who've interested me. The eligible ones have been bloodless number crunchers."

Iris encouraged me, opening my shirt and kissing my chest. I opened her robe and began kissing her breasts, running my tongue around her nipples.

"Umm ... slow down. That feels good, but I don't want to be just another of your conquests," she said. "What would Jane say?"

I was taken aback, but told the truth. "Jane and I became friends during a birding trip to Argentina, while Jimmy was out chasing birds. She and I hit it off and enjoyed some pleasant moments, but she was determined to stay with Jimmy. Jane says she's opposed to divorce."

Admitting my earlier affair with Jane was the hard part. I stopped to see how Iris felt.

"So you believed that she'd leave him if she really loved you?"

"Yes. I didn't want an affair. I wanted love. She may be having second thoughts now. She seems to want to take up where we left off in Argentina. She is desirable. I admit to being torn between desire for her and a wish to avoid becoming entangled in a brawl with somebody as unpleasant as Jimmy. I'm not in love with her now, but my body hasn't followed directions very well."

"Would you end the relationship if I asked you to?"

"I find you ravishing. I'll end the relationship tonight, if you wish."

"I find you very attractive, Jack Burnbridge. I think I could fall in love with you, but if I do, I want you all to myself." She kissed me forcefully, and the urge to please her overwhelmed me.

I looked intently into her gray eyes. I felt they were enveloping me. "I'll end my affair with Jane tonight."

She pointed toward the door. "You'd better lock the door just to be on the safe side. I'm not expecting anybody else, but who knows what Jane might do. She might come looking for you. She's obviously on the prowl. I can see the way she looks at you. If Jimmy wasn't so obsessed with his list, he'd see it too."

After I locked the door, she kissed me deeply again. She ran her fingers over me. We spent hours kissing and petting, but Iris halted me many times. Whenever she felt I was taking too many liberties, she admonished me as if I were some callow schoolboy. "Slow down. Be patient. You must prove you can be faithful," she said as she caressed my entire body.

It must have been ten o'clock when I joined Cameron at the viewing window. He was enjoying elephants and a wart hog. Hyenas were just coming out of the brush and heading toward the water.

"Are you having fun watching the mammal parade?" I said.

"If I'd known how amusing and comfortable it is on this couch, I'd have been here last night," Cameron said. "I like the elephants best."

Alice and Jane were watching the animals also. "Come and sit down with us, Jack," Jane said. "Here by me. Jimmy and Gabe are out looking for night birds."

"Thanks. I appreciate the offer, but it's been a long day. I won't stay but a few minutes." I sat down beside Jane, as far from the others as I could.

"I've missed you," she said, softly.

"I've made a decision. We've talked and talked about our relationship. You won't leave Jimmy. There's no future for us. I'm moving on." I spoke in a low tone to avoid being overheard.

Jane frowned. "I don't believe you."

"I mean it."

I stayed for a quarter of an hour to enjoy the animals. When I felt Jane's leg rubbing mine, I eased away from her. I was pleased at my being able to avoid temptation. After watching the elephants bathing their babies for a while longer, I rose and stretched. "I'm heading to bed," I said.

Jane looked disappointed. "I'll be here if you change your mind," she said.

Cameron looked surprised. "I'll stay here another half hour or so and keep Alice and Jane company, and then I'll be along. I'll try not to wake you," he said.

"By that time I should be sound asleep."

I went to our room feeling better about controlling my relationship with Jane. I resolved to avoid her whenever possible for the remainder of the tour.

Though I was in a state of frustrated arousal when I left Iris, she had intoxicated me with desire for her. Iris was the epitome of the liberated woman. My passion for her had eclipsed my attraction to Jane, although I suspected my body might make my decision to avoid Jane and win Iris difficult to enforce. Whenever scenes of my former encounters with Jane flashed across my mind, my body responded in a way my brain had decided not to pursue. Now, however, these flashes were pushed aside by pictures of what lovemaking with Iris might eventually be like.

I remembered the words from Robert Graves's poem "Down, Wanton, Down!": "Indifferent what you storm or why,/So be that in the breach you die!" It had applied to my relationship with Jane. I first encountered that poem as an undergraduate with raging hormones.

At the time, I thought this was just a problem for youth, but now I know the wanton can rise in beauty's name even for middle-aged men and refuse to be shamed into retreat by orders from the brain. I wanted more than what satisfies the wanton and thought that I might find it with Iris. In the meantime, I had to induce sleep using my own devices.

CHAPTER 14

For me, the drive to Samburu was uneventful. I was still tired. I spent almost all of the time dozing off, even though Iris was sitting beside me. When we arrived at the entrance to Samburu, she nudged me.

"Wake up, Jack, we're here. This isn't a well-watered place like the Abedarres.

I yawned and stretched, looking out the window. "We're in a very dry environment. Acacias and thornbushes cover the land. I think I smell animal spoor."

"It looks like a great place for photography."

Just then a flock of helmeted guineafowl ran across the road in front of the van. "Here's the welcoming committee," Sean called out. "Look to your left before they disappear into the brush."

"Hey, they're a lot like the ones we had in our chicken pen back home in Texas when I was a kid," Cameron said.

Jane and Jimmy Russo were sitting behind us, across from Cameron. Russo curled his lip in a sneer. "You have everything in Texas, evidently," he said.

"Yes, just about everything worth having," Cameron said. "Do you have any in New Jersey?"

"I couldn't say. I don't bird in barnyards," Jimmy said.

"We'll get our room assignments, stow our gear, and come back to the outdoor hearth for lunch," Sean said as the bus stopped in front of Samburu's headquarters. "The Samburu men put on a good show. You can take it in after you eat."

"We'll have an afternoon safari leaving from the main lodge at 4:00 p.m.," Terence said. "If you want to go, be on time. Until then you'll be on your own."

Cameron and I checked out our room and then headed to lunch.

"I certainly could use a Tusker," Cameron said.

"Me too. I'm planning to go to see the Samburu dancers. Sean says it's something we shouldn't miss. Are you interested? I've asked Iris to go with me too."

"Sure, I'd like to go. By the way, you seem to be spending a lot of time with Iris. Not that I feel neglected. I'm relieved to see you resisting your urge to fill empty space in Jane's life. That's dangerous territory to be riding through."

"I don't know where my friendship with Iris will lead, but I know I feel more drawn to her than I have to any woman since Susan. She's going to brighten our lunch. Not that I find you're dull company."

Cameron grinned and gave me a thumbs-up. "No, I agree. She's pleasant to have around."

As we crossed a stream, I noticed a kingfisher in a thorn tree. We stopped and had a close look.

"This stream doesn't seem big enough to hold many fish," Cameron said.

"That's something you have to get used to in Africa. Over half the kingfishers haunt the brush country, search for insects, and don't fish at all. Maybe this is one of those. Let's check the guide."

Turning the pages of the guide, Cameron pointed to the depiction of the gray-hooded kingfisher. "You were right. It says here it's a nonaquatic kingfisher of broad-leafed woodland and savannah. It's a pretty thing. Those blue wings and tail and a pink lower breast stand out. And that huge pink bill is really striking."

When we reached the verandah where lunch was being served, Iris had already found a table for us. Ordering a round of Tuskers, we headed to the buffet table and then to the huge round open-air fireplace where meats of various kinds were being barbecued. I chose some crocodile and antelope and some cooked vegetables. The aromas from the cooking whetted our appetites. We filled our plates. It wasn't long before we were enjoying a really tasty African lunch. I ordered a second round of beer.

"The tart but fruity taste of this beer is really refreshing," Iris said when we began to eat. "I prefer it to soft drinks."

As he lifted his Tusker, Cameron saluted Iris. "Yes, it's really good. Tuskers are one of my favorite things about Kenya," Cameron said. "Jack tells me that some of your photographs are excellent and that you often sell them."

Iris gave Cameron a radiant smile. "It's how I finance my birding trips," Iris said.

"That must give you a great deal of pleasure—creating so much beauty," Cameron said. "You should come to Texas and photograph our birds."

"I have. I will again. Looking back over my pictures, I live the trips all over again," Iris said.

"I see Alice Goforth and Jane Russo over there looking for a table. Mind if I offer to share ours?" Cameron said.

"Certainly, go ahead," Iris said, grinning at me. She leaned over to me and whispered, "It's not a test. Don't worry."

I didn't agree but kept silent. I worried that it would be a test I couldn't pass. I stood and helped Jane with a chair next to mine on the side opposite from Iris.

"You should sample the crocodile. It's really tasty, almost like chicken," Iris told her. "It'll melt in your mouth."

"It's like our Texas alligators, just a little drier," Cameron said.

"Are you going to see the Samburu dancers? Cameron and Jack have invited me to go with them," Iris said.

"I'd love to tag along, if you don't mind," Jane said. "We've heard they're really great. We have plenty of time. Gabe and Jimmy are out chasing life birds as usual. Sometimes I'd like to get rid of this whole Snetsinger contest."

I felt Jane's bare leg rubbing against mine. I reconsidered the wisdom of wearing short pants to beat the afternoon heat. I was responding despite my best intentions. Lifting my beer, I tried to ignore her overture. "I hear the dancers can leap off the ground higher than an NBA basketball player attempting to dunk," I said.

"This country is certainly different from the Abedarres. It's like going from Carolina to West Texas in one morning," Iris said. "We should have wonderful opportunities for photography here."

"How is the Snetsinger competition going? Who's ahead?" Cameron asked Alice.

"They are both close to seven thousand now. They're neck and neck. I think Jimmy is a few birds ahead," Alice said.

"That's a mind-boggling number, way over half the world's recognized species," Cameron said.

"I hope Maude and Jimmy don't get in each other's way," Jane said. "Maude seems to antagonize him."

Nobody ventured a rejoinder, though I am sure I was not the only one thinking that Jimmy did his share of antagonizing people.

Jane's efforts under the table were causing me to react despite my attempt to ignore her flesh. I became acutely aware that I had not completely conquered my attraction to her. My inability to control my body really bothered me. There Iris sat, beautiful and vivacious as ever. And I was falling in love with her. Still, no man is in complete control of his sexual responses. I was pleased that we would soon leave to watch the dancers.

Cameron came to my rescue. "I think we should leave now so that we can be seated and ready for the performance." He rose.

Punctuating his seriousness, and relieved, I jumped up, hiding my erection with my safari hat. "You're right. Let's go. We don't want to miss their entrance. Sean said it's a highlight." Moving off a little, I waited for the others.

Walking toward the dancing space, I saw the gray-hooded kingfisher again and pointed it out to the group.

"If that beauty stays around, I want to photograph it after we watch the dancers," Iris said.

At the dancing area, we found seating covered from the sun was available, so we all took places there, looking out on the dancing arena of smoothed, packed white sand.

"There are other things than birds to be enjoyed on birding tours," Iris said. Taking out her camera with a small lens attached, she readied to photograph the dancers.

"It doesn't seem natural to see you photographing without your big lens," I said.

Iris laughed. "These birds are way too big. And they'll be active. I need a fast lens. I'll use video too," she said, pulling out her camcorder.

Soon everyone had a camera out. Just in time. I heard rhythmic chants heading closer and closer to the dancing place. Then dancers outfitted in red garb and holding traditional weapons leaped into our presence, chanting. The leaping ability of the warriors carrying their spears was incredible. Any basketball coach would be pleased to recruit a team that could jump like these dancers. During the whole performance of mock battle movements, Iris busily photographed. I watched in amazement.

"You could almost believe they can leap tall buildings with a single bound, like Superman," Iris said.

Cameron clapped his approval. "I know a track coach in Texas who would love to have these guys to do the high jump."

"So would a ballet master," Iris said.

After the performance, I walked with Iris back to find the gray-hooded kingfisher for her to photograph. Luckily the bird was hunting in about the same place. She pulled out her telephoto lens and took several photos.

Finished, Iris took my hand. "Come on, let's go back to my room. I want to change before we go on the safari."

We didn't have far to walk. Inside, the faint aroma of lilacs permeated the room. Iris brought out cups and a small bottle of bourbon, then reached in her suitcase and pulled out a bottle of water.

"Pour a couple of weak drinks while I change."

She disappeared into the bathroom and in a few minutes emerged in khaki slacks and a long-sleeved khaki blouse. A broad-brimmed hat completed her safari outfit. She took a sip of her drink and gave me a kiss, slipping her wet tongue deep into my mouth, treating me to the taste to which I had grown addicted.

"I've been wanting to do that all day," she said when she finally drew back.

"Me too." I pulled her to me and returned her kiss to taste honeyed apples again.

"We'd better go now," Iris said when we broke apart. "We have just enough time to catch the safari vehicle."

I knew I had to avoid Jane. Losing Iris would be too much to bear.

CHAPTER 15

Maude and Jerry Buck, loaded with camera equipment, were standing in the front of the open platform on the safari vehicle. It was a large flatbed truck with the bed widened and the sides altered slightly to form a platform with a waist-high enclosure of metal bars to accommodate standing tourists. Algernon Wheatley, the Goforths, and the Russos filled much of the space toward the front of this viewing platform. Cameron arrived about the same time that Iris and I did. He found a place on the left front and Sean took the right front. Iris and I found places along the sides of the platform. Terence sat in the cab with the driver to give directions.

"We can see just as well from here," Iris said, "but it's harder to hold on when we hit bumps."

"It's like finding your sea legs on a boat," I said as we hit our first big bump.

Our truck moved through thornbush onto grassland past herds of African buffalo, giraffes, impalas, Thomson's gazelles (or tommies), and smaller antelopes called dik-diks. We stopped when we spied a strange antelope standing on its hind legs and stretching its long neck to nibble on the top shoots of a bush so high it could still barely reach it. "That's a gerenuk," Sean said. "Giraffes probably started that way and kept stretching."

"I wonder how long it will take." Iris focused her SLR. Cameras began to click on all sides.

I contemplated the eons involved. "Too long for any of us to see it happen."

Our vehicle moved on through thornbush, scattered palms, and grassland. Sean pointed out a huge, long-legged brown and white bird with gray neck and head stalking slowly through the grass.

"There goes a handsome kori bustard, the largest flighted bird, or at least it vies for the title with the ugly marabou stork. It all depends on your definition of *largest*. Marabous are taller, but koris are heavier."

"It's really large."

"Yes, a large male. Males stand almost as high as four feet and weigh as much as forty-four pounds. Their wingspan can reach nine feet."

"It certainly is handsome," Iris said as she snapped a series of pictures of the bustard. "I vote for it. Marabous are megaugly. This bird has a regal bearing, as if it knows how noble it is. Look at that black cap and white head and neck set off against its dark tan back. It is so photogenic."

"Can we get closer?" Maude said. "I would like to see it fly and get a shot of the world's largest flying bird in action."

All the photographers agreed with Maude. Filming the world's largest flighted bird actually flying seemed very appealing.

Sean gave us ample warning. "All right, but we won't flush the bird more than once, so you camera people must be ready for the first flight, because I'm not going to bother it again. I don't believe in putting undue pressure on the wildlife. Neither does Terence."

I turned to Iris. "Are you ready?"

She planted her feet firmly. "I am. I'm not letting Maude outdo me."

After a brief chase, the Kori took off and flew about a hundred yards, providing ample opportunities for pictures from cheering photographers.

"Did you get any good pictures?" I asked. Iris nodded.

"Here, look at this." She held up her camera's viewing screen for me to see as she showed several frames of the bustard.

"Congratulations. You really are good."

Iris whispered her reply. "I hope you feel that way about more than my photography."

"Look over to the left," Sean said, pointing. "You'll see several yellow-throated longclaws. They'll remind you Yanks of meadowlarks.

Beautiful birds with their yellow breasts with black *V*s across their chests. The two species not only look alike, they sound alike too. It's a prime example of what's called convergent evolution. Longclaws and meadowlarks are from very different groups of birds yet have evolved to be similar because they live in similar habitats.

While Sean was telling us about longclaws, Iris was busy using her camera to record them. "Yippee. They look just like skinny meadowlarks," Iris said "I got great pictures."

Scanning with my binoculars, I spied something at a distant clump of palms and acacias.

"Sean, would you ask Terence if we could go over to those palms. There's a bird in a tree, and I see some animals on the ground."

Sean beat on the truck cab. When Terence stuck his head out, Sean pointed to the grove of trees. When we moved closer, we saw that the bird in the acacia was a pygmy falcon, one of the world's smallest falcons, two centimeters shorter than a common starling. It was eating a grasshopper. The mammals turned out to be a small troop of olive baboons, including several mothers with youngsters. The head male was busy trying to produce another baby with one of the other females.

Jimmy laughed and waved. "Maude, here is your chance to get some X-rated baboon video. I have my pictures. You can take my place." I could not imagine why Jimmy was so obliging.

"I'm busy with the pygmy falcon, praise the Lord, but thank you," Maude said.

"I hope you're less squeamish, Iris," Jimmy said.

Iris laughed derisively. "Oh, I'm way ahead of you, Jimmy. I try not to miss opportunities to capture animal behavior, especially the behavior of our primate relatives. We can learn a lot about ourselves watching them. I already have all the video and stills I need."

Pointing at the baboon, Jimmy persisted. "Does that baboon teach you anything?"

"I read a lot of books, so I think I've covered that," Iris said with a sly smile. Looking at me, she winked as she moved to the other side of the platform to take more pictures of the falcon.

Sean signaled Terence to head over to a water hole where we might find some sandgrouse as well as some nesting blacksmith plovers and spur-winged plovers. "The black and white and gray pattern of the well-tailored blacksmith is very appealing. After we see the plovers, we'll go to trees where a leopard spends some time."

"Do you think we'll actually see the leopard?" Alice Goforth touched Sean's arm. "I really would like to see an actual wild one."

Sean nodded. "The chances are good. It's been seen there regularly," Sean said. "It's likely to be active in the evening."

During the excitement over the kori bustard, when Iris had moved to get a better shot, Jane Russo had switched places on the platform and was next to me, uncomfortably close.

Jane pulled her hat down as she turned her head toward me. "Afternoon, Jack."

"A beautiful evening. How are you?"

"Quite well. I'm sorta looking forward to seeing a leopard. Do you really think they can change their spots? I think some people can."

I assumed she was referring to me. Lowering my voice, I answered, "I haven't changed my spots. You refuse to leave Jimmy. I've moved on." Jane's face twisted in anger. I shifted the subject.

"Jimmy seems to have changed. He seems almost jolly today. What spot remover did you use?" I asked.

"I didn't use anything, though he's paid me some attention lately. It's amazing what a bit of jealousy will do. He even spent a whole night with me. He's ten life birds ahead of Gabe. That's what accounts for his mood."

I didn't miss her harsh tone or the fact that she was still rubbing her leg against mine, but Iris returned to my side and intervened.

"Jimmy seems to be in a better mood than I've seen before. He's even flirting with Maude and me. What magic potion did you give him, Jane?"

"He's ten life birds ahead of Gabe."

"Tonight, why don't you ask him if the baboons gave *him* any ideas? He seemed to be extremely interested in them," Iris said. "Maybe he's getting horny."

Jane gave her a sour look, turned away, and moved beside Jimmy.

"Thanks for the intervention. I wonder if there's another reason Jimmy's in such a good mood. He's been pressing people about buying stock. Maybe he made a sale."

In the grassland on the way to the water hole, I spotted several crested francolins. They wear a rakish reddish cap on their heads.

"These francolins are the chickens of the African savannas," I said.

"I expect they taste like chicken too," Cameron said. "I'll bet they'd do well in Texas."

"There were some francolins for a while doing well in Louisiana. I saw and heard one before they disappeared," I said. "Probably the Gulf Coast was too humid for them."

As we neared the water hole, we saw many spur-winged and blacksmith plovers. One blacksmith was incubating eggs. Sean was right about the blacksmith's beauty. It is a sharp dresser.

A flock of about fifty Lichtenstein's sandgrouse was drinking at the water hole. They are shaped a lot like our American grouse. They are striped black over light tan, camouflaged for a desert environment.

"These birds often flock in large groups," Sean said.

"What wonderful photographic creatures these sandgrouse are," Iris said. "They really do blend in with their environment."

She and the other camera buffs kept busy as these and other photogenic subjects appeared on every side. Burchell's Zeb-ras (many of us had adopted the British pronunciation), buffalo, giraffes, wildebeests, tommies, and several other species of antelope tempted photographers. The aromas of the grassland and the spoor of animals assailed us but did not diminish my pleasure at seeing so many animals spread out over the plain and close up at the water hole.

When we moved to the tree-filled spot where local people had reported a leopard hanging out, it appeared, as if on cue, climbing down out of its tree lair and walking past our parked vehicle, apparently unconcerned, stalking like the lord of all it surveyed and offering all of us excellent views.

"What a handsome creature; it's pure pleasure to see it like this," Alice said.

"And close enough to see its whiskers," said Iris as she changed from her camera to video.

"Maude, take lots of pictures—as many as you can. That's a beautiful cat," Jerry said. "Seeing this animal in the wild really beats views in a zoo."

I agreed. It was as if we were caged behind bars, and the leopard was a visitor enjoying a walk in order to contemplate the occupants of his zoo.

When the photographers were satiated, we headed back to the lodge. On the way, we made one more stop. Sean spotted a lilac-breasted roller perched on a bare snag close. "This is a beautiful bird. It looks like it just stepped out of a rainbow," Sean said.

"Look at that lilac breast set against the electric blue of the head, wings, and belly. The tan back just sets off the other colors. What a beauty," Maude Buck said as she photographed. "I think this is the best bird of the trip."

Everybody with a camera took a picture of this cooperative bird.

"It's obvious that Maude should be nicknamed lilac-breasted roller. She's usually dressed like one," I said.

Cameron agreed. "Jerry seems very happy with his lilac roller. She must be able to do something besides look pretty and take pictures."

"That's very naughty, Cameron. I'll bet your wife wouldn't approve," Iris said, laughing.

"Oh, I'm very happy with my double-breasted roller, thank you," Cameron said. "She finds me quite lovable. I'm just her pet talking parrot."

CHAPTER 16

"Watch your step getting down," Terence said as we prepared to leave the safari vehicle. "Come to dinner at the lodge anytime between six and nine. If you are interested, we'll be going out after nine to look for some owls."

As the group left the safari vehicle, Cameron pulled me aside.

"I'm looking forward to food. I just don't give a hoot for owling as long as I'm hungry," Cameron said. I laughed and gave a *hoo-hoo.*

"Owl hoots be damned. A hot shower comes before dinner."

"I'll be along after I walk Iris to her room," I said.

Cameron grinned "You obviously have a fight-or-flight situation bedeviling you," he said with true scientific aplomb and a twinkle in his eye. "Courting Iris is an obvious displacement action; I'm sure Jane would agree. I'll use the shower first. Take your time."

Evidently he approved of my new interest. Like a schoolboy, I held Iris's hand during the walk. She invited me in and fixed us a couple of weak drinks of whiskey and water. "I'm looking forward to the owling. Do you suppose there're many here?"

"I'd say the food the restaurant disposes of attracts rodents, and owls like to eat rodents. I think this place could support a good many," I said.

"Sounds reasonable."

Finishing my drink, I kissed her. "I'll come by and pick you up to go to dinner if that's all right."

"I'll be waiting," she said, returning my kiss.

* * *

After I showered, Cameron asked, "Do you want me to wait for you? I'll be ready to go to eat as soon as I dress."

"You go ahead. I'll pick up Iris and meet you at the lodge. Save us a table," I said.

"My bit for lovers."

After putting on dark jeans and a long-sleeved shirt, I walked over to join Iris. She was sitting outside, waiting. She had on a tight long-sleeved blue blouse and tight slacks that showed off her figure to my passionate gaze as I undressed her in my mind.

When Iris and I joined Cameron, he had already ordered a Tusker. I ordered two for Iris and me before we went to fill our plates.

The aromas from the barbecue pit whetted my appetite. It reminded me of home. We went over to the circular stone pit where the chef filled our plates with crocodile and antelope.

From the buffet table I took roasted meat cooked with spices called *Nyama Choma*, a rice dish cooked yellow with tamarack and other spices called *pilau*, and collards cooked with tomatoes called *wiki*. Anticipating a feast, I carried them back to our table.

"I'm really enjoying African barbecues," I said as I sampled the antelope.

"I still miss the raw vegetables of salads," Iris said, "but I'll follow our instructions to avoid anything uncooked, even though I hate doing it. This dish of peas mixed with potatoes is delicious. I wonder what spices they use. I thought I tasted cinnamon."

"They definitely use some cinnamon in this *pilau*," I said.

As he lifted another bite of antelope, Cameron agreed. "I taste cinnamon too. Avoiding uncooked food is a good rule for Africa, but who needs salads when the cooks are so skillful?" Then he shrugged and changed the subject. "I told Terence our suspicions about Algernon Wheatley."

"What did he say?"

"He said he appreciated the information, but Algernon had paid his fee for the trip and was entitled to write as many notes as he wanted. Sean will pass our information on to headquarters."

"Then I guess we don't need to fret about Algernon, if they aren't worrying about him," I said.

"I don't trust Secretary Bird, though," Cameron said. "He might do something underhanded."

"I think you two are a little hard on Algernon," Iris said. "He wants to see new birds as much as you do. He writes notes so that he can remember this trip. Just like I use my photos."

We all agreed the chef at the outdoor grill had worked his magic once again. Iris, Cameron, and I continued reveling in crocodile, antelope, beer, and the local dishes. It was easy to overeat. A walk-about to find owls would help digestion.

"To think there are people back in Texas worrying about my hardships on this trip," Cameron said, laughing.

"I see Alice and Jane coming in. Unless somebody objects, I'm going to invite them to join us," Iris said.

"It's okay with me," Cameron said. "What about you, Casanova?"

"If Iris wants to invite them, I won't object." I hid my reluctance. I knew I was being tested. I hoped I could at least get a pass.

Iris waved them over. I was sitting next to her, but Cameron made room between him and me for two women. Intentionally, I guessed. He and Iris seemed to me to be in league against me. I was not surprised when Jane took the chair next to mine.

"Are Jimmy and Gabe out hunting birds?" Iris asked.

"Yes, they didn't bother to shower. They just came here and ate and headed out. They'll be back in time for the owl prowl at nine," Alice said. "There are owls here they need."

"It's a good thing you and Jane get along so well, since you spend so much time together," Cameron said.

"Alice is a good friend," Jane said. "She's the only person who really understands my situation. Who else could appreciate just how much this Phoebe Snetsinger chase has disrupted our lives?"

I felt truly sorry for Jane, even though she was rubbing my leg under the table.

"There is an upside to our problem," Alice said. "We get to travel and see the world. It's a life full of adventure." She leaned back in her chair, obviously at ease.

In spite of my resolve, Jane's advances were beginning to arouse me. My resistance was less effective than I wished. As soon as we were through eating, I asked Iris to go for a walk with me.

"I'd like that," she said, sneaking a glance at the clock on the porch. "We both have our binoculars and cameras. We can walk around until nine."

"Don't leave without us. We'll be back to take part in the owl hunt," I said.

Cameron stood and stretched. "Okay, I'll wait here for you. I'll keep these ladies company and sip my beer."

"Let's go to my room," Iris said as we walked off from the table. "How are you feeling?" she asked as she opened the door.

"It's a relief to get away from Jane, even though I feel sorry for her. You and Cameron are being a little heartless providing Jane with opportunities to sit beside me."

Iris patted my loins and laughed. "I think you're doing marvelously. You deserve a reward." She turned and kissed me, then motioned me to sit down beside her on her small sofa.

I did as bid. "You can be cruel, but you seem to be the embodiment of the dream of love I've always had. I want to know more about you, my delightful tormentor."

Iris smiled, benignly, and patted my thigh. "You have to prove your trustworthiness. I'm not a mystery. I had a happy childhood, was the eldest of four children—a successful public school and college student."

"Did you have your career planned?"

Iris stood and pulled out her bottle of bourbon and a bottle of water from her travel bag; she poured a couple of weak drinks, and handed one to me. Then she sat back down beside me.

"Yes, I planned. I did my MBA and went from college to Wall Street. I worked my way up to where I am now. I didn't have much of a social life. Now, tell me something. Why did your marriage fail?

She gazed at me intently. I sipped my drink as I thought of how to answer.

"I think my marriage succumbed to empty-nest syndrome. Susan and I married in college. We had two children while I worked up the academic ladder."

This wasn't easy. I paused to take another sip of bourbon while trying to think of the best way to describe my failure as a husband.

"Susan continually accused me of having an affair with a female colleague whenever we argued. When the children left home, her jealous accusations grew worse. Angry, I finally had the affair she'd accused me of for so many years."

"But your unhappiness doesn't justify your adultery." Iris seemed to be taking Susan's side. She wasn't making this easy.

"I know. Maybe I had a midlife crisis a little early. I asked her to forgive me. Instead she sued for divorce, and I let her go. I gave her what she wanted."

"Have you been happy since?"

"I've been content during school terms, and chased birds during vacations. I've written poetry to occupy time, but I admit I've often been lonely."

"But you must have been sought after. You're very eligible. You're handsome. You have a sense of humor. You know what's going on in the world and can talk about interesting things."

"Even though I've had opportunities, nobody has come along to fill the void in my life. I guess I've become a little skeptical about finding the kind of love I've always believed possible."

Iris gave me a skeptical look. "You believe in true love?"

I squirmed mentally. "I'm a confirmed romantic. I've read too many novels like *Jane Eyre* and too much poetry by Keats and Shelley, I guess."

"Do you keep in touch with your former wife?"

"I have a decent relationship with Susan. We have our children in common."

Finishing her drink, Iris put down her glass, pulled me to her, and kissed me. I savored her luscious taste.

After a long pause, Iris ran her hand through my hair. "Maybe we can find the kind of love you want. Maybe it's the kind I want too. You might be the man I've been looking for, but I want to be sure."

I kissed her again to taste her honeyed tongue. I found it difficult to stop. "I hope to be able to give you that, a love without impediments, as Shakespeare called it, 'a marriage of true minds.'"

Iris stood and headed to the door. "Maybe we should go consult a wise old owl."

CHAPTER 17

Eager birders assembled with Sean and Terence a few minutes before nine o'clock. Everyone was there except Jane Russo, Alice Goforth, and Jerry Buck, who lingered in the dining area.

"We have located three species of owls close by the lodge and hope to find some of them for you," Terence said.

Algernon Wheatley took out his notebook. "What owls have you found?"

"Spotted eagle owl, white-faced owl, and African scops owl," Sean said.

"If we can't find all of them tonight, we'll try again tomorrow and tomorrow night," Terence said. "I like to quote Shakespeare's *Henry IV, I,* where Owen Glendower is bragging about his occult powers. Glendower boasts he can call spirits from the 'vasty deep,' and Hotspur jibes, 'So can I, and so can any man, but will they come when you do call for them?' We'll call and hope they respond."

We moved into the trees surrounding the lodge. Sean turned on the spotting light he was carrying and began a systematic search of the trees. After about five minutes, we heard a low but penetrating *hu-hoo* coming from a tree ahead of us. Sean moved his light to the tree from which the sound seemed to come. Flashing midway up the right side of the tree, Sean hit upon two yellow eyes. The figure of a large owl appeared. "It's a spotted eagle owl," Terence said. "It's smaller and grayer than some of the other eagle owls." Terence held the light on the owl for a few moments so that the photographers had a chance to record it.

Maude took a little longer than anybody else.

"Hurry up, woman. Don't take all night. You'll blind the bird. We have other owls to see," Jimmy Russo said, adding a "fuck the photograph" in a whisper that was audible.

"I heard that, Foul Mouth," Maude said.

"Quiet, you two. Successful owling requires stealth," Terence said. "Now we'll try for the smaller owls."

He led the group to trees on the other side of the lodge and repeated the procedure. This time Sean played a tape. We had no luck for a quarter of an hour; then I heard a fast *doo-doo-doo-doo-hoo* call twenty yards away. Moving that way, we followed Sean's light with our binoculars until it revealed orange eyes and a white face over a gray body. The head had ear tufts. This bird was about half the size of the eagle owl.

"A white-faced owl," Terence pronounced, as the photographers worked.

We searched for a half hour more but had no luck finding additional owls, although Sean's light located a fiery-necked nightjar on the ground in the parking lot and flying for insects in the lodge lights.

"I'll ask some of the locals to search for the African scops owl," Terence said. "It usually hangs out just outside its home hole during the day. Often it's easier to see them in the day than at night. But we've had great success with night birds, so sleep well. Early breakfast at six tomorrow before our morning safari."

As the owl hunters scattered, Iris grabbed my hand.

"Walk to my room with me."

I caught Cameron's attention. "Go on without me."

"Okay, Casanova. Have fun riding the range," he laughed. "John Denver would be proud of you."

Cameron's humor didn't always please me, but I made light of it. "I love John Denver's music. Iris fills up my senses, just like Annie's song says."

Walking to Iris's room, I asked her if any of her photos had turned out. "You didn't use a flash."

"Some of my shots turned out well. I didn't really need a flash. Sean's light gave enough for my camera."

"I wonder if Maude and the others had any trouble."

By this time, we had reached Iris's room. "I'll wait for the morning to find out. I'm sure Maude will tell us. She hasn't failed to brag yet. Just now I have another problem. I want your help."

"What's the problem?"

"Come in with me, and I'll show you."

After the door closed behind us, and as she turned a light on, Iris beckoned me with a smile.

She let down her hair. "My problem—you haven't kissed me for hours."

I tried to solve that problem. Then I unbuttoned her blouse and unclasped her bra, kissing her breasts before I spoke.

"Your beauty surpasses lilac-breasted rollers. You're a goddess, auburn haired, voluptuously formed, gorgeous, mesmerizing."

We kissed again as I ran my fingers through her silky hair, and she stroked my chest.

"Do you truly feel that way about me?"

"You're the incarnation of the love goddess." I suckled her breasts so passionately she began to moan.

"Oh, that feels so good." She drew away. "You're once again rather irreverent in your worship. Your goddess finds your attentions pleasurable but condemns you to sleep."

I found the African night unwilling to allow sleep. Tossing and turning me, my passions refused denial. I thought of beautiful yellow fever trees. Their yellow coating of bark is a remedy for the malarial sweats these trees are supposed to cause, or any other fevers. Fever trees appeal to elephants that gobble their leaves. Lovers thwarted, full of desire, burning with fever, use a tea made from the bark of these trees. I understood Iris's caution, but I couldn't help wanting her. I found relief in taking care of my desire without the aid of the fever tree. Complete exhaustion brought sleep.

*   *   *

Our six o'clock breakfast drew our entire group, ready for another journey through vistas full of large mammals spread across the plain. I sat down next to Iris, Cameron, and Jane. Jerry and Maude were across from us. Between bites, Maude was reviewing some of her recent photographs.

"I'm looking forward to a great day for photos," Iris said. "Are you looking for anything in particular today, Maude?"

"I guess I'll concentrate on the big animals unless I have another great chance at a lilac-breasted roller."

"How did your twinspot pictures turn out?" asked Jane. "You said you took some in the Abedarres."

"I haven't looked at them much yet. Just flipped through. They seemed pretty good. Why?"

"Jimmy has expressed a great desire for a picture of the twinspot. He and Gabe saw it, but Jimmy didn't get a photo."

Thinking back to the time they were taken, I guessed why Jane was particularly interested in them. I was curious, and apprehensive too. I remembered the day with regret, wishing I had shown more restraint. But that was TBI, or "Time before Iris."

"I haven't really gone over them yet," Maude said. "I know one was fairly good, but I haven't more than glanced at any of the rest."

"Jimmy wants a really good one."

"I might consider selling him one if he promises not to complain about my photography anymore. But you'll have to make the deal. I won't bargain with *him*."

Later, when we were alone, I made a request of Maude. "Would you let me look at your twinspot pictures?" I asked.

"When we have time. I don't see why not."

After breakfast, we boarded a safari vehicle and moved out to search for wildlife. The morning sun gave a golden glow to the savannah, thornbush, palms, and acacia. The air was still fairly cool. Cameron, Iris, and I managed to get a position up front on the platform. As the lodge became a small feature in the landscape behind us, we saw a long-legged slender gray and black bird striding along looking for prey; its crown feathers, like quills, were sticking out of its gray head. Bare red skin surrounded its eyes.

"There's a secretary bird," Sean said. "Look at those quills sticking up on his head."

I nudged Cameron. "Our secretary bird doesn't carry any quills in his head. Too bad. I guess he's not old-fashioned enough."

"What a great photo that'll make," Iris said as she took stills and video.

The gawky gray bird was still visible when Sean called our attention to a large bird atop an acacia. "That large hawk is a tawny eagle, a common raptor here," Sean said. Again the cameras clicked into action.

"I can't tell a bird tour from a photography shoot," Iris said. "My pictures will give me a great visual record of joy—not to mention money."

I agreed, but sometimes photography preserves a record of things we don't want recorded, even moments that, at the time, were pleasurable. I couldn't put those twinspot pictures out of my mind. They might show something to displease Jane and me, not to mention Iris—something that would anger Jimmy.

"Oh, there's another lilac-breasted roller. It takes my breath away. What fun to photograph that beauty," Iris said. It flew up after an insect, and she tried a flight shot. Iris snapped her camera and showed me the beautiful result.

Maude pointed her camera. "I hope I can get a photo to do it justice," she said as she tried for a flight shot to equal Iris's.

"I'm not sure any photo can. Its angle in the sun changes all the time. That full breeding plumage defies cameras," Iris said, marveling and winking at me as she lowered hers.

Looking at Iris, I thought of her as being in full breeding plumage with her gray eyes and deep auburn hair set off by her slender but curvaceous body in a blue outfit. My paradise flycatcher can hold her own with any roller, even a lilac-breasted one, I thought, mentally undressing her as she moved to get a better picture. My admiration of my thus-far-elusive paradise flycatcher ended abruptly as Jane pressed against me.

She brushed her hair back. "I'm worried about what Maude may have photographed in her films of the twinspot," Jane said. "Jimmy can be such a pain."

"No point borrowing trouble." I lowered my voice. "Maude said she would let me see her pictures. Once I know what's in them besides the twinspot, if anything. I'll let you know."

I reveled in the numerous mammals, including giraffes, elephants, wildebeests, impalas, and buffalo. The giraffes and elephants were grazing the trees, the buffalos and wildebeest the grass. A pride of lions eyed the buffalos and wildebeests from the shade. Once the vehicle stopped while a group of elephants passed by. On the savannah, elephants have the right of way. I was eye-to-eye with a big female. She stared me down before moving by.

"What's that awful odor?" Alice asked.

"You are smelling the pungent odor of fresh elephant dung, but lion dung puts these plant eaters to shame," Sean said, grinning.

As we drove through a buffalo herd, I saw more yellow-billed oxpeckers riding their backs.

"Still no red-billed oxpeckers," Algernon said. "I'm beginning to think we won't see any."

"Our chances of seeing them are better in South Africa," Sean said.

Jimmy interrupted with a curse. "How sure are you?" he asked. "I need that one."

"We rarely miss it at Kruger," Sean said.

"I'll be pissed off if we don't see it," Jimmy said.

"Shucks, we both will," Gabe said. "I'm sure Phoebe listed that one."

Despite having listing fever myself, I was beginning to tire of the obsessive attitude of our two companions. I had to admit, though, Gab's listing was much more tolerable than Jimmy's.

"I'm happy photographing the ones with yellow bills," Iris said. Yellow-billed oxpeckers riding buffalo provided her and Maude many photographs before we headed for lunch.

"Be careful. I saw a puff adder basking in the sun about ten yards to our left," Terence said, as we pulled up in front of the lodge. "They're very dangerous. They cause more deaths than black mambas, which are much shyer."

Iris pulled on my arm. "I'd love to have a picture of a puff adder. Come with me. I can use my big lens. We won't have to get close."

Apprehensive, I stared at her as I took her arm. "Are you sure? You heard Terence."

Iris pulled away. "C'mon. We'll be yards from it."

I started searching for the adder. The sooner I found it, the safer we'd be. Minutes later, I was pointing it out to Iris.

She grinned. "That's great. Now let's get about five feet closer."

Raising her camera, Iris steadied it and took a burst of shots.

Looking at them, I saw they were excellent, but Iris wasn't quite satisfied. "I really would like to have one coiled and rearing up as if to strike," she said.

"Damn, that's dangerous, but I'll rouse it—for you." I found a long, stiff dead weed and broke off its tip. "Okay, Iris, get ready." Walking closer to the adder, I touched it with the tip of my five-foot weed. My probe had the desired effect.

Iris yelled her joy. "Great, you're a honey. I've some sharp pictures."

Dropping my weed-stick, I beat a hasty retreat, glad to leave the adder in peace but happy to have gained Iris's favor.

"Let's get lunch," she said and slipped her camera to her shoulder and kissed me.

Instead of going back to our rooms, Iris and I made our way to the barbecue. I saw Maude and Jerry just sitting at a table by themselves, so I asked if we could join them.

After Iris showed off her pictures of the adder, I asked Maude for a look at her twinspot pictures. She was reluctant to let her camera out of her sight.

"It would be a great favor," I said.

She hesitated. "Well, since you and Jerry are fellow Wahoos, I'll stay and go through the pictures with you, if you don't linger over any."

I let out a soft Wahoo-wah. "Thanks."

"But let's get some lunch first," Maude said.

After we'd eaten quite a bit of food, Jerry and Iris left for their rooms.

Maude pulled out her camera. "Let's make this quick." First she brought up her still pictures of the bird. There was nothing but twinspot in her close-ups of the bird, but in her first shots, where much background was present, there appeared two figures in the background, a man and a woman close together standing behind bushes. They were of almost equal height—the man a blond maybe an inch or more taller, the woman auburn-haired. I wanted to curse but controlled my urge. Maude made no comment.

"Did you take any video of the twinspot?" I said.

"Yes, I did."

"Could I see that too?"

"If you don't ask me to stop. I don't want to miss our afternoon birding."

The video was even more revealing than the still pictures, since it showed more motion, but either was enough to suggest amorous activity.

As Maude quickly gathered up her camera gear, I pleaded. "Some of your twinspot pictures could cause trouble—if Jimmy Russo were to see them."

"Why should I worry about Jimmy? He's been nothing but trouble for me."

"They would be hurtful to Jane. They might cause me trouble too. Thanks for letting me see them."

"It's a good thing you and Jerry are fellow Wahoos. Let's get some rest," Maude said, stalking off without saying anything else, not even "praise the Lord."

Her attitude boded ill for Jane and me. I probably shouldn't have appealed to Maude's better nature. She liked me because Jerry and I were fellow UVA graduates, but she disliked Jimmy so intensely that she might think stirring up trouble for him so satisfying she wouldn't worry about other people. Christian compassion was unlikely where Jimmy was concerned, whether or not she said "praise the Lord."

CHAPTER 18

My mind was in a whirl. What should I do about the twinspot problem? I didn't want to lose Iris, but if she found out about Maude's pictures from somebody else, it might do more harm than if I told her myself.

I found Cameron and Iris at lunch and joined them. I kept wondering whether I should tell them what I had learned about Maude's twinspot photography. I felt sure I should tell Cameron and ask for advice. Iris was another matter. What would happen if she found out from somebody else? That might be worse. I kept imagining a negative reaction. Things had been going so well. I didn't want them to turn sour. It was a quandary.

I passed up more barbecue. After putting small amounts of the meat dish *Nyama Choma*, rice *pilau*, *wiki* collards with tomatoes, and banana stew on my plate to go with a Tusker, I settled down and began picking at my food, picking at my food without saying much. I must have seemed preoccupied.

Iris broke the silence. "You seem rather pensive."

Cameron gave me a searching look. "I agree. What's your problem?" he asked.

"Tell us what's bothering you," Iris said.

I hesitated, trying to decide.

Iris broke my silence. "Come on now, what's the matter?"

"If I tell you, I want you to promise that you, especially you, Iris, will remember that I've been trying to avoid Jane."

"I promise," Cameron said.

"I believe you. I think you're making progress. I promise," Iris said, her lips curled in a slight smile.

"Maude allowed me to see the twinspot pictures she took at the Abedarres. Some of them show Jane and me in the background. They will infuriate Jimmy if he should see them, especially the video."

"Too bad. I think I'll ask Maude to let me look at those pictures," Cameron said. "What did Jane have on?"

"Her blue outfit. I admit to being foolish, but I wasn't the aggressor. Jimmy won't consider that if he should see the pictures."

Cameron eyed the khaki outfit Iris had on. "Jane's blue outfit is just like yours, Iris, if I recall correctly," Cameron said.

"Yes, that's right."

I put my hand on Iris's arm. "It pains me to admit this to you, but I didn't want you to find out some other way. It happened before you and I became close friends."

"I'm not pleased, but I'm not surprised. Film can be a blessing or a curse. I hope I've convinced you to be more careful."

"You know what I think, Casanova?" Cameron said. "I've been warning you about Jane. If Jimmy becomes angry enough, there's no telling what he'll do. He might give you an unpleasant Russover."

I didn't relish his wordplay, but he meant well. Susan had called me much worse.

During lunch, Sean alerted the owl seekers of the night before that an African scops owl was available. "We'll meet outside in half an hour. Local Kenyans found one this morning while we were on safari." It took just a few minutes for the assembled group to have good looks at the bird. This time Alice, Jane, and Jerry tagged along, so all the group saw the bird.

"What a charming gray bird," Alice said. "He really looks like a wise old owl."

"Pretty dumb, if you ask me," Jimmy said. "Just sitting there."

Cameron laughed. "Chalk one up to the Kenyans. They don't eat owls."

"Add one to the life list for the Snetsinger challengers," Gabe Goforth said, raising his hand and making a mark in the air with his finger.

The photographers had a pleasant time taking pictures of the stolid gray bird with long feathered ear tufts—just sitting, posing for pictures, appearing unconcerned, if not wise.

The afternoon safari turned up some of the same birds we had seen in the morning plus a few additional ones, as well as many giraffes, elephants, Thompson's gazelles, and other antelope species. We saw female lions make a kill of a young impala—a dramatic chase and bloody meal caught on video by our photographers, although Maude feigned nausea and photographed the scene only at Jerry's strong insistence.

"I'm not sure how I feel about scenes like these," Iris said.

"Lions have to eat too," I said. "We live a sanitized life buying our meat packaged in grocery stores. I remember my dad telling about killing chickens for family dinner when he was a boy."

In a small grove of broad-leaved trees, we found go-away birds, large gray turacos, posing on bare branches for us. With them were several species of small birds, cisticolas and a friendly yellow-bellied apalis. Once again cameras were active. Jane situated herself close to me after Iris moved across the platform to get a better angle for her camera.

"Did you see Maude's photographs?"

"Yes. You don't want Jimmy to see them," I said. "He would be angry."

"Then they *are* revealing?"

"The shots including background reveal enough to anger somebody as jealous as Jimmy. Maude's video is even worse. Try to get her to show him only the close-up stills."

"Maybe I can persuade Maude not to show him any. But if she won't agree to that, I'll beg her to show only the close-ups."

"Good luck. From Maude's attitude, I'd say she won't be easy to convince."

"My life would be so much simpler without Jimmy." Jane grimaced and moaned. "It's horrible to say, but sometimes I wish somebody would kill him."

I moved away as quickly as I could. I felt sorry for Jane, but I was more worried about losing Iris.

After dinner and the ritual of the list, Terence announced that we would head back to Nairobi in the morning and fly to Johannesburg, South Africa.

"From there we'll see some of the birds we've become familiar with here but also many new ones for the list. Our first major effort will be in the Drakensburg Mountains, where we'll try to satisfy your desire to see lammergeyers. I know some of you are very eager to see them. Our chances of finding them are excellent."

"I long to photograph a lammergeyer," Iris said as we walked to our rooms. "It was the top bird species on my wanted list."

"It was high on my list too, though not as high as the rock fowl we're supposed to see in Sierra Leone."

"Come in and have a drink." Iris said as she opened her door.

Inside, the scent of lilacs enveloped me. In what had become a ritual, Iris poured a very small bit of bourbon in two glasses and added some water from a bottle.

Taking a glass from her, I lifted it in a toast, "Here's to our wonderful birds and our growing relationship."

"I'll drink to that," Iris said. "Let's see how the relationship is growing."

She hugged and kissed me and rubbed against me as I ran my hand through her silky auburn hair and undid it to flow down over her shoulders. I whispered in her ear. "I long to be like a robber bee stealing your honey." I kissed her as I unfastened her bra. "You taste like honey, and I long to eat your sweetness even though I know your sting will make forgetting impossible." I kissed her again, this time on her now-uncovered breasts. "I long to sip your flowing honey on love's altar, eating and dying."

"Oh, Jack, how beautiful. Kiss me some more. I believe we're falling in love."

*   *   *

The weeks passed quickly, life bird by life bird, one African location after another. Sean was now doubling as our driver. From Samburu we drove back to Nairobi and flew to Johannesburg. From there we drove to the Drakensberg Mountains as Terence had promised.

We motored through well-watered grasslands that reminded me of the foothills of the Rockies. In several hours of driving, with frequent stops for birds, we reached a large white building with dormer windows resembling a cottage that might have adorned an English moor. On a new building just going up next to the main house, thatchers were applying a roof. One man was handing up a new bundle of thatch to his fellow roofer just as we arrived.

"Our lodging is a structure built by rich English fishermen," Terence said as he handed out room keys. "You can see the magnificent Drakensberg Mountains in the distance. We go there tomorrow. You have just time to get settled, take a shower, and then come down for the evening meal. We are promised trout from the local streams. Local streams were stocked by the English."

Cameron and I found our room at the end of a long hall on the second floor. Iris followed us. It turned out that her room was one door before ours at the end of the hall. I couldn't help appreciating the convenience of the arrangement. I was thinking much more about Iris than about my ever-increasing list of life birds.

Now a bed and breakfast for well-to-do tourists, fishermen, birders, and globetrotting sightseers, the lodge offered comfort with a homey touch. The bedrooms looked as if the trout-fishing member of some well-to-do family had stepped out for only a day or two.

While Cameron showered, I knocked on Iris's door. "Iris, may I come in?"

"The door's open, Jack, but close it behind you."

Going in, I found Iris beginning to undress. I couldn't help admiring her beautiful figure, slender yet voluptuous.

"Has anyone told you lately how gorgeous you are?" I said.

Laughing, she tossed her auburn hair and continued slowly undressing, hanging up each garment in her closet. "That's the first time today. If I'm so gorgeous, why don't you come over here and offer me something besides words?"

I took a few steps and pulled her to me, kissing her with all the energy I could muster after the long ride. "You're a fragrant lilac. You taste like ambrosia. I don't believe you need to shower." She put aside my hands reaching to undo her bra.

"I need one to relax me. You wait. It won't take me long." Her lyrical laugh enveloped me. I sat down as she finished undressing, carefully removing her bra and then her panties. I enjoyed her strip tease, although my response left me full of desire. She noticed my look, walked across the room, and kissed me.

She tweaked my ear. "Don't look as if somebody stole your candy," she said. "You're still a little boy at heart."

She walked slowly back as I watched, entranced, put a shower cap over her hair, stepped in the shower, and looked back at me, laughing, as she pulled the shower curtain closed.

"This is magnificent country," I said, loud enough for her to hear me, pretending I'd only been watching the scenery outside.

"Those mountains are awe-inspiring." I heard her laughing. "Are you sure you're thinking about landscapes?"

After a long few minutes, Iris stuck out her hand to grab a towel. "I'm really looking forward to getting to the top of the dragon."

"Sean said the reserve people have put out a carcass for the Cape vultures and lammergeyers. The vultures are so persecuted by farmers they're almost extinct and need a little help."

"I'm eager to realize my top goal on this trip, to photograph a lammergeyer."

As she stepped out of the shower I thought again of Botticelli's Venus rising from the sea. "I worship your beauty, Aphrodite," I said.

"Like a sincere worshipper, kiss me, go shower, change, and come back."

"As you command." I kissed her and went out the door, still holding in my mind the image of Iris in the nude. Damn, she is lovely. I know physical beauty is ephemeral, but I can't help responding to it. Birds without their feathers lack beauty, but she's more beautiful without any adornments. That vision lingered during dinner. I couldn't keep my eyes off her.

The delicious grilled trout was complemented with the national dish of *Bobotie*, minced meat baked with egg-based topping. A *sambal* (think hot sauce) side dish helped spice cooked cabbage and other vegetables. The only sour note of the meal was Jimmy's vocal display of dislike for *Bobotie*.

"I want some steak, not fish and quiche," he said.

"Drink some lager," Gabe suggested. "That'll make you feel like going out for night birds. Drink two or three or four. Shucks, no telling how many life birds you'll find."

"Are you saying I list life birds when I'm half drunk?" Jimmy asked, glowering.

"You said that, not me," Gabe said, grinning.

"The food is delicious. Just eat and then go out birding, if you must," Jane said.

Jimmy gave her a withering look. "Nobody asked your opinion," he said as he raised his hand to reach for *sambal* to apply on his food. Jane bent away from him, as if expecting a blow, her face quivering. I think Iris and Alice saw Jane's movement too. I couldn't help wondering if Jane feared physical abuse from Jimmy.

"We saw lots of birds today," Iris said, changing the subject. "I took some great photos of cranes. "They're noble birds. The crowned cranes are splendid, but those blue cranes were even more elegant."

"I got some good photos too," Maude said.

"They're more gorgeous than our Texas sandhills," Cameron said, "but our whoopers are just as beautiful. All cranes are marvelous creatures."

I recalled with renewed pleasure the elegant blue cranes, the stately gray-crowned cranes with their elegant headdress we had encountered that day, and the blue gnus, a new breed of wildebeest for us, but I couldn't help thinking Iris's beauty outdid them.

The ritual of the list was short but full of new birds, most of them life birds for the entire group other than our leaders, Gabe, and Jimmy.

"Possibly tomorrow will prove exciting for those of you who so wish to see lammergeyers," Terence said. "If nothing else, we will see some beautiful scenery. Unless we have an unusually bad day, you'll see some extraordinary birds. In the blind on the mountaintop, the photographers will have opportunities to use cameras without worrying so much about the rest of us."

"We'll breakfast at six and load the van a half hour later," Sean said.

After eating, Iris, Cameron, and I walked outside. The sky was clear, and the stars in the Milky Way were spectacular—spread like diamonds across the night sky. Cameron found the Southern Cross and pointed it out to us.

"I feel as if I'm up there with the stars," Iris said. "They're so beautiful here. Without lights dimming their brilliance, they seem close to earth."

I agreed as I put my arm around her. "It's no wonder primitive people were awed by them."

Frogs were calling from the stream at the foot of the hill and goatsuckers were emitting calls as they hunted insects overhead. The freckled nightjars were yelping *whip-wheeu,* and our old friend from Samburu, the fiery-necked nightjar, was calling what some people say is "good lord deliver us." That's the reason it's called the litany bird.

The breeze brought the fragrant scents of the grassland to us— hay and flowers mixed with animal odors.

We spent about twenty minutes finding all the constellations we could recognize. I relied on Cameron to point out the southern star clusters. He identified Cygnus, Leo, and Hercules for us before he yawned and said he was heading to bed.

Iris and I and went with him. At our doors, I left Cameron and went with Iris.

"Don't wait up for me," I said.

Cameron winked. "Just be quiet when you come in."

"I hope you want to stay for a while," Iris said, when we reached her door. "I want some company."

Inside, Iris kissed me, running her tongue in my ear. "The stars were so lovely. I could have stayed longer looking at them," she said.

"I still hold a vision of you entering your shower," I said.

"Good, I'm trying to fill your mind with positive images of me. I hope to replace all previous female vignettes in your mind," Iris said, smiling, reminding me of Da Vinci's inscrutable Mona Lisa.

"I'm thinking of you coming from your shower like a goddess. Only you're more beautiful."

"I'm glad I affect you that way, but I'm flesh and blood, remember. Give me another kiss."

Savoring the taste of her mouth, I found her demand pleasant to fulfill. She remained both irresistible and yet, like fruit on a high branch, just a little beyond capture. I longed for more of her, but I knew she was wise to be wary of somebody with my history.

She wanted something more than a casual affair. That was what I wanted also. I hoped to survive the testing. I went to bed, my desire again unquenched but my hopes high that I would eventually win her trust.

CHAPTER 19

Next morning, we traveled over red dirt roads past the round mud huts of Zulu villages to the reserve where we had reservations to use the upscale hide at the top of the mountain.

After we boarded our van to leave, Terence prepared us for our morning in the hide. "We'll be in a nature preserve set aside primarily to protect persecuted Cape griffon vultures sheep farmers have decimated. They're becoming very rare. The carcasses the caretakers put out attract lammergeyers as well."

"Do you think we'll see them?" I asked.

"Yes. The vultures dine on carcasses put out to attract them. If they eat in the reserve, they are less likely to be killed by sheep farmers. Visitors like us pay fees to provide the corpses that also attract lammergeyers after the vultures have stripped them to reveal some bones."

We were able to drive part of the way up the mountain but had to walk the last three hundred yards. As the group came in sight of the summit, large gray Cape griffons flushed from a carcass as we approached the building.

"There's a new bird for our lists," Gabe said.

"Not quite as beautiful as a lilac-breasted roller," Alice said. "I don't get pleasure from seeing them."

"I'll be happy to add it to my list," Jimmy said. "Beauty is greatly overrated." I thought I saw Jane give him a nasty look.

The carcass was decayed sufficiently to provide an acrid odor, but still had much flesh covering large sections of the bones.

"It stinks," Iris said. "I hope we don't smell it inside the hide."

"I don't think we will. The hide is well built," Sean said.

Terence nodded. "The carcass is too new to be greatly appealing to lammergeyers, but we should see a few." An octagonal structure, the handsome hide had glass windows on all sides, except part of one side where there was an entrance.

Cameron whistled. "This is the Taj Mahal of hides."

Inside, we found a tile floor bare except for a supporting post in the middle of the spacious room. Large glass windows faced every direction except above the entrance door, where there was a convenient water closet. The windows offered splendid views. We could look at mountain ranges stretching blue and red and tan and purple as far as we could see. The sun was playing hide and seek with clouds creating a panorama of fierce, shifting color. Hawks of various species were visible soaring on the updrafts created by the ridges.

Iris echoed my thoughts. "The scenery alone is worth lots of photographs. The colors on the mountain ranges shift constantly from blue to gold to purple to red to orange as the clouds move. It's a photographer's dream landscape."

Terence and Sean pointed out a black and white jackal buzzard with its red tail. Then a blue and reddish-brown European kestrel flew in and hovered like a helicopter on beating wings, looking for a rodent just beyond our hide, justifying its nickname of windhover. A rook, a svelte black crow, flew in. Small birds landed on the rocks on the edge of the mountain just beyond the hide—a black and yellow shrike called *bokmakerie* and a blue and red Cape rock thrush—two beauties.

Iris, Maude, and everyone else with a camera kept busy. A whirring of automatic lenses complemented expressions of excitement at every new bird.

But after an hour, Iris became frustrated. "Drat, all these beautiful birds but no lammergeyers."

Sean caught her eye and explained. "They prefer carcasses from which the meat's been stripped. They take bones to great heights and drop them to the rocks far below to be crushed. Then they eat the marrow. I think our carcass still has too much meat. The vultures haven't worked the carcass enough. But don't give up hope."

"I won't," Iris said. "I've plenty of subjects while I wait for the bone crushers."

Fifteen minutes later, Terence pointed to large birds soaring effortlessly in the distance, heading our way. "Young lammergeyers," he said, raising his fingers in a V.

Four birds came in, lighting at the carcass. These youngsters were all varying shades of brown and black with what looked like Halloween masks for faces. They reminded me of something out of a Hollywood horror show, although I was awed by their weird beauty and flying skill, their ability to soar without seeming effort.

"How wonderful!" Iris pointed her camera. After taking many still shots, she switched to video and filmed for about ten minutes, when the lammergeyers departed, undoubtedly unhappy with the status of the carcass.

I was amazed at how well Maude, Jimmy, and Iris did their photography without arguing. Perhaps it was the ambiance of the hide, its plethora of windows, and their not having to work around the rest of us that muted the antagonism of Maude and Jimmy.

Their halcyon period ended abruptly when the lammergeyers returned. Jimmy got in front of Maude's video camera just as she was filming a lammergeyer landing. "Darn you, Russo, you ruined my shot of the approach. And to think you have the nerve to bark at me."

"You foolish pissant witch. I hope my picture breaks your camera. You've messed up plenty of my shots, you sanctimonious bitch." Nobody could miss Jimmy's loud voice.

Appearing from behind, Jerry Buck landed a blow to Jimmy's side that doubled him up. "Turn around, and I'll give you one on your chin."

"You son of a bitch." Jimmy straightened and threw a punch at Jerry, who ducked and landed another blow to Jimmy's midriff. Jimmy bent forward again.

Terence and Sean intervened before more blows landed. In a few seconds, a call to see a great view of a male Cape rock thrush eased the tension.

Then another lammergeyer came in, an adult. I could see how it got its other name of bearded vulture. More handsome than the youngsters, this one indeed had a black beard hanging down from a white head. It merged with a reddish-tan neck and breast and belly. It was uncanny how handsome it seemed. I raised my camera and clicked.

"Come photograph this elegant creature, Iris," I beckoned her to take my place. She was soon taking picture after picture.

We stayed in the hide another hour enjoying the birds and the panorama around us, feeling as if we were on top of the world. Then Terence told us we had engaged the hide only for the morning. So we headed back to the vehicle and then down the mountain.

On the road away from the park, along a stream, Sean spotted a giant kingfisher. We stopped to enjoy this huge fisher and admire his gigantic bill, red breast, and checkered blue and white back. A photographic orgy ensued.

Following the creek to a place where it became fairly wide and slow, we saw an African fish eagle perched on a dead snag. Its white head and tail and brown body reminded me of bald eagles back home, but its tail was shorter and its beak smaller.

I managed good views of birds despite Jane's rubbing close against me in the hide and grabbing a seat next to me in the van, a feat she managed while Iris was packing her camera away before getting in. Iris had to sit with Jimmy, who, I guessed, was seething with anger in the seat behind Jane and me.

"Are you enjoying your ride up there, Burnside" Russo inquired, mangling my name, after we'd been riding ten minutes or so. His voice had a tense, nasty edge.

I tried to reduce the tension. I turned and spoke to Jimmy. "I'm just looking for birds and enjoying the scenery. I believe Iris would be quite willing to trade seats with Jane, if you'd like."

Iris nodded her head. "I think that's a great idea. Jane, how about trading seats with me?"

"Jane, come back here and let Iris get up there," Jimmy said.

Jane expressed surprise. "All right, I didn't think you wanted me near you."

"What gave you that idea?" Jimmy asked. He jibed at me. "That okay with you, Burnside."

"Sure, Jimmy, if that makes you happy."

The trade was made, and Iris sat beside me, smiling. "You're doing well, sweetheart," she whispered. "Maybe you missed your calling. You'd do well in politics."

CHAPTER 20

We reached Mkusi National Park early in the evening. After a long drive from the mountains, we were in flat coastal country. The bare branches of the huge baobab or upside down trees simulating roots seemed like sentinels guarding the approach. A long, sprawling tan building set in an opening in the brush greeted us. It housed the administrative office of the reserve as well as accommodations for tourists.

Terence gave us our room assignments. "Get settled and come back for a welcoming dance—-in the large front room where the reception desk is located. Only after we are properly welcomed will they serve our dinner. Our bags will be brought to our rooms as usual."

So Cameron and I dropped off our field gear and made our usual inspection of the facilities to see that everything worked. Then he headed back to be welcomed. I went to Iris's room to escort her. We were among the first of our group to arrive. The native dancers were just setting up their drums. Workers at the reserve had covered their shirts and pants. They now appeared in animal skins and colorful traditional garb, carrying spears and shields.

Soon our entire group had assembled, and the drums began to beat. The dancers leaped forward, pointing their spears at us while chanting in keeping with their actions, simulating the movements of warriors fighting or hunting big game. Forward and back, side to side they flowed in unison, coming close with their spears. The performance continued for about twenty minutes before their final charge, at the end of which they greeted us with a great shout of welcome.

Then they ushered us into a large room where we found a buffet table loaded with food. Besides barbecued meats, there were various dishes made from maize and milk. I was particularly fond of *isibhede*, a fermented porridge, and their grain beer called *amehewu*. Corn on the cob, beans, and cabbage were served with *amasi*, a kind of yogurt, and a crumbly porridge called *phutu*. There was also a yam dish called *amandube*. A vegetable relish called *chakalka* was offered to spice all the food. I loaded my plate and enjoyed the bounty.

Outside a sudden afternoon storm had developed, and the rain poured down, beating noisily on the tin roof. It was comfortable inside. The food was delicious, so nobody hurried through the meal. Everything seemed calm, and the group's contentment with the meal led to much discussion of it and our colorful reception.

After we ate, and Terence conducted the ritual of the list, our group scattered. I noticed Jimmy and Maude at the end of the tables looking at some of her pictures. Jerry was sitting between them. Alice and Jane were sitting across the table from them. *There's trouble*, I said to myself. To Iris and Cameron I said, "Look down at the far table. Get ready. I think Maude's showing Jimmy the twinspot pictures. If she shows them all, there's bound to be a blowup."

I could see that Jimmy was engrossed with the pictures. Maude continued to change from one shot to another. Jimmy was becoming more and more agitated. Then Maude switched to her video.

When Maude turned her screen for Jimmy to watch, he studied for a while and then grabbed for the camera. Maude drew it back out of his reach as Jerry intervened with a clenched fist.

"Maude didn't heed Jane's pleas not to show him the video, evidently," I said. "I'd like to wring that woman's neck. Pretending to be so frigging pious. She's just getting even with Jimmy. She doesn't give a damn about anybody else."

"I wonder what he'll do to Jane," Iris said.

"I wonder whether he'll try to attack me," I said. "I'll fight if I have to."

Cameron gripped my arm. "You keep calm, Casanova. I'll stand between you and him. It's a situation that requires tact. I'm glad Maude showed *me* those pictures."

"I don't want you to get into trouble," I said. Jimmy was rising from his seat, and we could hear his growling and see him shaking his fist at Jane. I could make out a "pissant" now and again. Maude was sitting quietly, grinning like the Cheshire Cat of *Alice in Wonderland*.

"Maude seems really smug," Iris said. "I guess the Devil made her do it."

Jimmy started moving rapidly toward us. "Burnbridge, you two-timing pissant, I'll beat your sorry ass," he said, waving his fist at me.

"Slow down, Russo. Just *what* is your problem?" Cameron asked as he eased between us.

"That slimy little pissant has been making out with my wife," Jimmy said, halting. "I don't let anybody mess with my woman."

"Just how did you come to this conclusion? Jack spends most of his time with me or with Iris. He can't be doing much with Jane," Cameron said.

My friend's cool demeanor and reasonable analysis seemed to deflate Jimmy's ire.

"Maude Buck has pictures that prove it," Jimmy said. "You've no right to butt in. My business is with Burnbridge."

"No, those pictures don't prove it. I've seen them. They just show a blond man embracing a woman with auburn hair. They could as easily be pictures of Jack and Iris as Jane and Jack. Jane and Iris are about the same height. They both have auburn hair. To top that off, both women have identical blue outfits."

"Okay. I'll admit that's true, but I don't appreciate your butting in, you frigging busybody pissant."

"I don't think calling me names helps," Cameron said.

Somewhat disarmed, Jimmy continued glowering and clenching his fists.

"Old man, you're a fucking busybody. If it weren't for your gray hairs and glasses, I'd teach you to mind your own business."

"Fighting won't solve your problem. It's not Maude's pictures. It's your guilt for neglecting your wife." Cameron took off his glasses and handed them to Iris. "Don't let my gray hairs stop you."

"It's tempting, you damned pissant, but you'd probably sue me." Jimmy was clenching and unclenching his fists.

"Why don't you calm down and forget about those pictures," Iris said. "You can see that Jack is interested in me, not Jane." Jimmy glared at her but made no more effort to begin a fight with me. Finally, he turned and went back to Jane and continued his tirade.

"Thanks. You certainly handled that well, Cameron, although we owe an apology to Iris," I said.

"No need for an apology—I don't mind having my name linked with yours romantically. After all, if those pictures had been taken a few days later, they could well have been of us, though we try to be more discreet."

"I'm happy to have helped you two lovebirds," Cameron said. "Don't stay out too late, Casanova," Cameron said, laughing as he winked at Iris and turned to go to our room.

When Iris and I went outside, the rain had stopped. The setting sun was shining. The rich hues of a bright rainbow were arched over the building where I had just escaped Jimmy's wrath.

"Nature is creating a beautiful evening sky. It's a good omen," I said as Iris reached in her carrying bag for her camera. We spent our next quarter of an hour enjoying the rainbow as Iris took many pictures of the sun bathing the landscape in an ethereal light. I felt as if I'd been granted a heavenly reprieve.

"I agree that rainbow is a good omen. It promises a better time ahead. You certainly received a lesson in why to avoid Jane."

We walked hand in hand to Iris's room. The rain had refreshed the land. I savored its redolence mixed with Iris's lilac scent.

"Did you know that the Greek goddess of the rainbow was named Iris?" I asked.

"I thought she was a messenger of the gods."

"That's true, and when she brought the rainbow, she announced good news. Cameron's a true friend, and a real diplomat, but you're my best protector," I said. "You're bringing good news to me."

As we entered her room, she turned to kiss me. "I hope this is part of the good news," she said. One kiss wasn't enough.

CHAPTER 21

Next morning our safari began with another English breakfast. Terence spent time describing problems on past trips from which people had had to go home early. He mentioned some where sickness required early withdrawal. The one that impressed me was that of a woman who developed what Terence termed *birding overload.* She had been advised she wasn't ready for a strenuous trip to eastern Brazil, an area with so many endemic birds. She had a nervous breakdown after two weeks and had to be loaded on a plane and sent home.

Terence ended by suggesting another reason for sending a client home. "There are other reasons that clients are asked to leave trips early. If people make the trip too unpleasant for others, we might ask them to leave. I warn you that, whatever conflicts arise, you are expected to maintain civility in dealing with others of the group. I hope this reminder will prove sufficient."

He looked about before continuing. 'We still are using the Toyota van in which we've come to the reserve. It offers plenty of room, so remember my caution." Sean was driving, Terence told us, and we could exit the van only in designated areas, because of the danger of animal attack. I missed the freedom that the vehicles we used in Samburu had allowed us, but we were able to get out of the van at water holes specifically built with large hides or blinds to allow us to watch the animals coming to drink.

At one of these hides we found a prized white rhinoceros family: a male, female, and young. They dwarfed the other animals coming for a drink. A herd of Burchell's zeb-ras and several species of antelope, including a beautiful male kudu with its striking twisted horns and white stripes, came in to drink. So engaged in looking at the animals we became, we almost forgot the odors of animal spoor and even, for a bit, the birds. Then I spied something as colorful as the rainbow Iris and I had seen last evening.

In the trees, I saw a bird larger than a crow creep out on a limb over the water and drink after the limb bent low enough.

"Look at that beautiful big bird with the purple crest. It shows almost every color in an artist's palette," Iris said. "What is it?"

"That's a purple-crested lourie, a really good find," Sean Selkirk said. "More striking than those glossy starlings and gray-headed sparrows crowding the water's edge."

Jimmy Russo was elsewhere when Iris and I spotted the lourie. Back in the van, when he learned of the sighting, he became almost apoplectic.

"Why didn't someone let me know—before we moved on? You pissants wanted me to miss it."

"You are showing paranoia, Mr. Russo. The bird disappeared before anybody else had a chance to see it. Nobody slighted you," Cameron said.

"Don't talk to me, you medical quack. I should have been told. I could have searched for it. Did Gabe see it?" Jimmy looked intently at Alice.

"I think he came by before the bird left," Alice said. "If I remember correctly, it left while he was watching. It was iridescent. Watching it was pure pleasure."

Jane intervened. "You're still ahead. It was just bad luck."

"Damn. Yes, but he's getting closer. And this isn't an easy bird to find. You pissants are conspiring against me," Jimmy said, pointing a finger at Cameron, Iris, and me.

"I think you're reacting out of all proportion," Cameron said. "First, we don't consider your list every time we see a bird. Second, we didn't know you needed it for your list. Third, we were busy identifying birds and animals we'd never seen. Fourth, we were enjoying the beauty of the natural world, not worrying about our lists—or yours."

I could see from their smiles and nods that many others in the group agreed with Cameron. Maude and Jerry were stifling laughter. Though Jimmy continued to glower and mutter, he made no more accusations.

I said a silent bravo for Cameron. He had put so well the case for nature study as opposed to artificial constructs we force upon the natural world. Though listing is a sport, Russo's behavior was insufferable—as obsessed as football fans attacking fans of rival teams. I felt certain Russo could not understand that our pursuit of wildlife is justified because our money gives the local people a reason to protect the animals, not because of any intrinsic value in our listing of species.

We went on to search for birds at several other watering places, including some lakes. We found striped kingfishers, whose lineated white breasts contrast with the blue and black of their heads, backs, and upper wings; white-backed, yellow-billed, and red-billed ducks; wooly-necked and yellow-billed storks; and—most prized of all by me—I have a special love of owls—a close look at a huge Pel's fishing owl, whose tawny-gold beauty prompted oohs and aahs from all of us. A nocturnal hunter, it was perched at its daytime roost.

As Iris and Maude leaned out the van window to photograph, Jimmy jumped out of the van over Terence's objections and moved another fifty feet closer to the owl before shooting pictures.

Maude complained, "He's ruining my shot. I thought we had to stay in the vehicle."

"Russo, get back in the van immediately." Sean yelled his order. "You know there are dangerous animals in this park. This particular area is noted for problems with hippos. A man was killed here recently. Getting out of vehicles here is absolutely prohibited."

Sheepishly, Jimmy returned with head lowered like a recalcitrant schoolboy, but I noticed a grin lurking on one side of his face as he sat down beside Jane.

"Russo, possibly you know it's strictly forbidden for you to be outside the van except in designated areas," Terence said. "We told you just a few hours ago. You remember every bird you've seen or missed. Possibly you might try to remember a few simple instructions. Sean and I could lose our permits over this. If you do this again, you won't be allowed near the front of the van anymore," Terence said. "Just last week a hippo killed a worker here."

Sean pulled the van up slowly to where Jimmy had taken pictures of the owl, and all of us were able to photograph from as close as Jimmy had been.

Down the road from the owl, a huge goliath heron was standing in the lake, patiently watching for fish. We could see why people think of it as gigantic, like an American great blue heron on steroids. We moved on to areas with brush and woods and saw many other very different birds, including several species of weavers. Overhead we saw white-backed vultures soaring.

Cameron joked. "The way those vultures are circling, maybe they're coming for one of us. I wonder if they think Jimmy is carrion, the way he's been stinking things up."

Iris and I laughed, but I defended Jimmy. "If they go by smell, you can't be sure. It's pretty hot, and we're all dirty sweaty."

As we moved on, we saw southern red-billed and yellow-billed hornbills, species split from those we saw in the north, but looking just as weird as they flew by. They offered us great looks at their strange heads. "The DNA splits from the northern birds give us some new life birds," Gabe said.

Jimmy laughed. "I'll take my lifers anyway I can get them."

In brushy patches we found beautiful sulphur-breasted shrikes and green woodhoopoes as well as a red-backed scrub-robin and a white-browed coucal. Late in the evening, we happened upon a wary group of crested guineafowl. I was delighted to see these birds. They looked to me like exotic dancers in a weird Hollywood floor show shaking their feathered headdresses.

These gray-black birds covered with small white spots are notable for their curly black feathers standing up on their crowns. They are as odd looking as their uglier, more common relatives, the helmeted guineafowl I had seen several times on our tour. These curly-headed crested fowl reminded me less than their cousins did of the barnyard guineas of my youth that my dad had kept to warn our barnyard chickens and ducks about what he called marauding chicken hawks.

After dinner, the ritual of the list went well until Terence Stavens reached the louries. Jimmy was still griping about not seeing the purple-crested lourie. He jumped up and interrupted Stavens. "A bunch of pissants kept me from getting that life bird."

"Mr. Russo," Terence said, "it is impossible to be in all places at any one time. Had you been with Sean instead of with me, you possibly would have seen the lourie. But you saw a Sabota lark and a swallow-tailed bee-eater, which the other group didn't." Jimmy became quiet as Jane pulled him to his seat.

After the list was done, I told Cameron to go on without me.

"I'm going to walk Iris to her room."

"Okay, I won't wait up," Cameron said, grinning.

CHAPTER 22

Huge Kruger National Park was having problems when we arrived. We didn't know of the trouble when we enjoyed the brilliant purple of a mariqua sunbird at the park entrance. We entered a dry area of woodland known as bushveld, relatively dense and scrubby mixed broad-leaved and small-leaved, often thorny, trees and bushes. The sun was blazing hot, and groups of elephants and buffalo were plentiful.

When our group reached park headquarters, there were few people to be seen except the park warden and his wife.

The warden greeted us. "Our Zulu employees are out on strike. There's almost no one on hand to do the many everyday tasks needed to keep the park running. The workers are in their villages conferring about their wage demands. You can hear their drums beating, sending messages."

The warden's wife apologized for their poor hospitality. "The two of us and a few upper-level staff are trying to hold things together until the strike is over."

"We'll give you all the help we can," the warden said. "We can provide some food, but you'll have to fix your own meals in our kitchen or cook out on the grills. You'll be responsible for cleaning up after yourselves."

Terence asked for volunteers from our group to help with the cooking. Alice, Jane, Iris, and Algernon volunteered to help get our meals together during our brief stay.

"What the hell are you planning to do in the kitchen, Algernon?" Jimmy asked. I heard incredulity in his voice.

"To be sure, I know how to cook. I used to be a chef. I may be out of practice, but I'm sure I can manage a simple meal or two."

Iris gave Algernon an approving glance. "I think it's marvelous you're willing to help."

The park warden and his wife provided us with fish and antelope meat, potatoes, and fruits for evening meals, and eggs and bread to make toast for breakfast. Stavens and Selkirk had brought with us food for our lunches, as they usually did.

The park officials offered plenty of coffee, tea, soft drinks, and—-for a modest extra sum—-beer. We spent the evening eating antelope steak and potatoes with pineapple and apples for dessert as we listened to the Zulu drums beating. Drinking iced tea or beer, we sat around after dinner discussing the situation.

Iris pointed out what a good meal we'd had. "I think Algernon should get a round of applause." Everybody agreed. Even Jimmy clapped. Then those not involved in cleanup went outside to enjoy the night air.

"I never experienced a labor strike on a birding tour before this," I said.

Sean agreed it was unusual. "A new experience for all of us blokes, I suppose."

"What do you expect from a group of dumb asshole Zulus?" Jimmy Russo asked. "The worst part is we have to listen to those fucking drums instead of going out on a night drive to see animals and birds."

Jerry Buck grunted. "That's a pretty nasty remark. They have a union, and they're bargaining for better wages. That sounds like a reasonable thing to do. I think they're up to date. You just don't see the working man's viewpoint."

"It's too dangerous for a night drive. The warden has told us that's off-limits," Sean said.

"Have it your own frigging way. If nobody objects to my using a spotlight, I'm going to see what birds I can find in this compound," said Jimmy, stomping off.

"You two fellows seem to have achieved a decent level of civility, Jerry," Cameron said, laughing.

Jerry grinned and held up crossed fingers. "It sure makes life more pleasant. I hope it lasts. I admit I root for Gabe to win their competition."

"I give any tips of good birds to Gabe, not to Jimmy," Cameron said, laughing. "I'm afraid I'm not much help."

I went to find Iris, who was helping with the cleanup. She, Alice, and Jane were just finishing. They gave me the trash to dispose of. When I finished my chore, Iris was waiting. We walked to her room.

"There's something about those drums that's eerie. I feel like I'm in darkest Africa with Dr. Livingston."

I pulled her to me and kissed her. "Did that feel like Dr. Livingston?"

Iris laughed. "No, that felt a lot like a guy I'm falling in love with."

*   *   *

The next morning, after a breakfast of eggs and toast fixed by our cooking corps—with cleanup by each individual—we headed out to see what we could find. Once again, we were required to bird from the van for safety.

Large and dangerous mammals are plentiful in Kruger. The panorama of wildlife was difficult to comprehend. Giraffes, buffalo, elephants, lions, gnus, and smaller antelope of several species were easy to see from the van. The spoor of the wildlife accosted my nostrils, but I was too enthralled with the sheer numbers of animals to pay much attention to the odors.

"Look to our left," Sean said in a loud voice as we drove through broad-leaved mopane woodland. "There's a pack of wild dogs. They're very rare now because of susceptibility to diseases spread by tame animals."

"Are you sure these wild dogs are very rare?" Algernon seemed skeptical.

"Very rare. Canine diseases have made great inroads in the population of wild dogs. They may disappear," Terence said.

We were very lucky. We saw another pack of wild dogs an hour later. I thought their multicolored bodies and their huge ears strange and comical.

"What weird-looking animals," Alice Goforth said. "It would be a pleasure to don an outlandish outfit on Halloween and have a dog like that to take along for trick or treat."

"Look at those big ears sticking out," Maude said as she tried snapping a picture out her window. "Could we stop to look at these wild dogs longer? They don't stay still."

"We're after birds, dammit," Russo growled. "Why waste our time with your photography? You should take a photography trip."

Jerry Buck shook a fist at Jimmy. "Why don't you shut your negative mouth?"

"Pipe down," Terence said. "I think the dogs do deserve some time. This is a safe area. We'll get out and give them a longer look. They move constantly except when they have young."

Jimmy groused but kept his complaints to low mutterings about pissants and camera nuts. He even took his own camera out and used it to record the pack.

"What a hypocrite you are, Jimmy," Gabe said. "You should be trying to find birds. I just added a grasshopper buzzard to my life list."

"So what? I already have that. I'm still ahead."

Gabe grinned. "Enjoy the lead while it lasts."

I was rooting for Gabe, who was much more pleasant than Jimmy, and also a better birder. He lacked Jimmy's completely obsessive approach to their contest. But I was glad we stopped for the dogs. Their weird appearance made it easier to understand the great variety of dog breeds human beings have developed. I had always thought of dogs looking like ancestral wolves. I used my camera too.

Dark brown yellow-billed kites were skimming low above the administrative compound and along the roads we traveled. Occasional elegant, gray, dark chanting goshawks sat on snags along the roads looking for prey while long-crested eagles soared above us screaming *kee-ah.*

I pointed another out to Iris. I never tire of seeing these eagles. "They're common, but I really like their elegance."

Iris agreed. "They are very cooperative photo subjects too."

On high perches, we found purple and broad-billed rollers hawking insects, both beautiful but neither as showy as their lilac-breasted cousins.

Iris took many photos. I noticed Maude took very few.

"Don't you like all these rollers we're seeing?" I asked her.

"I'm unimpressed. I've taken a few shots of them, but I've photographed a lot of the occasional lilac-breasted rollers hawking insects. Now those are beautiful birds."

Large numbers of wire-tailed swallows and other swallows and swifts were flying around us hunting flying insects. You could imagine a horde of acrobats performing as they scraped insects from the sky.

A group of swifts flew overhead. "Aren't those African palm swifts?" Gabe asked.

"Yes," Sean said, "but keep your eyes open. Other species are possible."

Our group found Swainson's and Shelley's francolins roaming grassy areas. Ground woodpeckers appeared where rocks invaded the grassy areas. Anthills were common there. The only woodpecker in the region appearing often on the ground, these reminded me of flickers in the States. Like colorful flickers, these birds' pink breasts and rumps create a very colorful bird.

Iris had her camera pointed. "Look at that. A woodpecker on the ground, just like our flickers back home. These are prettier and very photogenic. I think I have some great photos."

Cameron agreed about the beauty. "These woodpeckers are good-looking, but you expect peckerwoods to have a little wood to peck. There's not much here in this open country."

"Probably they're after the ants. Besides eating them, they use them to ease the itching when molting feathers," I said. "The ants produce acid and that reduces the itching of new feathers breaking out."

Where streams and water holes occurred, flocks of sacred ibis probed for snails, worms, and frogs with their down-curved black bills. Flocks of noisy hadeda ibis hunted the same spots. Herons and egrets were common around the water. We stopped for strange black and white knob-billed ducks swimming in a water hole.

Maude lifted her camera. "Look at those funny ducks. Some of them look like they have some kind of tumor on their heads."

"Those aren't cancerous growths," Sean said. "They're sexual lures on the males to attract the females to a polygamous relationship."

"Some male ducks have all the fun," Cameron said. "I didn't know African ducks were promiscuous."

"They're setting a bad example for some of our group," Maude said. She looked over at me. I noted the disapproval in her turned-down lips out of the corner of my eye as I watched the ducks through the leaders' scope.

Where stops were possible as we drove through broad-leaved mopane woodland, we found black-collared barbets, bearded woodpeckers, southern black tits, black-headed orioles, plum-colored starlings, a group of chinspot batises, and olive bushshrikes—-a very desirable bevy of life birds, I thought, despite the arguments between Goforth and Russo.

At one stop late in the morning Gabe and Jimmy had almost come to blows over an identification of scrub-robins. Jimmy insisted one bird was a brown scrub-robin, but Gabe had identified it as a bearded scrub-robin, a more common bird that Jimmy had already listed.

"I saw the rufous flanks and upper tail coverts," Gabe said. "Those are definitive for an ID."

Jimmy scoffed, "How could you see those field marks in that frigging low light?"

"There was plenty of light. The problem is you've seen a bearded scrub-robin and not a brown scrub-robin. Brown scrub-robins like drier habitat than this."

"You damn pissant—are you accusing me of fudging field marks just to list another species?"

"No, I'm just saying you're letting your itch to see a brown scrub-robin mislead you. You're seeing what you want to see."

"You no-account tree hugger. I've half a mind to kick your sorry ass." I noticed that he was clenching and unclenching his fists.

Luckily, Sean overheard them and set things straight. "There was a bearded scrub-robin calling from the underbrush. I saw one there. The habitat isn't dry enough for brown scrub-robins, so I think you're mistaken, Mr. Russo."

Jimmy glowered and muttered his displeasure but backed down.

I was glad not to be the object of Jimmy's ire. I asked Iris how she felt about scrub-robins.

"I'm amazed anybody gets so upset about them. I'm enjoying our success. There're a lot of beautiful birds and other animals here."

"I've added at least ten life birds today," I said, "including a bearded scrub-robin."

"To be sure, there are a lot of birds here," Algernon Wheatley said, as he and Iris and I got back in the van after enjoying the batises and bushshrikes expressing their ire at the small owlet lured in by Sean's imitation of its call.

Surprise bordering on astonishment lit up Iris's face at Algernon's sociability.

"Do you keep a life list, Algernon?" she asked.

"I do keep a life list, to be sure. I like to make notes on bird behavior too. That makes the memories more complete, but I do enjoy adding birds to my list."

"I thought those fussy batises were cute," Iris said.

"Now that you mention it, I did write words to that effect in my notebook. They're comical."

"Don't you find it's difficult to write in a van moving over rough roads?" I asked. I wasn't altogether happy to see Iris and Algernon so friendly.

"To be sure, I do, but the effort's worth the trouble."

I listened, surprised. Algernon was one of us listers after all. Maybe I had misjudged him. He had won Iris's approval, so I reconsidered my opinion of him. He wasn't a bad cook either.

A pleasant morning of birding passed quickly, offering many photographic opportunities and life birds. Jimmy Russo caused little more trouble that day. We were soon stopping in a safe area for another of Fantastic Flights' tasty field lunches. For once, under orders from Terence on account of the possible danger, Gabe and Jimmy stayed with the group for lunch.

Not to be deterred from pursuit of birds, Gabe spied a lanner falcon hunting nearby for all of us to see. Larger than peregrines, lanners are lighter in color and almost as fast. Then Gabe located another strangely shaped hammerkop a hundred yards from us.

"I can't get over how crazy those strange birds look," Iris said. "It's not easy to catch their oddness of headdress in photos."

"You're right," Maude said, "but I keep trying."

Just before lunch was ready, I pointed out a magnificent black goshawk chasing a longclaw into the brush, where the prey escaped.

"That goshawk was a beauty. I wish I had a photo of it," Iris said. "What a wonderful example of nature's fierceness."

"Sometimes you have to settle for a great view. That's not one I'll forget anytime soon. I'll bet that longclaw is still diving deeper into the bushes."

CHAPTER 23

I recalled my view of Iris preparing for the shower. I would've paid for a photograph of that. I wouldn't forget that sight either. Every time it intruded upon my thoughts, I felt my longing for her grow. I had to convince her to trust me.

Our afternoon drive took us north to the Limpopo River, on the border with Zimbabwe. There we saw a beautiful bushbuck and a waterbuck feeding on reddish-brown bushwillow leaves. The striped beauty of the bushbuck stood out from the willows and the yellow fever trees decorating the riverside.

"Be sure to look at the rear end of the waterbucks," Sean said, grinning. "The white ring around their rumps earns them the nickname of toilet-seat antelope."

A distance from the river we again encountered gigantic baobab trees, whose bare limbs look like roots and cause people to call them upside-down trees. It is a plant that offers man and animals many benefits—fruit, leaf, bark, places to hide and nest, and lumber.

Farther away from the river in grassland we saw elephants, buffalo, blue gnus, giraffes, lions, and cheetahs as well as impalas and steenbok. Though our group was searching for birds, the panorama of mammals seduced me into forgetting our main quarry now and then. The big animals kept the photographers busy.

Maude patted her camera lovingly as she aimed it at the wild animals. "I'm ecstatic. I can't get enough of the wildlife. The many wild landscapes I've seen on television can't compare with the real spectacle."

"Those cheetahs are graceful animals," Alice said.

"I've caught them with video. They look like shafts of sheet lightning moving over the veldt," Iris said. "Look at that one chasing an impala." She moved her camcorder, trying to keep up with the action.

Alice tried to follow the action with her binoculars. "It's swift. It changes directions really fast."

Iris bent to the right. "I know. I can't follow it with my camcorder."

The cheetah tired. The antelope just barely got away. I had to admit I was glad, though I know that cheetahs need to eat.

We found some tamarinds, mobula plums, and other fruiting trees, where we discovered flocks of African green pigeons and brown-headed parrots feeding. In the same area we saw red-chested cuckoos and a crested black and white Jacobin cuckoo. In brush under the trees a large black, white, and tan Burchell's coucal showed itself, all no doubt drawn to fruit in the trees and on the ground. And finally, in open country, riding a buffalo, red-billed oxpeckers appeared—to be joyfully added to our lists.

"Algernon, do you see those birds?" Cameron asked. "You were worried about whether we would see one."

"Yes, I can see their red bills," Wheatley said.

"But are you sure?"

"Yes, Dr. MacDonald, I can see the red of their bills well. I am quite sure." Algernon took out his notebook and began writing. His patience was remarkable.

Jimmy flashed a middle finger at Cameron. "The man says he sees them, pissant. They're not British redcoats. Leave him alone. They are definitely red-billed oxpeckers."

"Oh, yes, Mr. Russo, I certainly agree they have red bills," Cameron said, grinning while returning Jimmy a middle finger and then a fist imitating cow horns.

Jimmy didn't seem to notice the sign of the cuckold.

"I wonder what Algernon will put in his notebook," Iris said. "Despite your dislike of him, he does seem to enjoy the birds. His notes serve the same purpose for him that my photos do for me. They help him relive the trip."

"Maybe I've misjudged him," I said. "You're a good judge of character."

That night, as I returned to the kitchen after disposing of the trash, I overheard a conversation between Alice, Iris, and Jane as they finished cleaning up and putting food and utensils away. I stopped at the doorway and listened, a little guilty about eavesdropping.

"Helping to prepare a meal for others provides me with needed practice for the new lifestyle I'm contemplating," Iris said.

Alice stopped putting away dishes. "What lifestyle are you planning?"

"What you two are already, being married. I've been on my own for a long time—you know, the liberated professional woman. I'm used to doing things my way. Not asking anybody's opinion. Being married and having to consider another person's wishes in decisions will be a new thing for me."

"You have to give a lot sometimes. More than you'd planned," Alice said. "If I had known what I'd have to do to keep my marriage with Gabe, I might never have married him, even though I love him dearly. This competition he and Jimmy are engaged in is a real trial, though Jane and I have banded together to deal with it."

Jane nodded. "It's difficult to adjust when the person you've married suddenly turns into somebody you have a hard time recognizing. Gabe is obsessive, but Jimmy is completely obsessed with the idea of surpassing Phoebe Snetsinger."

Iris questioned, "Have you ever thought of leaving him?"

"Lately he spends so little time with me I've thought I should. But leaving Jimmy might be even more difficult than staying with him," Jane said. "He's got a short fuse. We used to have some loving times, but now he doesn't seem to need me except when he gets jealous."

At this point, I decided to stop eavesdropping and announce myself.

"If you ladies are finished, I'd like to take a walk with Iris."

"We're just about done. Jane and I can close up. Go on, Iris," Alice said.

As we walked to her room, Iris told me her opinion of what Jane had said.

"I think Jane is afraid of Jimmy. She's reaching out in desperation. I think she might try to get rid of him if she can find the courage. He doesn't seem to her to be the man she married, and she dislikes what he's become. I wonder if she'd poison him."

"You may be right, but that might create trouble for me. Her pursuit of me is a misdirected cry for help. I can't fulfill her need. She might decide to do something drastic if she's afraid of what he will do if she leaves."

"I know, Sweetheart. I'd be the last person to ask you to act the part of savior. I'm doing everything I can to prevent your playing that role. I feel sad for her, but the answer to her problem is not an affair with you." She kissed me passionately, and I returned her passion, happy in the knowledge that she was thinking about marrying me.

The kiss lasted a long time. She sighed. "I've been wanting that all day."

"I have too." I wanted more. I loosened her blouse and bra and began kissing her breasts, but when my hands wandered lower, she called a halt.

Kissing me again, she pushed me away. She said I had to wait. "I still haven't decided whether or not you can be faithful to me."

I had a lot to think about before going to sleep that night. Iris was considering me as a husband. I was jubilant and, at the same time, apprehensive and very frustrated.

"Don't blow this one, Burnbridge," I told myself. I tried walking off my frustration before heading to my room, my heat bringing to mind the fever trees encountered at the river. A cool breeze helped calm me enough to seek my bed. Sleep didn't come easily. Finally, I solved the immediate problem with my libido.

CHAPTER 24

Our flight to Capetown was uneventful. It was early morning. We could see the flat expanse of Table Rock Mountain rising up from the coast and gleaming in the sunshine as we left the airport. I could imagine the migration of the Boers, the Voortrekkers, who took their wagons over this height to found their own state on the other side.

"The next few days we will spend traveling around the Cape, sampling its many habitats," Terence said as Sean loaded the van. Sean was to be our driver again.

Cameron asked what we were all wondering. "Where are we headed first?"

"We'll go down to the Cape of Good Hope and see the southernmost part of the continent, then up to Bontebok Park and over Table Rock to the Karoo," Terence said.

Algernon wanted more information. "I thought the itinerary said we were to do a boat trip."

"After the Karoo," Terence said, "we go back down the coast at Lambert's Bay and out to sea for a boat trip before flying to Sierra Leone."

Soon our Toyota van was heading down to the Cape of Good Hope through magnificent scenery as the highway rose high above the ocean. The road snaked through rocky inlets reminding me of a drive along the Pacific Coast of the United States. Iris and I kept pointing out breathtaking views of rocky inlets below—some of which she photographed. We were able to identify a few of the birds we saw. There were many soaring hawks circling lazily in the sky, taking advantage of the thermals rising from the steep slopes along the narrow inlets. We distinguished booted eagles and black eagles soaring on the updrafts, perhaps searching for rock hyraxes, one of which I spied on a rock ledge close to the road.

I pointed to the hyrax. "Did you know these small creatures the size of guinea pigs are related to elephants?" I asked.

"No, that's hard to believe—something so small related to something so large," Iris said, waving her hand as if brushing a fantastic idea away and then slapping me lightly.

"Some people won't admit we're kin to other primates," Cameron said, chuckling and giving me a thumbs-up.

"Lots of people accept science that adds to their bottom line. They love science that increases their wealth with new discoveries. Just look at how they pile into biotech stocks though they don't believe in evolution," Iris said, pressing her hands against her cheeks. "You'd be amazed at how some people who deny science as inconvenient truth ignore their accepted beliefs. They drop their objections when science produces a lucrative stock like Apple."

Cameron laughed and turned away. "They think God approves science that makes money—a strange view for people who're supposed to believe money is the root of all evil."

Iris tried filming a rock hyrax. "I don't think any of these hawks are as strong as the great roc of *The Thousand and One Nights.* It could carry off an elephant."

I nodded in agreement and stretched. "At any rate, these eagles wouldn't turn down a meal of hyrax, but I don't think any of them will tackle an elephant, no matter how close to the hyrax their DNA says elephants are."

When we reached our destination at land's end, I noticed a troop of chacma baboons lurking in the rocks above the parking area. To me, they looked even more formidable than the olive baboons we had seen farther north. They are a third larger.

Everybody in the group went down to see the sign marking the end of the continent. Kelp gulls loitered around it, and a Cape cormorant perched on top. All the photographers vied to get the best shot of the marker with the cormorant perched on it. And then several of us had someone take our pictures beside the sign. When our group returned to the van, it was evident that the baboons had mounted a raid. The biggest one was still sitting on the van's roof. He was eating Jimmy Russo's hamburger, bought at our last stop to use restrooms. Jimmy had been saving it for an afternoon snack.

He ran toward the culprit. "Look at that damn thieving baboon."

The miscreant didn't want to give up his loot. He headed for the rocks, hamburger in paw.

"Damn pissant baboon; I'll teach him a lesson." Jimmy snarled his anger. He looked for a weapon. He found a large rock and ran after the wrongdoer hurrying farther into the rocks. Cursing in anger, he threw the rock, just missing the baboon; and then Jimmy picked up a big piece of driftwood. He continued chasing the thief with raised stick ready to strike.

Sean yelled, "Don't do that! You'll be sorry if he turns on you. You're no match for an angry baboon."

Luckily for the avenger, Terence thrust himself between Jimmy and the baboon. "Put that stick down. We should have closed the van better. It's too late to change that. Hitting that baboon would be folly."

Jimmy paused but kept the stick.

"Dammit," Sean said. "Drop the fucking stick! We don't want to be cited for molesting the wildlife. And we don't want to take you for medical attention."

Growling, still hesitating, Jimmy finally let go of the stick, shaking his fist at the guilty primate.

Laughing as she lowered her camcorder, Iris expressed what I was thinking. "Jimmy really didn't want to give up that burger. What a silly way to act. But what great video."

"Observing Russo's behavior, I easily admit we may be closely related to that baboon," Cameron said.

We were soon on our way inland, headed into Bontebok Park. Its fields were full of flowers of many colors whose blooms always turn to face the sun, so that if you look at them the wrong way you cannot see any color at all, while looking at them from the other side you see vivid colors. Among this rainbow of sun-seeking flowers, colorful antelopes named bonteboks and gigantic gray ones called elands were roaming and grazing together with zeb-ras.

Among them we found what I thought a most interesting life bird. Not much to look at, just a little brown bundle of feathers, the cloud cisticola put on an unforgettable show for us. The tiny bird flew up so high it was out of sight in the clouds though its singing could still be heard. Then it zoomed straight back down to where its mate waited in the grass.

I turned to Iris and grabbed her hand. "I would like to be a cloud cisticola soaring for you, only I can't fly like that bird. It puts skylarks to shame."

"I think I'll like the way you fly," Iris said. I was pleased she felt that way. I was all-too-eager for flight with her.

The rest of the group listed the cloud cisticola but were less impressed with its performance. Almost everybody soon seemed ready to move on, but Maude and Jimmy were still trying to photograph a black, white, and chestnut male bontebok.

"Get out of my way, woman," Jimmy said, pushing ahead of her.

Maude shook her fist at Jimmy. "I was just ready to take my shot when you got in the way, you pest."

Jane came up behind them. "Try to realize other people want photographs too, Maude."

"Yes, they do. And they may never see copies of the twinspot they want so badly, if they don't act a little more politely," Maude said, turning and walking away.

Jane pursued her. "You witch. You showed those twinspot photos to Jimmy just to cause trouble."

"I made a bargain. Your husband was willing to pay my price, praise the Lord,"

"And 'pass the ammunition.' You go to hell," Jane said, making a move to hit Maude. Jerry Buck's hand stopped her arm in midair.

"We've enough trouble with Jimmy. Don't you get involved too, Jane," Jerry said as he lowered her hand.

By this time Jimmy saw what was happening. He ran over with raised fist to enter the fray. "Get your hands off my wife, you damned pissant ape."

Terence and Sean had become aware of the altercation. They rushed to the rescue, stepping between the belligerents.

"You people are always creating trouble. From now on please try to at least be civil to each other," Terence said, shaking his head. I could well believe he was exasperated.

"Watching them, you can see why some birders become annoyed at photographers," Iris said.

Before we left the park, we saw a few other new birds for our list. Sean pointed out a dainty rufous-eared warbler with its red face and black chest band, a small, drab Nanaqua prinia, and a nomadic black-eared finchlark male, all black except for its brown back—all small birds Iris caught with her camera.

A martial eagle soared overhead, its black head and crest visible, perhaps seeking a hyrax, watching as the van headed for Swellendam, where we were to spend the night.

Before dinner, Iris and I took a walk in evening light from a glowing setting sun. Close to our lodging we saw a pair of Cape buntings, with their zebra-like black-and-white heads; a gray-and-yellow Cape canary; and a group of beautiful endemic orange-breasted sunbirds sampling the flowers in several yards we passed.

I grabbed Iris's arm. "Look at those orange and green sunbirds. They're electric—spectacular in the sunlight. That's a great life bird for us."

Taking advantage of the waning light, Iris took pictures of all of these birds, as well as of Cape weavers sewing their rounded hanging grass nests. "It's amazing how well these birds build their grass homes; I wish I could sew like that," she said as she finally lowered her camera.

The dinner of local fish was delicious, reminding me of the buttery taste of Tidewater Virginia's Norfolk spot melting in the mouth. We washed the meal down with an excellent local table wine, fruity and not too dry. After dinner and the ritual of the list, I invited Iris to join Cameron and me in our room.

"I want to celebrate tonight."

"What are we to celebrate," Cameron asked.

"That's a surprise." I flapped my arms and whistled.

In the room, I poured wine into three glasses and handed one to Cameron and one to Iris. "The orange-breasted sunbirds Iris and I saw before dinner were my life bird number four thousand," I said, lifting my glass. "Here's to the sunbirds."

"How wonderful. That's a lot of species. And you haven't become obsessive like Goforth and Russo," Iris said as we sipped. When the three of us touched glasses again, she toasted me, "To your four thousandth."

"Congratulations; I didn't think you'd make it this soon," Cameron said.

"Thanks. This is good wine. We should drink the rest."

"That sounds like a great idea. That won't take long. I've reached three thousand life birds recently, but it's not too late to celebrate." Cameron proffered his glass for more wine. "The lammergeyer was my three thousandth life bird."

"Here's to lammergeyers," Iris said as we touched our glasses.

We made short work of the bottle. We found other things to toast. My admiration of Iris was high on the list. "To my auburn-haired, gray-eyed goddess," I said after we poured our last glassfuls.

As we ran out of toasts and wine, Iris stood up. "It's time for me to leave. Good night, Cameron. Jack, walk me back to my room, please."

Telling Cameron not to wait up for me, I followed Iris.

"Come in for a while. I miss not being alone with you." Inside, she poured some whiskey and water. "We'll use this one glass if you don't object." She took a sip and handed it to me. I took a sip and handed the glass back to her. "I think our relationship has progressed to the point that we can have a communion drink. I've fallen deeply in love with you. I want to believe you can be faithful to me."

I sipped the bourbon. I licked my lips. I felt happy. "I'm sure I will be. I'm sure I'll never love anyone more than I do you."

"I want to believe that."

Pulling her to me, I kissed her. "I'd hate to lose these delicious kisses." I was reluctant to say how much more I longed for.

CHAPTER 25

Famous Table Rock loomed up over Capetown ahead the next morning as we reached the highway for the climb up the mountain. When we reached the top, Terence pulled the van off the road and parked. Outside he explained our stop would be brief.

"The *fynbos* ecosystem holds a special collection of plants with special birds. Here in the *fynbos* we will look for three birds found in this vegetation: the Cape rockjumper, the grassbird, and Victorin's warbler. We'll try to find them along the dirt track you see here.

"Is this where the Voortrekkers crossed the mountain?" I asked, pointing to rocks higher up on the ridge.

"It's where one group came over. While we're looking for the birds, keep your eyes open for ruts cut in the rock by Boer wagons. Those were made by some of the Voortrekkers leaving to set up their own state beyond the Cape."

Later, looking at the deep tracks in rocks where a Capte rockjumper was perched, I could imagine thousands of wagons crossing Table Rock, fleeing British rule in the Cape and then again in Natal, fighting against overwhelming Zulu numbers at the Battle of Blood River and emerging victorious, only to succumb to the British in the Boer War, and then diminishing their heroism in apartheid. I was glad that had ended. It reminded me too much of troubles we'd had at home.

With some effort walking the dirt track and moving into the fynbos when necessary, we located all three of the target species, although not everyone saw all three well enough to list them. All of us saw the perky rockjumper well, as it perched in the open frequently, moving from rock to rock, flicking up its tail and thrusting out its striped black and white chest. Iris was able to get good photos. The other two species are skulkers, especially the warbler. Not everyone saw the drab Victorin's warbler well. Jimmy Russo was one of those.

He had strayed from the group and had caught up just in time to get a glimpse of the warbler.

"I'm afraid our schedule demands we move on," Terence said after we had spent an hour searching for the birds. He began walking toward the van.

Jimmy stood still, crossing his arms. "I haven't seen the Victorin's really well. I want to see that bird better. You should let us stay longer. What's so important that we can't spend a little more time here?"

Terence placed his hands on his hips. "You should have stuck with the group. We've spent ample time here. Almost everyone has seen the warbler very well. We need to reach Ceres in time for supper. We've spent all of the time here that our schedule allows."

Jimmy muttered about damned schedules as we climbed into the van.

Shaking his head, Gabe couldn't resist having a little fun at Russo's expense. "That warbler was certainly a skulker. Shucks, you had to be in just the right place to see it scuttling through the thick growth. I had some brief but perfect views."

I wondered at Gabe's willingness to goad Jimmy. He must have known when to stop.

Jimmy looked out the window, pretending lack of interest. "Have your fun, Goforth. I saw enough to count it."

His voice lacked conviction. He grumbled to himself, rubbing his chin and consulting his bird guide. I assumed he was wrestling with himself about whether or not to count the warbler as we continued on to Ceres, a town on the edge of the Karoo, a famous semidesert area noted for its endemic water-storing succulent plants and endemic animals.

A few miles from Ceres, we located large groups of succulents amassed in what is called a podocarpus forest composed of a species called halfmens, which grows as high as thirteen feet. *Pachypodium. namaquanum* flowers suggest human form and its common name. Its flowers attract many nectar-eating sunbirds, including the beautiful iridescent green malachite sunbird.

Terence stopped to let us have a close look at the succulent forest. While we explored the stand, I had a close view of one of the scintillating green malachite nectar eaters.

I turned to Iris and pointed. "Look at this beauty."

Iris took photos. "It seems to glow as if it is made of shiny crystal. I hope I can catch that in my photos." She looked at her camera's viewing screen and held it up for me to see.

"I think you caught that glow."

In the town, we found palm trees and sunshine and many flocks of doves of three species: Namaqua, Cape turtle, and laughing doves. Despite our warmth in the sun-baked streets, we could see snow shining in the sun on distant high mountains.

Grabbing Cameron's arm, I pointed to the snowcaps, hoping I had found something that would not pass muster. "Look at that. Does that remind you of Texas?"

Before Cameron could answer, Jimmy interrupted. "If it doesn't, I won't have a beer with dinner tonight. Everything reminds him of Texas."

I resented Jimmy's butting in. I turned and gave him a nasty look. "Maybe you're jealous that you don't live in Texas, Buttinsky."

"In fact, looking at those snow-covered peaks, I think of viewing the mountains from Big Bend National Park on a sunny winter's day," Cameron said. "I guess you can have your beer, Jimmy."

I must have spoken louder than I intended. Jane had overheard and came over to intercede. "Come on over where Alice is, Jimmy. We want you to identify a small bird that we've found."

*   *   *

The Karoo is a place where little rain falls, but a place of undeniable beauty—stony flat-topped hills and low mountains with stunted scrubby vegetation and little grass. The afternoon sun colors the hills and mountains with purple and red merging into black shadow. Here and there I saw a few ranches where a little low vegetation remained, yet ranchers were still trying to raise sheep.

"I don't see anything here a sheep could eat," Jerry Buck said. "It certainly doesn't look like the green, rolling hills where my father raised them in Virginia. How can sheep survive in this inhospitable place?" He shook his head in disbelief.

"You're correct. Sheep ranching fares poorly here. That fact has become evident to many ranchers, who have quit sheep raising and now are harvesting wildlife for the European market," Terence said, pointing to two antelopes running through the brush.

"Is that legal?" Alice asked.

"Yes, and ranchers have to work to improve their land for wildlife. Keep in mind that the major predators have been eliminated. Grazers tend to proliferate. The deer populations in the United States could support a reasonable commercial harvest."

"Antelope survive much better than sheep," Sean said, "so these ranchers are attempting to exploit a sustainable wildlife harvest. More and more ranchers are moving from sheep to wildlife. They're working with the environment, not against it. Besides, they're making more money catering to the European market."

"That's usually the way," Gabe Goforth said. "I've tried to persuade Jimmy that efficient use of resources is more profitable than working against nature. Like pollution, overgrazing is simply a waste of resources, lost money."

"I don't give my clients an environmental lecture when I sell real estate or stock," Jimmy said. *"Caveat emptor,* I always say. Screw the unwary." Jimmy gestured with his middle finger for greater effect.

"Your poor translation is one reason I have a problem with you. That and your list." Gabe said. "I've almost caught up with you."

"Just because you're an environmental nut doesn't mean I have to be one. I'm still ahead despite your environmental clap trap."

Sean changed the subject. "The Karoo sustains a specialized group of animals that've adapted to its harsh conditions. Birds are no exception. There are innumerable plants and animals endemic to the Karoo—a Karoo lark, a Karoo chat, a Karoo rock martin, a Karoo prinia, a Karoo bustard. We hope to see almost all of them."

"Look around. Forty percent of the plants here are endemic. There are numerous species of aloes. Twenty-eight species of plants here are pollinated by two species of endemic long-tongued flies. Other endemic animals include the golden mole and many species of scorpions. So watch your steps," Terence said.

"The Karoo should add birds to your list. Besides endemics, red-winged starlings do well here, as do trac trac chats and chestnut-banded plovers," Sean said. "We may even see scarce greater kestrels here, as well as southern penduline tits and their hanging nests. I saw a black harrier an hour ago while we were traveling, but it was too far off to stop. At a water hole we might find a flock of Namaqua sandgrouse."

"Look at those purple mountains," Cameron said. He shaded his eyes as he looked at the landscape. "They remind me a lot of West Texas—riding west in the evening, viewing the purple mountains in the evening sun—with different birds here, and without oil wells, of course."

"You say that about every dry place we come to," Jimmy Russo said, kicking a rock toward Cameron and thrusting a middle finger at him.

Cameron grabbed the rock and tossed it back. The missile landed at Russo's feet. "So a lot of dry places remind me of West Texas. What's that to you? Texas is so big and varied that almost any hot, dry spot offers something similar to a place in Texas. We have plenty of wet areas also, not the least being the Gulf of Mexico."

I guessed Cameron was really pissed off. He usually repressed his dislike of Jimmy better.

"Comparisons get old after awhile," Russo said.

Cameron passed his finger over his throat. "So do people who find fault with everything. Maybe they're begging to be put out of their misery." His smile did not convey friendliness.

It was my turn to calm Cameron. "Hey, buddy, come on over here and look at this bird. I think it's new for you."

CHAPTER 26

Leaving Ceres, Sean drove from the Karoo to the coast, to Lambert's Bay. Our first stop was at the Cape gannet colony, where black and white Cape gannets and jackass penguins, black bank cormorants, and Cape cormorants were breeding. Set on rocks jutting out into the ocean, nesting birds often were wetted by the waves crashing froths of white foam around and throwing spray on the rocks and the birds nesting on them. Gangs of young flightless, roly-poly, downy gray gannets eager for adults to bring them fish, and adult white gannets with black wing tips going and coming seemed to be everywhere. Black and white kelp gulls and gray Hartlaub's gulls wheeled overhead, robbers searching for opportunities to seize unguarded eggs or helpless young. Jackass penguins lumbered about, occasionally braying in the way that prompted their naming.

"What a sight. How do the parents recognize their young?" Iris asked as she took photographs with several cameras and lenses, still shots, and video.

I was just as baffled. "Nobody knows for sure. Some scientists think they recognize individual voices."

Her fellow photographers were busy also. So many opportunities were available that even Maude Buck and Jimmy Russo did not clash.

Looking around, Iris lowered her camera, laughing. "Those penguins look and act like clowns as they waddle about on land."

"They're funny, but those kelp gulls aren't. They prowl about displaying a nasty disposition. They're a perfect bird for Jimmy Russo," I said. A kelp gull screamed over my head, defecating and narrowly missing Iris and me as I ducked and pushed her to safety.

Iris walked away. "That was a narrow miss. It was almost like the gull tried to hit us on purpose."

I patted her back. "I told you. Those gulls are a lot like Jimmy."

We spent the afternoon visiting various beaches and mudflats and inland estuaries. Among our finds were lesser and greater flamingoes.

"They remind me of pink swans on stilts with bills shaped like Australian boomerangs," I said as I trained my binoculars on them.

Iris turned to Sean, "Yes, they walk around on red legs resembling toothpicks. How do you tell lesser from greater?"

"If they're side by side, the greater flamingo appears much larger," Sean said, pointing to a close group where the two species mingled.

"Other than that, look at the color of the bill. The lessers have all-dark bills."

Sean's lesson faded under the loud voice of Jimmy Russo. He was shaking his fist at Maude.

"Out of my way. Can't you see I'm trying to photograph both species together, you dimwit woman?" He slapped his thigh.

"You're not the only one who wants that shot, you loudmouth. I just raised my price for those twinspot pictures," Maude said, waving him away.

I had to wonder what the final price for those pictures was going to be. They had already caused me a great deal of trouble. I was tired of hearing about them.

Sean turned to the noise, frowning. "Let's keep it down over there. Arguments about photography must not interfere with our seeing and identifying the birds."

White African spoonbills were also feeding at this spot. The pink flamingoes demanded an immense number of photos, yet the spoonbills enticed photographers to film their huge spoon-shaped bills.

"I prefer our pink Texas spoonbills," Cameron said, lowering his binoculars.

"Everything's pinker in Texas?" Iris asked.

Cameron laughed. "Maybe not; we're a conservative anticommunist heterosexual bunch, but spoonbills seem to look better pink." He raised his binoculars for another look.

"I know somebody who looks really great in pink," I said. "She claims to be a bird man."

Jimmy overheard. "Man, I am so tired of hearing that joke. It's really stale."

"Then mind your own business, Buttinsky, and you won't be bothered. I still like it."

Iris ignored the interruption. "I see a man in khaki field clothes and behind him lots of pink birds in gorgeous field clothes. Smile, Jack." Iris snapped a picture of me with the spoonbills in the background. She scored a figure one with her finger.

Three-banded plovers, Cape teal, and Antarctic terns worked the shore waters. Listers and photographers kept busy interacting all day long with the panorama of species old and new for the tour.

After dinner and the ritual of the list, Terence told us what to expect the next day.

"Tomorrow we'll board a boat to take us off the coast. On our pelagic trip, we'll seek the offshore fishing vessels and the hordes of seabirds that tend to gather round them. When we return, we'll take a flight to Freetown, Sierra Leone, for the final leg of our tour."

Sean raised his hand and gave us advice. "Don't forget to take your medicines for seasickness. And you blokes be careful what you eat in the morning. Eat nothing heavy or greasy, or you'll end up providing a lot of chum for seabirds."

Jimmy looked glum. Gabe was smiling.

"We may see lots of seabirds tomorrow. I can hardly wait," Gabe said. "I'll bet I catch up with your list and pass you."

Jimmy made an obscene gesture with his middle finger. "Go screw yourself, meathead."

*   *   *

As our group waited to board the *Southern Lady,* I watched and photographed kelp gulls and smaller Hartlaub's gulls that came so close I couldn't resist pulling out my camera.

Once our group was on board, the crew presented us with life jackets as the captain gave out printed safety information. He told us where water and soft drinks were available, and where to find and how to use the head.

"G'day, mates. Our facilities are bog standard. Don't put anything big down the head that doesn't come from your body or you'll cark it. Use the trash can," the captain ordered, gazing intently at the women.

Alice and Jane exchanged glances and laughed. Iris joined in.

After the captain headed to the wheelhouse, Sean instructed us, "Keep in mind that we may see seabirds before we clear the harbor. So don't be surprised. Don't fail to look for birds before we get to the open ocean. We'll see some right away."

Within fifteen minutes after we boarded, we were under way. Hardly a mile from the dock, I heard Sean shout, "Albatross dead ahead; get ready."

Stationed at the stern facing our trail of foam, I saw a giant bird flying by on my right. It was a huge white bird with black upper wings and mantle and a yellow bill, a bird large enough to be a killer drone flown by our military.

"Black-browed albatross," Sean yelled. Soon after came another shout, "Southern giant petrel."

A huge gray-brown bird with a gray-brown head and pale bill was off our bow. It was almost as large as the albatross we had seen.

After the excitement prompted by the albatross and petrel, I noticed that Jane and Maude had joined me at my post at the stern. They were not interested in me. They were busy depositing their breakfasts in the ocean. The acrid odor was nauseating.

I couldn't help feeling glad I wouldn't have to worry about Jane's advances that day. A gray pallor covered her usually pretty face as she tried to adjust to the rocking of the boat and get her sea legs.

Gabe had joined me also. He was scanning for birds. He watched the seasick approvingly. He showed little sympathy for their suffering.

"Birds have a very poor sense of smell. The people who throw up will provide chum to attract more birds," Gabe said, grinning. The sea breeze took the unpleasant smell of the chum away. "I hope Terence and Sean brought some real chum."

Shortly afterward, while we could still see land, perhaps drawn by the chum the ladies had provided, much smaller black birds with white rumps began feeding in our wake, swooping low like swallows and then fluttering just over the water, legs dangling, looking for food.

"Wilson's petrels," Gabe pronounced. "Mother Carey's chickens, the sailors dub them, coming to take the souls of drowned seamen to heaven. See how they patter over the ocean as if they're walking on water like Jesus."

"You seem to know your seabirds. Have you been on many of these boat trips?" I asked as I grabbed the rail with one hand to steady myself and protected my binoculars with the other.

"Yeah, you don't get to seven thousand species without doing some pelagic trips. Look on your left. A Cory's shearwater is coming in. See how it skims the ocean without a wing beat."

A large brown bird, three-fourths the size of the giant petrel, came flying low over the water without moving its wings, seemingly without effort moving past our boat like a glider on an updraft.

"Cory's shearwaters are among the first sea birds you see when you leave land. We're out of sight of land now," Gabe said, pointing to the horizon. Following his hand I could see nothing but ocean. A sense of loneliness came over me.

Wondering where Iris might be, I was about to seek her when she appeared, camera in hand, as if summoned. Her khaki blouse and slacks set off her figure well. Her matching wide-brimmed blue straw hat with a chinstrap sheltered her from the sun.

"Have you come to add your breakfast to those of Jane and Maude?"

"No, I'm feeling fine. I followed Sean's advice not to eat anything heavy or greasy and to wear a hat or cap. I came to see if I could get good pictures back here," Iris said.

Just then, Jerry Buck rushed to the rail and added his breakfast to the ocean. Jimmy Russo was not far behind.

Gabe looked at them with a smirk on his face. "The Bucks and the Russos didn't heed Sean's advice. Jimmy never listens and always gets seasick. Shucks, he hates pelagic trips, but he can't afford to pass them up for fear I'll get ahead of him," Gabe said. He was grinning, obviously happy about his advantage.

"I think I'll catch up with you today, Jimmy," he yelled at Russo, who was just finishing throwing up breakfast and was still leaning over the handrail.

Jimmy stood and looked back as he weaved unsteadily forward. "No you won't, you frigging pissant. I've added life birds."

"It doesn't look like you're enjoying them very much. I'll bet I get four or five birds ahead of you. You don't look like you could hold your binoculars up for long."

Jimmy shook his fist unsteadily at us. "Shut the hell up, you braying jackass."

Gabe and I laughed as Jimmy weaved away forward and into the ship's cabin.

Gabe shook his head. "A hot, stuffy cabin is the worst place he could go."

Just then, another shearwater, living up to its name, sailed effortlessly by. It was a bit smaller and grayer than the Cory's. "What's this one?" I said, pointing at the new seabird.

"Look at the black cap and the white collar extending around the neck. That's a great shearwater," Gabe said.

"I got a picture, sharp, full frame," Iris said. "This is an excellent spot to photograph."

Gabe left for a time; he headed forward but soon came back, glowing.

"We've found the fishing fleet. We're in for a real show now. We won't need any chum," he said.

The next few hours were full of activity. Fish parts rained down from the ships. Seabirds were all around us feeding on the detritus cast off by the fishing fleet. The fleet did not consist of small boats like our American shrimping vessels I had seen in Virginia and other coastal waters. These were huge ocean-going fish processing plants dwarfing the *Southern Lady*. These ships were taking in tons of fish and casting out huge amounts of fish detritus.

Huge numbers of seabirds soared to the feast and dropped to the water to feed. Luckily for me, Gabe stayed with Iris and me much of the time. He knew the seabirds so well that I didn't need to bother Sean or Terence to confirm my sightings. Iris remained with me, convinced I had found the best place for her photography. "There are so many birds I wouldn't have much time for dolphins and other marine animals," she said.

More albatrosses appeared. The huge wandering and royal dwarfed the other birds, even the more common shy, yellow-nosed, and black-browed albatrosses.

Iris pointed. "Look at those beautiful birds."

A number of black and white Cape pigeons or Pintado petrels about the size of a small crow and white-chinned petrels, black except for their white throats, landed around us to feed.

The fishing fleet was providing us with all the seafood offal we needed to entice a mob of seabirds. Loud cries and foul odors abounded, but the sea breeze dissipated them quickly.

"I'm glad I followed Sean's advice about headgear," Iris said. "Do you suppose this tumult will attract sharks?"

I patted my field hat. "Me too. I haven't seen any sharks, but no doubt they're down there."

Dark sooty shearwaters and light gray Antarctic fulmars were joined by several species of white-bellied prions of several sizes. These blue-backed, crow-sized seabirds have a bow-shaped gray-black line running across their light blue wings. Hungry for life birds, I feasted on this cornucopia of seabirds.

"Most of these are broad-billed prions," Gabe said. "But look at that smaller one. See its tail. It has a broad black tip, not like the narrow band on the broad-bills. That's a rare fairy prion. The prions are new birds for me."

Iris was elated. "Wonderful. I have a sharp picture of a fairy prion." She spoke this into her electronic notepad where she kept her list of photographs.

Our intense effort to identify all of the seabirds continued for several hours. Then the *Southern Lady* turned back to land. We had fewer and fewer birds around us until all but gulls were gone, when finally we reached the harbor.

I took Iris's hand as we descended the platform to leave *Southern Lady*. "I added at least fifteen life birds today. I'll bet you added at least that many to your photographic list."

"You're right. And I didn't get sick at all."

"Me either. I'm glad I followed Sean's advice. It's hard to sympathize with Jimmy and the rest who didn't pay attention."

*   *   *

As we rode to a restaurant in the van, I leaned forward and asked Terence his opinion about the fishing operation we had seen raping the sea life.

"Do you think that fishing fleet can continue to put such pressure on the fishing stock without depleting the fish beyond recovery? The process brought us birds but seems very wasteful and unsustainable."

He turned slightly, keeping his eyes on traffic. "Yes, I agree with you. I don't approve of the overfishing, but since they are doing it, I see no reason we shouldn't take advantage of it. It's up to the South African politicians to deal with the problem. We can only offer advice."

I nodded in agreement, but I couldn't resist a comment. "Human beings are greedy and too concerned with the present. Many fisheries have been decimated by overfishing."

"Yes, but there's no denying it's a spectacular show," Iris said. Leaning back in her seat, she patted her camera. "A feeding frenzy inciting my photographic frenzy."

A feeding frenzy—that's just what Iris incited in me, but of course Jimmy had a negative comment to make.

"You bunch of environmentalists make me sick. I think I'll buy some stock in South Africa seafood companies," Jimmy said.

Iris gave him an intent stare. "If you do, you'll lose money. It was the boat ride that made you sick and miserable. You aren't being realistic. Jack's right. This fishing pressure is unsustainable."

After a lunch during which a number of poor appetites were in evidence, we boarded a plane for Sierra Leone.

CHAPTER 27

An uneventful flight brought us to Freetown, capital of the Republic of Sierra Leone, a West African city famous as a former hub of the slave trade and then a destination for freed slaves from all over Africa. The airport was noisy with activity and people offering to help us.

Our local agent, Kenneth Oshabi, a tall African with aquiline features, met us, accompanied by a beautiful young woman he claimed was an intern with his touring company. That description piqued my credulity. I knew polygamy existed in Sierra Leone. Adorned and coiffured as if she had stepped from a fashion magazine, she was to help smooth our way through the gauntlet of insistent hands and voices seeking to take our luggage and money when Kenneth wasn't around. Whatever her role, Kenneth and his men guarded us well.

Freetown was well into recovery from a bloody civil war, but our airport had a seedy look. Its bars and shops hadn't recovered from the years of warfare. "Like the rest of the city, our airport shows bullet holes and other ravages of civil war," Kenneth said. He gathered us and led us outside. As I breathed the cooler night air, a variety of pungent odors assailed me—exhaust fumes, motor oil mixing with odors of unwashed bodies and food smells from vendors' stalls.

Then Kenneth broke the bad news. "The airport is a most improbable distance from the city. That adds to your long trip, but it was a good thing during our late disturbance. You must go by helicopter or water taxi from here. Tonight it's water taxi."

He ushered us toward a bus where his men were waiting with our baggage. "You'll board this bus to take you to the boat. Do what my men tell you. Sometimes there is danger about."

There was some grumbling as our group walked to the bus. Jimmy complained the most vociferously. "Hurry up and wait. It's the army all over again. You have to put up with a lot just to see a few new birds."

Others nodded agreement, but everyone was silent once they took their seats. The irony of Jimmy's complaint did not escape me. I assumed the others were like me, too tired to say much.

Iris sat next to me on the bus. "What a horse's ass Jimmy is, complaining about Kenneth's helpers. I'm relieved to have Kenneth and his crew look out for us. There're too many hands out. Some of them are attached to mean-looking men. Their looks made me shiver." She snuggled closer.

I was thrilled that she was so comfortably close to me. It seemed a sign that she was feeling at ease with our having an even closer relationship. Maybe I should tell her I wanted to marry her.

The water taxi turned out to be a hovercraft. Near the boat, a crowd was milling around under a rough shelter. Underneath a tin roof held up by rough posts, there were tables and benches. Kenneth's men told us to stick together and pay no attention to people trying to sell us things. Whenever someone harassed us, one of our handlers intervened. Kenneth's aides saw to it that our group made it through our wait for the taxi without being bothered by people trying to find some pretext to persuade us to part with money.

After about a quarter of an hour, boarding began. On the hovercraft, we found seats, but Iris and I stood next to Cameron to enjoy the cooling wind on our faces as the hovercraft picked up speed.

"Without Kenneth's organization, this would have been a very difficult arrival," Cameron said. "Except for his employees, all the people we see have their hands out. They linger like vultures over a dead carcass. I'm glad Kenneth's men are watching over us. Some of the fellows who tried to bother us looked very hungry. And we still have 'miles to go before we sleep.'"

I yawned. "Luckily we don't have a horse or snow to deal with." I laughed. "I'm surprised you're able to make an allusion to Robert Frost at this point. You must not be as tired as I am."

"The night air is refreshing. Water taxi is a new addition to my transportation list," Cameron said.

"Mine too. I hear they give a smooth ride," I said as Iris pressed against me and took my arm in hers. I took her hand and squeezed.

"It's new to my list also," Iris said as she moved even closer.

My expectation proved correct. The water taxi ride was pleasant. Sitting down, Cameron, Iris, and I kept a watch out the window as the lights of Freetown crept closer and closer. The wind against my face told me we were moving fast.

"Look at all the lights ahead. Freetown must be a large city with plenty of electricity. They evidently have recovered somewhat from the warfare," Iris said as she smoothed her hair blowing in the wind.

A half hour later, we arrived at the city, and more of Kenneth's people met the hovercraft to guide us and our luggage to waiting vans. Through circuitous roughly paved streets, they transferred us to our hotel, reportedly the best available—once the pride of the capital, though now it showed signs of decay. Evidence of the war damage— broken places in the walls around its terrace and peeling paint on its sides, marred the hotel. Here and there glimpses of its former glory showed. Inside, we walked on worn carpets of high quality.

Terence gathered the group in the lobby and distributed keys. "You have thirty-five minutes before we meet for dinner down on the terrace overlooking the ocean. It's late, so just dump the stuff you're carrying in your room. Kenneth's boys will get your luggage in as soon as they can. It should be in your rooms before you eat or shortly thereafter. No need to worry now. You can feel safe here."

When we had our keys, Cameron began walking up the flight of steps to our room rather than waiting for the elevator.

"I'm waiting with Iris. I'll ride up with her," I said.

"Okay. Be sure to wake me up in time to eat."

As we entered the elevator, Iris took my hand. "Come to my room with me."

Despite our long journey, Iris seemed full of energy. She bustled about, unpacking what she had brought with her in her hand luggage, assigning me small tasks such as checking the fixtures. Her room seemed comfortable. The lights and toilet worked, and her bed was clean.

When she was satisfied with her arrangements, she thanked me, pulled me to her, and kissed me. I was delighted to sample her delicious taste again.

"We still have a few minutes before we meet for dinner. I know you like me, Jack, and I'm wild about you. You must stay away from Jane. Remember, she's married to a jealous man. His anger at you is unmistakable."

Warning delivered, she kissed me again. Like Milton's Adam, fondly overcome by female charm, I again admitted to myself I found her irresistible.

"You're my best defense against Jane's advances."

"She hasn't come on to you lately, has she?"

"She hasn't had the opportunity. She couldn't today." I couldn't help smiling. "Jane was very seasick."

"Don't seem so delighted. You should be ashamed of yourself." Smiling, she ran her fingers through my hair.

"Jimmy's been a real pain since Maude showed him those pictures of the twinspot. She did it out of spite. She certainly didn't take into account its effect on other people."

"Her being a religious hypocrite doesn't absolve you of keeping your vow to avoid Jane." She refused to kiss me, playfully pushing me away.

"No, I shouldn't worry about Jimmy and Jane. I don't even worry about my bird list any more. I'm in love with you. I want you to marry me. I want you to stay in my life. I'll settle for whatever relationship you're comfortable with."

"Come here, lover; kiss me."

"As many times as you want."

"Maybe a little more than a few hundred."

The next few minutes passed too swiftly. I hated to leave, but I had to check on Cameron before dinner.

Thinking of how lucky I was Iris found me attractive, I walked to the room Cameron and I were to share. I had proposed. I had to wait and hope. I found my roommate stretched out, resting, fully clothed, his eyes shut. His binoculars and other field gear lay in a mound on the floor at the foot of his bed. My backpack quickly found the floor beside his.

Trying not to wake him, rubbing the back of my neck, I combed my hair, washed my hands and face, and then walked around the room, finding evidence formerly excellent accommodations had suffered from lack of attention. The light in the bath hung loosely from its socket flickering fitfully, offering sporadic glimpses of a beautiful shower with no handle on one of its water faucets. Fortunately, the air conditioning, though not working well, cooled enough with the aid of ceiling fans to bring the room to a comfortable temperature.

Cameron began to stir, so I woke him.

"Well, our room isn't quite as pleasant as the one they gave Iris. I guess they believe men can deal with subpar conditions. It's time to go to dinner. I'm hungry. We can shower later, if the thing works."

"Suits me," he said. "I admit to being hungry." He got up, combed his hair, and we went to dinner out in the moonlight on a terrace overlooking the bay.

The night air mixed odors on the sea breeze with the smell of our evening meal. I happily sat by Iris in the seat she had saved for me.

The dinner of local fish and shrimp with pasta that she and I ordered went down well with the local beer and wine. It was a welcome ending to a long journey. Everyone expressed satisfaction with the food, even Jimmy.

After four beers and a Bloody Mary, however, Russo became belligerent. I was wary of him and kept count. We were all seated around large round tables, and he was sitting across from me, so it was easy to guess his mood. He began looking at me intently.

"You eat well, Burnside. Trying to keep up your energy level for all of your bird sightings and other activities?"

I ignored his sarcastic corruption of my name. "I'm just enjoying the tasty meal and the local beer," I said. I tried to remain calm and speak softly. I didn't want to rile him.

"You *do* like to enjoy things. What else have you been enjoying, you educated pissant? Female birds without feathers?"

I couldn't help rubbing my arms. I was trying not to irritate him, but a sarcastic remark came out anyway. "I like birds with feathers. I'm just not as obsessive as you."

"Obsessive? I'm bothered by other people fucking with my unfeathered bird." He cracked his knuckles.

I felt my chest tighten. "I thought you were interested only in feathered creatures."

Jane looked at him, her face pale with anger. "I'm tired. It's time for us to get to bed." She rose from the table. "I'm going now, Jimmy. Are you coming with me or do you plan to look for night birds again?"

"Don't go off in a huff. I'm coming." He got up. "Gabe, I'll get today's list from you." I was glad to see his back.

Iris touched my arm. "I warned you," she said, grinning.

Gazing at her, I responded to her enticing auburn hair and gray eyes—portals of a gorgeous soul—more beautiful than any bird. What a fool I'd been to succumb to Jane's charms. As far as I could see now, I had been simply a handy alternative to Jimmy's neglect. Or maybe just a means of Jane's getting his attention. My dinner became less tasty than earlier. I couldn't eat any more but ordered another beer.

I tugged Iris's sleeve. "He's nursing a grudge. I'm trying not to antagonize him."

Iris smiled and patted my cheek. "That's wise."

Her lilac scent aroused my desire, but also increased my anxiety.

I cursed my luck. If it had not been for Maude, my flight from Jane could have been made without much incident. Damn those twinspot pictures Maude took. Since seeing them, Jimmy had grown from unpleasant to hostile. Jimmy's jealousy hadn't prevented Jane's making more advances, but, worried about losing Iris, I had managed to fend them off. It wasn't that I wanted to hurt Jane, but I wanted Iris to marry me. For a while, I was having some difficulty digesting my dinner, but gradually my anxiety faded as I feasted my eyes on Iris.

As we finished eating, Terence announced that we'd leave the day's list for the next night. "It's been a long day of travel. We'll be birding around the capital a couple of days. Tomorrow morning we leave very early. In the afternoon we'll go for a boat ride. Cold breakfast at four-thirty—we load the van at five. Try to get some sleep."

He left, as did most of the group, including Iris.

She took my hand. "Are you going up now, Jack?"

"I'm going to have another beer before bed. I need it to ease my angst. Please think over what I asked."

"I will. Don't stay up too late."

Sean stayed on to have another beer when I offered to buy a round for him and Cameron.

"What are the chances of seeing a rock fowl tomorrow?" Cameron asked.

"Not tomorrow. Maybe next day or the day after," Sean said. "There're many other good birds to see. No need to rush. If we don't see them here, we still have another chance."

"I hope we won't need a second chance," Cameron said.

"Me too," I said. "It's one of the reasons I came on this trip. You know I missed the other rock fowl species in Gabon. I need this one to list the family."

Sean grunted. "This one's more reliable. I hate to think about the one in Gabon. That's where we lost Wandering Willy," Sean said.

"I've heard. Just how did that happen?" I asked.

Sean told us they had split into two groups. Willy insisted on going with the first, faster group. They cautioned him against doing the fast group. They didn't know his reputation for wandering then, so he persuaded them he would be all right, and they allowed him to go. When they were about halfway to the rock fowl spot, it had become obvious Willy couldn't keep up. Finally he agreed to wait by the trail for Terence and the second group. Sean stressed more than once that Willy should stay right there on the trail and not leave. Then the first group went on.

Terence and Sean never found him. They made a big search. Sean took the group on to their next stop while Terence stayed to look some more. They never discovered anything but his hat—beside a stream about five hundred yards off the trail. They found out then that he was called Wandering Willy back home in Canada. His family caused an international stink. Even though it obviously was not the fault of the tour company, his family threatened a lawsuit.

Sean concluded. "It was a big mess."

"It doesn't pay to wander off in the jungle," Cameron said.

"Especially here in Sierra Leone. The civil war took its toll on this place." Sean tried to soften this observation. "We'll be fine as long as we stick with Kenneth. He knows everyone and what's safe and what isn't. But we need to be careful. Some places will be quite primitive. You don't want to stray."

"Even here in our hotel there're signs of hardship," I said. "Our room needs attention. But there's a good view off our balcony. I've already heard some pied crows."

"I think we'd better get some sleep now," Sean said as he downed the last of his beer.

"No doubt about it. I'm tired," Cameron said. He and I followed Sean to the elevator and rode to the second floor.

Cameron put his arm on my shoulder as we entered our room. "Jimmy's more jealous than ever. I would ignore his anger if I were you."

"You're right. I've been trying hard. I don't want to give him any more grounds for jealousy. Besides, I want Iris, not Jane. But Maude showed him those damn pictures. He just won't let it go in spite of your reasonable explanation." I looked up and was relieved to see the ceiling fans were still working.

As we surveyed our room again, Cameron shook his head. "I think we may be roughing it a lot here, if it's this bad in the best they have to offer." Just then, the flickering light in the bathroom went out. Cameron found a flashlight in his waist pouch and went into the dark.

After his inspection, he gave some positive news. "At least the frigging john's working. I'm going to see if I can find a way to turn on the hot water." After a bit of cursing and searching, Cameron found a handle for the faucets. He turned the hot water on. "It's not hot, but it is warm. I'm going to try a shower in the dark."

"I'm going to brush my teeth. Go ahead and shower. I'm turning in as soon as they bring our luggage."

Cameron didn't linger. He soaped and rinsed and dried in quick order, brushed his teeth, and came back to the main room.

By that time the luggage had arrived. I was already in bed, barely awake, wondering if Iris would agree to marry me as I drifted into sleep.

CHAPTER 28

Yawning, I dressed and stumbled down to breakfast with my equipment, ready for a day of birding in West Africa. I was well beyond reaching my goal of four thousand species of life birds. The intensity of my birding had diminished due to my attraction to Iris and my attempt to avoid conflict with Jimmy, but our group was seeing so many new birds I couldn't help adding many species. Despite distractions and my lack of sleep, the prospect of finding new birds was high in my mind.

Sitting down beside Iris in the breakfast room, I noticed she had camera in hand editing yesterday's pictures. She was fully awake.

I pointed to her camera gear. "Are you ready for new pictures?"

"More ready than you are for new life birds apparently. You look sleepy." Her tone was soothing.

I grinned. "It takes us old fellows a while to get our bearings."

"You stayed up too late."

"Just time for one more beer. Sean told us about losing a client in Gabon nicknamed Wandering Willy."

Downing a continental breakfast of tea and pastry, I took bananas and apples and followed Iris out to the van. We weren't the last to load up with fruit. Maude and Jerry Buck clambered aboard with their hands full.

After they boarded, Terence said. "This morning we will be birding above Freetown in an undeveloped wooded area protecting the reservoir that provides the city's water supply. The van will take us to the top to hike down. We'll meet it at the bottom and have our lunch in the field today. After lunch we'll take a boat trip." Then Terence told our driver to get under way.

"When do we go for the rock fowl?" Algernon Wheatley asked. His tone was a bit querulous.

"Tomorrow afternoon, if all goes well, Mr. Wheatley," Terence said.

Jimmy frowned and glared at Terence. "That damn rock fowl better show up."

Terence crossed his arms over his chest. "Kenneth has found them reliable. But we can't guarantee them. You know well enough from your experience in Gabon that these birds are shy."

I hated to admit that Jimmy and I had a Gabon miss in common. I secretly felt as eager as he did.

Our Secretary Bird Wheatley had remained secretive and unwilling to mix with the group, but he chatted with Iris. I sometimes saw him speaking with Jimmy during the infrequent times when Russo wasn't chasing life birds in his competition with Gabe.

Jimmy had not opened his lead over Goforth again, but he spent a little more time hawking stocks and bonds. Though he made some effort to sell stock to Cameron, Algernon appeared to be his main target. Cameron overheard them discussing a deal one day after Jimmy had approached him.

"Anything to avoid spending time with me," was Jane's unhappy assessment when Cameron brought up the subject in her presence.

Alice tried to console her. "Honey, just be glad he's not chasing something in skirts."

Unhappily for me, Jimmy's neglect of Jane left her time to pursue me, even though it should have been obvious to her by now that I was preoccupied with Iris. Making Jimmy jealous was really what was behind her pursuit of me; I did not find that flattering. In any event, I was determined to rebuff her advances. I didn't want to irritate Jimmy further. Or give Iris reason to doubt me.

It was still dark when our leaders made a stop to get food for lunch. Iris got out to look at what the shop had to offer. The smells of food cooking in the shops whetted my appetite. I savored the smell of cooking sausage but made do with a banana.

My enjoyment ended suddenly. Jane grabbed the seat next to me.

"That's Iris's seat. Find yourself another one."

I kept my objection low to avoid a scene that would alert Jimmy to the situation.

"No, I like this one."

I didn't want to attract attention. Iris had to find another seat. With a raised eyebrow, she gave me an incredulous but knowing look as she passed by, hunting a place. When the van started off again, Jane made an attempt on my privates. I firmly pulled her hand away.

I kept my voice low. "Jane, I don't want to anger Jimmy more. It's no telling what he might do to you—or me. And it wouldn't please Iris, either."

"Are you a coward?"

"No, but I'm not foolhardy. I don't want a fight. And I'm in love with Iris." I commended myself for taking firm action, but I was apprehensive. It was obvious Jane had not given up her pursuit even after Jimmy's outburst the night before—or perhaps because of it. I knew I had to redouble my efforts to avoid her. I moved as far from her as I could and placed my backpack between us. The rest of our trip up the mountain was uneventful.

At the top of the mountain was a building with restrooms surrounded by picnic tables. Iris looked at me with raised eyebrow.

"Did you enjoy the ride up the mountain?"

"Not much. I missed you."

"You had company."

"That wasn't my choice. I didn't want to draw attention to the change." I made a peace offering. "Let's share some of this fruit I brought for a second breakfast."

Terence must have read my mind. He passed out yogurt. "We have a long walk ahead of us. You should have some more to eat, and you should use these restrooms. I repeat, we'll have a long walk."

While the group was waiting for everyone to take Terence's advice, I looked around us at the scenery. I ate more of the cold breakfast I had brought and some of the yogurt our leaders provided. The view from the top of the ridge showed us a deep valley filled with a reservoir created by damming a river. The fog was lifting from the trees. Here, high above the city, the air was clear, and the scents were of the forest, not the crowded city streets the van had traveled earlier.

The clouds were lifting from the surrounding heights as the van driver made ready to leave us. It was a scene of wild nature, contrasting starkly with the congested streets of Freetown. In every direction my eyes gazed on a large wooded area preserved to maintain the watershed supplying the reservoir. As I breathed in the cool, clear, morning air, a small African pied hornbill flew by, its black back contrasting with its white belly. Following the hornbill in my binoculars, I spotted a brown-hooded kingfisher perched in a dead tree on the far side of the reservoir—an auspicious beginning for our morning.

Maude was inspecting Jerry. Loaded with her camera equipment, he looked like a walking photo shop. She turned to Sean. "Just how long a walk will it be?"

Sean eyed Jerry. "A couple of miles, all downhill. I recommend leaving some of your equipment in the van."

"I guess Jerry can carry it," Maude said. Jerry groaned loud enough for Iris and me to hear.

"Oh, all right, I'll leave a couple of things in the van. Are you sure they'll be okay?"

"Our driver will look after them." Sean signaled the driver to stop as the van headed by us, and Maude put a large bag aboard. Jerry's load was lighter and his face less unhappy.

The hike down the mountain proceeded at a slow walk with frequent stops for birds. One of the first halts was for a resplendent yellow-billed turaco with a lime-green crest tipped with white and red. The lime green of the crest extended to the breast, belly, and neck, where it met the electric blue of the wings, back, and tail. It reminded me of lime sherbet under black cherry ice cream.

"You have to get a picture of this bird," I told Iris. She was looking through her binoculars as if in a daze. She dropped her binoculars and was soon at work with her camera, moving rapidly like an eager kid snapping shots as she sought the best angle.

"Thanks, Jack. Sometimes it's hard to break away from the joy of watching beauty to indulge in the enjoyment of photography. As Alice says, 'It's just pure pleasure.'" Iris waved goodbye to the turaco as we moved on.

Our next birds were dull brown, not beautiful photographic subjects. Sean and Terence spotted a group of birds the size of an American cardinal skulking in roadside brush and retiring into the forest. Very drab, these mostly brown forms were prized finds for us listers with the exotic names of brown and red-winged illadopsis. Iris was less excited than I about seeing them. She didn't even lift her camera. "What drab birds," she said, but she did look at them.

Muttered curses floated in the air as the group tried to see these birds well enough to count them. Maude was moving about attempting photography despite Jimmy's rudely expressed irritation and the rule about not photographing before everyone had seen the birds.

"Get the shit out of my way you fat bitch. You're scaring the birds."

Maude did not respond, but Jerry Buck did. "Hold your filthy tongue, or I'll deck you."

After much effort, in spite of the noise and movement, all of us claimed to have seen the birds well enough to count them.

Then Terence called the group together. "I remind you that there is a cardinal rule we all must follow: life birds first, photography *after* everyone has a satisfactory look. However, loud comments to a person breaking this rule do not aid in identifying the target birds. I hope you, Maude, and you, Jimmy, will try to remember this. I hope the rest of the group will help you remember."

"If these blokes don't, I will," Sean said.

Cameron laughed. "I'll be glad to remind them."

Just then I sighted a bird and heard it tapping on a tree. I butted in the conversation.

"What's that woodpecker?" I asked, pointing to a bird working its way up a tree.

"A new bird for all of us," Sean said. "A melancholy woodpecker, a recent species split. Good spotting. It's a new life bird for all the group, including Terence and me."

Finding a new life bird prompted joy rather than *melancholia* despite its being a drab, olive-backed bird with a dull, striped breast, unremarkable except for its brilliant red cap. Like other listers in the group, I examined it as if it was a rare precious stone.

Iris laughed at my excitement. "I'm glad to see a new bird, but I'm not as happy about listing the bird as I am about getting a sharp photo of it. It's not a great beauty except for its head."

"To a nonlister, our excitement must seem silly. On some days I wonder about the thrill of life birds myself. My list has definitely become less important to me since I met you."

The change of mood was helped also by the appearance of two handsome kingfishers, the gray-hooded and the chocolate-backed, both with huge red bills.

"It's difficult to adjust to finding all these kingfishers in the middle of woodland," Cameron said. "What would they eat? There're no fish. Mosquitoes? I don't see how they'd catch mosquitoes with those big beaks."

"They must depend on things like dragonflies and woodland frogs or lizards," Iris said.

"Yeah, but it's still hard for those of us used to our New World fish-eaters to adjust to kingfishers in the woods away from water and fish," I said.

Iris laughed. "Some of us have many things to adjust to on this trip."

Cameron snickered.

I managed a weak grin. "Some of the adjustments are very pleasant."

"I'm glad to hear that," Iris said, giving me a loving pinch.

As the morning sun rose higher and thermals began rising over the ridges, we began to see soaring hawks. Sean pointed out a Eurasian honey buzzard calling. It gave a sharp *screeer*. A lizard buzzard shouted *wee, wee, wee*, and, best of all, a Cassin's hawk eagle soared low over the forest canopy screaming just above our heads.

Many birds later, we reached our van without further hostilities between Maude and Jimmy, though they glared at each other and muttered to themselves.

Cameron told Iris and me he heard Jerry tell Maude he'd "kill the son of a bitch for half a dollar and a good draft beer," a fee that Iris and I agreed was creative and not excessive.

"I might demand more. I would be tempted to do it for a case of good beer," Cameron said, grinning.

"I think you should be paid at least two cases," Iris said, clutching me and laughing. "A tough job should demand a great reward."

CHAPTER 29

Hauling food out of the van and setting up a table under shade, Terence and Sean prepared another tasty field lunch out of the hot sun, a feast for which Fantastic Flights is famous among birders. Our meal consisted of a gourmet tuna salad spiced with cinnamon and pineapple chunks, juice, palm hearts, and sliced bananas topped with caramel sauce. The scent of ripe pineapple added to the ambiance of the meal. We had our pick of soft drinks, water, or beer from a cooler. Kenneth Oshabi's view of beer differed from that of Fantastic Flights. For him, there were times when it passed for nonalcoholic drink. I approved his humane attitude.

Cameron, Iris, and I found a convenient rock to sit on to enjoy our meal while ready for any birds that might appear. Iris welcomed Alice and Jane when they asked to join us, since Gabe and Jimmy were taking their lunches to a place away from the group.

"Jane, Jimmy doesn't seem as upbeat today as he has been lately," Iris said.

"Gabe has narrowed the gap again. Jimmy's sour because his lead is slipping."

"I'm surprised Gabe and Jimmy still haven't come to blows," I said.

"They've come close," Alice said. "So far Gabe has exercised restraint. I've encouraged him to be patient. Jane and I have helped keep them apart."

"I'm a lister myself," Cameron said, "but I could never pursue a list with such intensity. They may actually break Phoebe Snetsinger's record at this pace. Where do they stand?"

"Gabe's reached seven thousand species, and Jimmy is two species above seven thousand. They both should be well over seven thousand before this trip is done," Alice said.

"Phoebe had over eighty-seven hundred species on her list," Jane said. "They still have a long way to go, but DNA splitting of species will help them."

Cameron whistled. "Are many new species determined this way?"

"DNA research is creating many new species and altering our understanding of avian relationships. Not many birders are as close to Phoebe's record as Jimmy and Gabe are. And none of them are competing for the prize they're seeking."

"It becomes harder and harder to add birds as their lists grow larger. It takes time and money to chase new birds," Alice said.

Jane waved her hands in a triumphant gesture. "You know, Jimmy and Gabe depend on us to plan trips. They want the maximum new species, so Alice and I have become experts on the geographic distribution of birds."

"Gabe's so loving when he's with me. It's like having repeated honeymoons," Alice said.

"Jimmy's like a husband bringing home work from the office. He won't leave his birds in the bush," Jane said. "I can't stand this damned listing competition much longer. Jimmy was poor growing up. He succeeded in business because he worked hard. Cut corners. Made money. I've made lots of allowances for Jimmy's hard youth and his drive for success. But sometimes I'd like to shoot him."

"Just what causes the intensity of their contest?" I asked. "What's the reward?"

"Well, for Gabe it's just pure pleasure," Alice said, "but the winner will get to choose what conservation cause will receive a huge grant, plus a prize of $20,000 for the winner himself. The runner-up gets five thousand. Gabe worries that Jimmy won't choose a worthy cause if he wins, because he doesn't value nature."

"Now I understand. That's a tempting incentive," Cameron said. "It could be fun. Too bad Jimmy's so obsessed. Who finances these awards?"

The American Birding Association and the Royal Society for the Protection of Birds set up this special award in honor of Phoebe Snetsinger. They've collected donations from companies around the globe. Gabe and Jimmy are so far ahead it's almost certain one of them will win."

"The prize will be decided by who comes closest to Phoebe's record after this trip ends, whether or not they break Phoebe's record," Alice said. "That explains why Jimmy is extra nasty. He wants that money."

Jane cursed in exasperation. "He's got enough money. He doesn't need more, but he can't stop trying to prove he can be a winner."

I looked at Iris, who was gazing away from us. I wondered what she was watching. "Terence and Sean know how to whip up a good lunch," I said, changing the subject.

Iris turned back to Alice. "I think you and Jane should take up photography. It would give you a hobby of your own. You could balance the scales with your obsessed husbands. You're already doing the planning work. You might as well cash in on it. I believe women don't need to ride in the backseat."

"I like the sound of that," Alice said. "You're quite a photographer. Could you give us tips on what we would need?"

Iris smiled like a fisherman whose prey has taken his bait. "I'd be glad to, if you decide you're interested."

I felt a pain in my ribs as I controlled laughter. My already-great admiration of Iris increased. She wanted to turn Jane's attention to something other than Jimmy's neglect of her.

Terence allowed half an hour for lunch and fifteen minutes for cleanup. At two-o'clock it was time to board the van for our trip down to the river's mouth. There we would meet the boats for our afternoon ride through tree- and mangrove-covered islands to find rare endemics. A light breeze cooled us. In all of our African trips, I hadn't experienced heat and humidity comparable to that in coastal Virginia and coastal Texas during the summer.

On the beach, walking toward the boats, I saw a variety of waders, gulls, and shorebirds. At the water's edge, there were two small boats waiting for us, and the leaders divided us: six of us with Terence and four with Sean. Cameron, Iris, Algernon, and I went into Sean's boat. The Russos, the Goforths, and the Bucks went in the other with Terence.

I noticed he had Alice and Gabe sit in the middle, separating the Russos from the Bucks. "That way Maude and Jimmy will have more opportunities for photos," Terence said.

Our boats eased along routes through the islands. The water reminded me of the Okefenokee, especially where the island growth shadowed the water. Iris bathed her fingers in the clear water and dried them on my shirt.

Accumulated debris of branches and leaves in the clear water showed under our boats as we slipped quietly along channels between islands covered with small trees resembling willows and mangroves to find rare birds. We stopped to look carefully at white-browed forest flycatchers, mouse-brown sunbirds, and blue-billed malimbes, small black birds with red chests and huge blue bills—all birds endemic to this specialized habitat.

All the while we flushed squawking purple herons, western reef herons, and little egrets. Great egrets lifted off with grunts and croaks—their beauty added to the enjoyment of our boat ride. As the afternoon wore on, the shadows of the trees lengthened over the water and cooled us. The boat ride ended too soon.

"To be sure, those blue-billed malimbes were the highlight of this boat trip," Algernon said.

"Yes, but I found all of those herons and egrets more satisfying for photography," Iris said.

Algernon grinned. "You are a connoisseur of beauty. How appropriate, since you're so lovely."

My muscles tightened. I wished I'd said that. Though envious, I definitely approved of Algernon's taste in women.

"Thank you." Iris smiled her appreciation.

I wished that smile had been intended for me.

Back on the beach, we disembarked and headed to the van, scattering flocks of birds—whimbrels (small curlews with down-curved beaks), smaller shorebirds such as redshanks and greenshanks, lesser black-backed gulls, and several species of terns—all flushing and producing a cacophony of shrill and guttural cries and screams of alarm—before reaching our van.

"We certainly have seen a lot of birds today," Cameron said. "But evidently we must wait for the rock fowl. Perhaps tomorrow will be the day. Our leaders are like cooks who encourage delight in their work by delaying gratification."

Jimmy overheard. "You must be a frigging cousin of Pollyanna. I've had enough delay. I want that damned bird."

Gabe shoved him into the van before he could continue. Jimmy protested. "Let go of me, you pissant."

Gabe ducked as Russo tried to land a blow and succeeded in pushing him to a seat. "Dammit, let go of me. I'm in the frigging van."

Iris winked at Cameron and me. "Consider the source."

We returned to our hotel and what promised to be another delicious dinner. Cameron, Iris and I chose the seafood and pasta again to savor the sweet and sour local sauce. We washed it down with some of the very good local beer that reminded me of Kenyan Tuskers. I couldn't resist having three of them.

When the dinner was nearing its end, Terence took us through the ritual of the list. Many people clapped when he reached the blue-billed malimbe.

"In the morning we will bird the Freeport Golf Course and a few other choice spots. In the afternoon we will seek the elusive, almost mythical white-necked rock fowl, *Picathartes gymnocephalus.* We cannot guarantee this elusive species, but we feel that our chances of seeing several of them are good."

Jimmy interrupted. "I thought it was almost a sure thing."

"Kenneth has pinpointed a nesting spot. If we wait near it and remain still and quiet, we should get some decent views. We'll start a little later tomorrow, so we'll have a hot breakfast."

Cameron, Iris, and I departed for our rooms in high spirits.

"I'm going to sing my version of an old politically incorrect song, 'Carry Me Back to Ole Virginny,'" I said. "I call it 'Carry Me Out to My Ole Rock Fowl.' Listen. 'Carry me back to Sierra Leone/That's where the rock fowl sing sweet for the birders.'"

Cameron interrupted. "Man, you call that singing?"

I persisted despite poor singing ability. "'That's where I've labored so long for my bird list/day after day in the African jungle.'"

I felt rewarded when Iris laughed so hard she held on to me.

Cameron laughed too. "You're no Caruso."

Iris agreed. "Stop singing, Jack. It's not your strong suit. Come spend a little time with me."

She turned to Cameron and said, "You can spare this songster for a little while, can't you?"

"Take the young man for as long as you want. That way I get the first shower."

CHAPTER 30

I was delighted to go with Iris. All day I had wanted to be alone with her. Besides, her room was more pleasant than mine. Everything in her room worked well, including the shower.

Inside her room, the scent of lilacs permeated the air. Iris turned, put her hands around my neck and kissed me. When she released me, she began unbuttoning her blouse. "Would you shower with me?"

I was surprised but eager and happy to please. I was overjoyed she was inviting me to fulfill my prolonged desire. "I'd love to shower with you. Do you have enough towels? Cameron and I have only one apiece. I guess the civil war's to blame."

She laughed. I heard bells tinkling. "I'm sure I do. I was planning for us both to use the same one. They did give me a hand towel too. But no singing in the shower."

"Whatever you say, dahlin'. Do you mind my calling you dahlin'?"

"Not at all. I think we should use more terms of endearment, my love. I like the way *darling* sounds in your Tidewater Virginia dialect." Iris took off her hiking boots and socks and put on slippers. Her bathroom was open to the main room, just like Cameron's and mine. She turned on the shower and regulated it. Then she smiled at me.

Hands on hips, Iris waited. "Now, my dear, disrobe."

At that moment I was very happy I had not let my body go after my divorce but had continued to run and exercise to keep in shape. I still had the slim body of a younger man.

While I carried out her command, she assessed me with her gray eyes. When I finished, she inspected me with a twinkle in her eyes, feeling my muscles and lightly punching my stomach.

"You're as fit as I imagined. Now undress me. Take your time. Don't rush."

I started with her shorts, dropping them to her feet, then took off her blouse slowly and unfastened her brassiere. I ran my hands over her freed breasts, cupping them and kissing the nipples, running my tongue around them. Then I ran my hands down her sides and legs, sliding her panties to her feet. As she stepped out of them, I moved up the inside of her legs and thighs. I kissed her many times as I went, saving the best kiss for her lower lips. I felt as if I was in thrall to beauty and eager to surrender.

I stood. "I think you're ready for our shower now."

"Yes, I believe I am." Leaving her slippers and clothes, she took my hand.

Entering together, we soaped and washed each other. Iris was pleased with my reaction. "You respond well to my touch, and your hands are driving me crazy."

We rinsed off. Then Iris handed me a tube of body lotion. "Rub this on me. Then I'll give you a rubdown."

I followed directions, spreading the lotion over every part of her body with long lingering motions.

She ran her fingers through my hair. "Umm. Oh, don't linger too long down there. I don't want to rush. You have great hands. It feels wonderful."

When I finished, she took the lotion and worked the magic of her fingers over my entire body slowly and gently. My arousal became even more evident. Then she twisted herself back and forth over me and hugged me.

Her touch inflamed me. "I didn't know hugging could be such fun."

Turning to face her, I knelt and gave her another long, intimate kiss.

Iris sighed. "Ah ... this feels so wonderful."

After a few minutes, she pushed me away. "I don't want us to be hasty."

"Venus come to earth, I obey." I placed my hands on her hips as I stood.

She smiled. "I'm no goddess—very much flesh and blood. I don't want you to be guilty of idolatry."

"I can't help feeling worshipful."

"I've decided to take a chance on your being faithful to me. Tonight I'll give myself to you completely, without reservation. But you must give yourself completely to me also. Promise?"

"I do. I swear. I admire your beauty, your brains, and your independent spirit. You are butterfly, brainiac, and angel. I still can't believe you love pedantic old Jackson Burnbridge."

"If you keep saying things like that, my boy, I'll wash your mouth out with soap and give you a whipping to boot. Come to think of it, the whipping might be fun."

She reached out and grabbed her cotton bathrobe belt. She peppered me with it, laughing as it hit some tender places and I put my hands down to protect myself.

After softly whipping me to her satisfaction, she gave me another kiss. "I find you young at heart—a sweet, lovable man with a body someone twenty years younger would envy."

We used the same towel. Then she led me to her bed.

Gently she pushed me back onto it. "Sweetheart, lie down."

I did as she instructed.

Soon she was astride me, placing me within her, bending low and kissing me. Her warmth enveloped me.

"Babe, you're showing me what bliss is."

"I will marry you, Jackson Burnbridge. Consider yourself engaged. We'll just have to work out a few details."

As we became one, she moved up and down, lingering, whispering how much she'd longed to be with me like this.

"We've waited so long. I feel like I've waited years and years for this," she crooned.

She lowered herself to kiss me again, murmuring. "I've wanted a man who loves nature, who sees the beauty surrounding us, a poet, not a number cruncher. I love you."

I drank her honey, eager, trying to match her ecstasy, feeling as if I had been taken to a higher plane of existence, surrendering myself to joy, imagining lilac petals drifting down upon us.

After midnight I dragged myself to my room and entered with a minimum of noise, trying not to wake Cameron, but as happy as I could recall being for many years. I felt like I was the luckiest man in the world, even though I must have been the most exhausted. The wait had been long, but the reward was marvelous.

I congratulated myself on my patience. The intense longing of our courtship had rendered the final consummation of our desire exhausting mentally and physically—as well as glorious—even more wonderful than my fantasies. I dropped on my bed and slept soundly until my alarm went off.

The hot breakfast of eggs, bacon, sausage, beans, toast, jelly, and lemon tea tasted even better than I had imagined it would. But then, my whole world shone brighter to me this morning.

I could face Jimmy's taunts with equanimity now, and I would avoid Jane's advances gently but firmly. I wanted to tell Cameron that Iris and I were engaged, but I knew I should ask her before telling anyone.

"You look unusually chipper this morning, Casanova," Cameron said as he helped himself to more bacon.

"I feel great. I think we'll see the *Picathartes* today. I really believe it will happen."

"I hope you're right. I want to have it in my sights, and it was one of your main reasons for coming on this trip."

Just then Iris joined us, still looking like a goddess. "Good morning, Venus," I said, taking her hand and kissing it.

"I think I want to photograph you today, Iris. You look prettier than ever," Cameron said.

She gave a low laugh. "Do you think I'll get to put a *Picathartes* on my photographic list today?"

I nodded. "I believe you've done so many good deeds lately you absolutely deserve to have it on your photo list."

"Cameron, I want you to be the first to know. Jack and I are engaged. He'd *better* behave himself now. But I want you to keep this news to yourself for the time being."

"Congratulations, Jack," Cameron said. "Your secret's safe with me. I can't decide whether I should congratulate Iris or not, but you better treat this gal right. She's better than you deserve."

"I agree." I was happily aware he had not called me Casanova.

In the van, I found a mood of anticipation. This was going to be a great birding day. The *Picathartes* was high on everybody's desired-birds list. But first we drove through the city traffic to the Freetown Golf Course. After our slow progress through poorer, more crowded sections of the city, the wide four-lane to the golf course was an introduction to how the more affluent residents of the capitol lived.

Once out on the course, we birded toward the edge of the golf fairway next to the wetlands where the city disposed of its sewage.

"I guess you have to take your wetlands where you find them," I said, holding my nose with two fingers.

Cameron laughed. "No shit."

Cameron's joke prompted a soft laugh from Iris. "You two need to clean up your act."

Laughing, I objected. "No. Birds are keen of sight and hearing, but their sense of smell is less acute. So sewage disposal areas are often notable birding spots."

Cameron backed me up. "Build your sewage disposal right and the birds will come."

At the edge of the course, we entered a stand of trees and brush. Sean pointed to a large bird sitting motionless in a huge tree almost directly above us. As we all focused our binoculars on the gray bird, Terence said in a very low voice, "It's a banded snake eagle."

As we examined and photographed the hawk, a commotion off to our left turned our attention to a small flock of birds. Among them were several cardinal-sized birds with gray heads, olive backs, pink breasts, and yellow bellies, and a smaller black and white bird displaying white feathers on its back. They enveloped almost its entire body.

Sean pointed, "Look, you blokes. Here're some gray-headed bush-shrikes and a very unhappy northern puffback," he said. "It doesn't like their intruding on its territory."

Jimmy Russo came to my mind. "It reminds me of some people I know," I said, chuckling.

Cameron grinned. "I can think of at least one person on this tour."

Iris tried to place herself to take a good photograph. She knelt and pointed her camera up, first at the puffback, then at a bushshrike. "That bushshrike is a gorgeous bird. It doesn't rely on stealth in hunting."

A little farther on, Terence told us to listen to a bird calling *boo-boo* many times in succession. "That's Turati's boubou," he said.

Gabe moved quietly to his left to begin a search. "He'll list that bird, so it won't be his boo-boo," Alice said, grinning.

Sean squeaked a bit to excite the bird's interest, and a bird the size of an American thrush appeared. Its black back and white underparts reminded me of a man in a tuxedo. Careful not to make a sudden motion, I pointed it out to Iris.

Jimmy almost knocked me down in his haste to see the boubou.

"Keep out of my way Burnbridge."

I gave him a dirty look, but I kept silent as he brushed past, bumping me with the camera slung over his shoulder.

Sean directed us to a pair of seedeaters building a nest, taking turns carrying nesting material—twigs, leaves, and fibers—into the bamboo at the edge of the wetland. "Try to get a look at these crimson seedeaters. It's a rare species."

"This sure is a birdy place," Jerry Buck said. "Golf courses can be good birding spots, but this combination of golf and sewage disposal area seems like a real winner."

Maude agreed. "And it's a great place to photograph.

I've got terrific shots of a snowy-crowned robin chat, a gray-headed negrofinch, and that rare crimson seedeater, the red male, praise the Lord.'"

Ignoring the tension, Iris added a footnote. "I agree, Maude, but I think this venue lacks something in ambiance," she said, giggling.

Nobody objected to this enthusiastic endorsement except Jimmy. "You'd think this was a photographic tour, to listen to some people."

Jerry Buck eyed Jimmy, clenching and unclenching his fist several times. "Get a life, Russo."

Maude pulled him away. "Don't pay that jackass any attention. He's angry because he didn't see the crimson male."

It took quite awhile to get views of a seedeater for the entire group, but since these birds seemed to be nest building, they passed back and forth in front of us a number of times. Finally everyone had listed the seedeater, though not everybody saw the brilliant red male well enough to engender satisfaction in Jimmy and a few others.

Despite its lack of ambiance, the sewage disposal area produced an immaculately white Egyptian vulture, many herons and egrets, and shorebirds of several species.

Lured by the potential feast, a small bird hawk, a shikra, and a large peregrine were working the area, looking for brunch.

Bird after bird appeared to fill up our binoculars. I stayed very busy all morning.

As the day wore on, a few golfers began to appear on the course, and golf balls began to fly.

"I'll take birds over birdies on a golf course any day," Cameron said as an errant ball flew in our direction, just missing Cameron and landing in the rough, far from the cup. "I don't have the patience to deal with a small ball flying askew. I'd rather exhaust my patience watching what nature offers."

Thinking of my life devoted to impressing on students the joys of literature, I agreed. "I understand. Why waste your life waiting for an inanimate object to perform correctly when you can deal with something truly meaningful," I said. "That's why we love nature. That's why I keep trying to teach literature."

Cameron grinned. "Yes, that's it. I guess I misjudged you. You think as well as chase birds and women."

"I see a parallel between golf and my relationships with women. A golfer hits his ball as true as he can, hoping to reach the cup in as few shots as possible. I wanted to believe I had aimed true with Susan. I was patient, waiting for her to believe in me. But she never did."

"I hope you're aiming true with Iris."

"I think I am. Susan's accusations angered me. Finally I bogeyed badly, like a nervous golfer. I had the affair she accused me of, and she left me. We had trouble achieving par."

Cameron shoved his hands in his pockets. "But even Tiger Woods has bad days with golf and women."

"Don't lump me with that philanderer. I need a woman's affection, but relationships of convenience don't satisfy me. I want a real love, one without impediments. I think I've found it with Iris."

"I'm surprised a golf ball's flight prompted so much philosophy," Cameron said, shaking his head and laughing.

CHAPTER 31

The much-anticipated afternoon trip to find rock fowl required a lunch in the field. So Terence Stavens and Sean Selkirk put together another of their luncheon feasts with palm hearts, tuna salad, and plantains with a caramel topping. When all of us were well occupied with the meal, Terence told us about the afternoon.

"We should see some new birds this afternoon, but you won't be overwhelmed by numbers of species. Our major effort will be to see the rock fowl. Until we do, we won't bother greatly with anything else."

"How tough is this going to be?" Algernon asked.

"Not tough at all, but we must be careful walking in and out, since there isn't a maintained trail. We must go to a spot and wait. To get there, we ride in the van and then walk not quite half a mile to the hillside where we'll have to sit for a long time. If we're unlucky, it will be a very long wait. If we're lucky, we'll see them soon and well."

Sean added a reminder. "No photography until all you blokes have counted this species as a life bird. Is that understood?"

Nobody admitted doubt about his meaning. Everybody looked at Maude.

"Don't stare at me. I understand," she said, rearranging her camera gear.

Shaking his fist, Jimmy growled. "I hope so. This is a megatick. Some of us missed the other rock fowl species."

Lowering my voice, I leaned close to Iris. "Jimmy and I have a missed bird in common."

Turning toward me, Iris whispered. "You have more than that in common with Jimmy." I was glad she was grinning.

"That was before I was smitten, Aphrodite." Taking her hand in mine, I gave it a light squeeze.

I saw Jane gazing at us with hands on hips. *Uh-ooh.* I felt a twinge in my stomach, but I brushed aside my apprehension.

The long van ride allowed only an occasional brief stop. We viewed cattle egrets from the vehicle, but got out of the van when Sean spotted a bateleur eagle soaring in circles overhead.

"Look at the hawk wheeling directly overhead," he said, when we all were out of the van, glad to stretch our legs, escaping the heat by standing in the shade of the bus.

"It looks as if it's a flying wing with little tail and less head," Iris said. "Its flight appears effortless."

Sean nodded as he pointed at the eagle. "That's an apt description."

After a rest stop, it was an hour and a half before we finally reached our departure point for the hike. Everybody was ready for birding activity in the cool forest.

"I hope that damned bird shows itself," Jimmy said while we were stretching.

Sean grimaced. "We have a good chance. Kenneth saw them yesterday. It's imperative to be quiet. Understand?"

There followed a thirty-minute foray over rough terrain to reach a hillside looking down on a broken rock face surrounded on three sides by growth. Two-thirds of the distance up the gray rock face, at either end, a couple of mud and fiber nests hung suspended like new moons.

"Find places where you can sit in enough comfort so that you can remain still and quiet," Terence said.

It took us awhile to find spots on the hillside to sit in something approximating comfort, but in about ten minutes we were all sitting without movement like Easter Island statues, waiting for a rock fowl to appear. We waited and waited and waited.

Russo began to glower and give Sean and Terence dirty looks. Finally, he shattered the silence. "Are you sure these damn birds exist?"

"Quiet, you ass!" Terence kept his voice low, but the venom was evident.

Twenty more minutes passed. No rock fowl.

About ten minutes later, Sean held up his hand, a signal to be alert. He must have seen or heard a rock fowl.

Then several people on my right slowly lifted their binoculars. Following their lead, I raised mine. I could see a yellow head sticking up above the top of the rock face—-a rock fowl looking at us.

"I'd like to see more than a head," Iris whispered. I squeezed her hand.

At least the wait seemed less boring now that we knew a bird was around. Eyes focused on the nests, everybody became more alert, binoculars up at the ready. Soon I saw a white body behind trees to the right of where the bird's head had appeared earlier. Having seen all of the bird, I wanted a look at head and body together, but the skulker disappeared.

After another half hour, a bird appeared moving at the other end of the rock. I raised my binoculars. Briefly, very briefly, I saw the entire bird.

"Did you see it?" I whispered to Iris. She pressed my hand yes.

Searching for another view of the bird, I noticed Jane glaring at Iris and me. My apprehension resurfaced, but I brushed it aside again.

We waited another hour, but no further activity offered an entire bird, only glimpses of parts.

"I think we've seen all that we are likely to see today," Terence said. "We'll have another chance later in the trip. How many of you feel you viewed enough to count the bird?"

Everyone agreed they'd seen enough to count it except for Alice and Jerry.

"But we've had no photographic opportunities," Maude said. "I'm not as enamored with my list as some people, praise the Lord."

Jimmy gave a snarling laugh. "Praise as much as you want. This is a trip to see birds, not to photograph. Praise the devil, I've added a rock fowl to my list."

"As I told you, we'll have another chance," Terence said. "Given our impatient noise, we were luckier than we deserved. At our second opportunity in the Gola forest, we should see them well enough for photos." Terence turned, motioning us to the trail. "We have a long hike back to the van. The men will go on ahead and allow the women to have a rest stop. We'll wait up ahead for you to catch up. Good birds are possible on the return hike, but we are beginning to lose light, so we don't want to tarry. In the dark, the walk might be dangerous."

Sean pointed to the path. "Be careful—we don't want any turned ankles, or worse, a broken leg or arm. We'll do more birding after we reach the van."

The return hike went slowly because some of our group lacked the ability to move fast on rough terrain. We didn't stop for any birds until after we had done the most difficult part of the walk.

Then Sean said he heard the *fuuu, fuu, fuu, fju-weh* whistle of a fire-crested alethe, a thrush-like bird with a brown back, a white breast, a gray face, and an orange-red cap. We came to a halt. After a short search, Sean found it and pointed it out on its perch just as it sang again in the fading light, sending a chill up my neck, a poetic pang similar to what I felt the first time I read Keats's lines about hearing a nightingale sing.

I whispered to Iris. "I feel as if I've heard an African cousin of the nightingale. Its song brings to mind Keats's "Ode to a Nightingale" about "magic casements, opening on the foam/Of perilous seas, in faery lands forlorn."

Iris clasped my waist. "Yes, such a romantic sound. It makes me wish we were alone."

Our hike didn't stop again until we reached the van. After boarding, we moved to a part of the forest where a large opening afforded brilliant light. We found a number of forest birds. I saw a golden greenbul, a red-tailed greenbul, and a violet-backed starling— well-named birds whose colors appeared glowing in the fading yet piercing sunlight.

Two people had missed a great look at the rock fowl, but there were many happy birders in our group—numbered among them Cameron, Iris, and me. Even Jimmy Russo radiated happiness despite the reprimand he had received.

I felt as if the load of my rock fowl jinx had vaporized. I added a bird family to my list, no small feat for those of us seeking to see at least one member of all of the world's over two hundred bird families. For me, the rockfowl, one of the only two species in the family *Picathartes,* was number 201.

Back at the hotel, getting ready for dinner, Cameron told me he had overheard a conversation between Secretary Bird Wheatley and braying Hadeda Ibis Russo.

"Jimmy was reassuring Algernon about a stock deal. He evidently had promised it was sure to make a 30 percent gain in six months. Algernon asked, 'Are you sure?' Jimmy made the same pitch to me, but I turned him down. Maybe Wheatley bit."

"A stock like that sounds too good to believe. I think Algernon is too cautious to fall for that line."

I went to Iris's room to go with her to dinner. After a long kiss, I told her I wanted her opinion on an investment matter.

Iris laughed. "I'll charge you another lengthy kiss."

I eagerly paid my fee. "Cameron says he overheard Jimmy talking to Algernon about a stock he claimed would gain 30 percent in six months. What do you think?"

"I like to find those stocks for my fund. The trouble is few exist. There are many more that lose 30 percent."

"I wonder if Algernon bit."

"Sometimes even careful people become greedy," Iris said.

"I'm greedy. I want another kiss before dinner," I said, pulling her to me.

She held her lips away. "I don't want to ruin your appetite with too much dessert."

"I feel like throwing caution away. Give me another taste of your honey."

After we had eaten our meal, Terence embarked upon the ritual of the list. As he called out the rock fowl, there were loud cheers and clapping. Terence took a bow, and then continued. List completed, he outlined the next day's program.

"We're leaving early, around 4:30 a.m. Try to get some sleep. Please try to be ready to board at four. We'll have breakfast on the road and hope to see and hear night birds as we drive and then boat to Tiwai Island."

CHAPTER 32

Climbing aboard our bus in the dark, we began the trip to Tiwai Island. Soon over half the occupants of our large Toyota bus were returning to their interrupted sleep in their comfortable seats. Iris cuddled up to me as I nodded off. Kenneth was our driver again.

"Heads up back there, Burnbridge." I heard Sean through my napping. I had asked him to wake me once we were out of the city and traveling roads where night birds were likely. Making myself open my eyes, leaning forward, I began watching for night birds.

Ten minutes later, nightjar eyes flashed in the road ahead of us, and as the bird took off at our approach, Sean called out, "long-tailed nightjar." We flushed several more before we saw a huge lump in the road.

It flushed, carrying a rodent, as the bus approached it. "It's an eagle owl," Sean said, "a grayish eagle owl, close kin to the giant eagle owl."

We made a stop about ten miles farther on. Terence led those awake out of the van to listen. I woke Iris. Yawning, she followed me. After ten minutes, I heard a barking *woo-woo-woo-roo-roo-woo.*

"That's an African wood owl," Terence said.

The cool night air and a slight breeze helped me wake up. The aroma of nearby wood fires reached me as we waited for another call. After I heard the owl again, Terence ushered us back into the bus. I lingered to be last on board to hear the cry once more.

I was enthusiastic about hearing the owl so clearly. "There's something about owls calling that always gives me a pang. They seem so mysterious. I feel as if they're voices from another world. Their hoots are a summons."

"I know what you mean, but I'm too sleepy to wonder about owl mystery," Iris said as she yawned, snuggled against me, and went back to sleep. I thanked my luck, blissful to feel her heartbeat.

A few more nightjars appeared before sunrise. Once the sun was up, Terence found a convenient place to pull off for us to have breakfast. We had a cook with us now. Sean introduced Sandy, who served us a cold breakfast of buns, yogurt, hard-boiled eggs, and plenty of hot tea and coffee to go with them.

Half an hour later, Sandy packed up breakfast, and we once again headed for Tiwai Island, set in the middle of the Moa River. Another hour brought us to a landing, where a crowd of local folk dressed in a rainbow of colorful garb had gathered to see us off. Milling about, the villagers shouted enjoyment at the excitement we offered, their entertainment for the day.

Laughing and joking, helpers took our gear and loaded two boats at Kenneth's direction. Afterward, we stepped into the boats for transport to the island.

Sandy, her utensils, our provisions, and the leaders' equipment went in the first boat with the Bucks, the Goforths, and Terence. Sean and the rest of us followed in the second boat despite Jimmy's protests.

"Jane and I should go in the first boat. I may miss a bird that Gabe sees. The Bucks can wait. They don't care about their lists."

"Things go better when you and the Bucks are apart," Sean said. "Maude asked to go in the first boat to get pictures of the island."

Jimmy glowered but contented himself with a few muttered curses about pissant frigging photographers.

On the trip to the island, we saw white-winged black terns diving for fish and clownish-looking African skimmers fishing by flying with the lower mandibles of their huge orange and black beaks skimming the water. As we approached the landing, shorebirds—including a common sandpiper with its stuttering, stiff-winged flight, and a greenshank with upturned bill—flushed and flew off.

While the unloading of the boats took place, Iris and I had a chance to look around. We walked the track from the shore. It led to a clearing. Fronted by a grassy lawn were two large rustic brown clapboard cabins backed by woods. We were to room in the rustic buildings, the men all in one building and the women in the other, but Sandy would cook for all of us with the help of the Tiwai Island Wildlife Sanctuary cook.

"I suppose we won't get to see each other alone while we're here," Iris said. She held my hand as we walked to our quarters. "Two buildings—segregation of the sexes is mandatory."

I squeezed her hand. "Maybe we can take some walks alone in the evenings if there aren't any birding activities."

Iris sighed. "Let's try. I'll miss you. I'm getting accustomed to having you around. You could write out one of your poems for me. I'll read it when I miss you."

After the group had selected beds and stowed gear, we met with Terence and Sean on the porch of the men's building.

"We'll take a boat trip this afternoon. Our chief target bird will be the Egyptian plover, but there are many shorebirds and other water birds to see," Terence said. "First we'll rest and bird around here while Sandy prepares lunch."

Sean offered a quick birding hike. "Those who want to go birding for about thirty minutes should come with me."

With the exception of Jane Russo, Alice Goforth, and the Bucks, everyone followed Sean as he headed down a woodland trail. The first bird we encountered was an African pied wagtail, a friendly black and white bird about six or seven inches long that fluttered ahead of us, searching for insects. Two hundred yards down the trail, Sean pointed out a yellow-rumped tinkerbird, searching under tree bark for grubs, and a form skulking in the brush. The skulker turned out to be an oriole warbler, a twelve-inch yellow bird with a black head.

"That warbler is a good-looking bird, but it's not eager to be seen," Cameron said after he finally managed to get a good look.

I was still trying to see it. "I agree. It reminds me of some skulking warblers like Swainson's back home. I like the challenge stealthy birds give."

Sean was determined to get everyone a view of this bird. It took some time, but I had a really good look. In situations like this, I always think of my first Lincoln's sparrow I chased along through the brush on a ditch bank on my parents' farm. Finally I saw it. I felt triumphant. I was only thirteen and proud to have found it.

By the time everyone managed to get a view of the shy African warbler, it was time for lunch. As we exited the woods, Sean pointed out several species of swifts flying over the clearing, hunting insects. "They're having lunch too," Sean said.

Sandy had squash soup and chicken salad sandwiches ready for us. The others were already eating with obvious enjoyment. After lunch, Iris and I wandered about the edge of the clearing. We passed by Jimmy Russo and Algernon Wheatley conversing, evidently about investments. The word "stock" and the question, "Are you sure?" made me wonder whether something was worrying Algernon.

The boats came for us at two o'clock. Iris and I ended up in the same boat with Jimmy. Looking at Iris, Jane hesitated to board.

Jimmy motioned to her. "Get in the boat."

Scowling at Iris and me, Jane refused. "I think I'll stay here."

"Get in. You'll enjoy the ride."

"No, thanks." Jane turned and walked away. Alice followed. "I'll stay with Jane."

I felt a twinge of apprehension, but it soon passed as Iris took my hand. With everybody but Jane and Alice on board for the river trip, we headed upriver.

Sean alerted the group. "Look carefully at any sandbars we see. That's where we'll find an Egyptian plover and other shorebirds—and maybe some river terns and new animals."

The evening sun gave a golden glow to the river. Our boat ride up the Moa River would have been enjoyable even without birds, but I saw large numbers of terns and shorebirds. Finally, on a large sandbar building up around large rocks, I saw birds perched, some flying off, hunting insects, then lighting again.

"What are those birds with dark faces and large white throat patches?" I asked. "Their backs are tan and their breasts gray. They're graceful flyers."

"Rock pratincoles," Sean said. Then he pointed to the other end of the sandbar. "Look over there. That's an Egyptian plover. That pattern of black cap, white throat and breast, black chest band, and pink belly is unmistakable."

In the other boat, away from Jimmy, Maude was busy photographing the plover. "What great photos I'm getting."

Not to be outdone, Iris was madly photographing also. "What a beautiful shorebird."

Our target bird seen well by everyone and photographed by many, we headed back down river in the glow of a setting sun. Pratincoles swooped over us as the trees cast shadows across the river. In the canopy of large red ironwood and kapok trees, I saw green monkeys and western red colobus monkeys.

Sean pointed them out. "Those colobus monkeys are supposed to harbor the Ebola virus. Chimpanzees hunt them and become infected. Then human hunters eat the monkeys or chimpanzees and become infected. At least that's the theory."

Iris shuddered. "Ugh, I couldn't eat a monkey, much less a chimpanzee. It's cannibalistic."

Deep in conversation at the back of our boat, Jimmy Russo and Algernon Wheatley paid little attention to the scenic beauty, monkeys, the pungent odors of the jungle, the swirling currents of the river, or the bird flocks flying to roost.

I reveled in the beauty. "The Moa is a splendid river." Nobody demurred.

Iris couldn't resist photographing. "The beautiful pratincoles and the plover would have been enough to please me. This evening scenery makes the trip even more satisfying."

"Look there, over by the river bank." Sean pointed to a large animal and a smaller one coming out of the water. "It's a pygmy hippopotamus with young. They're leaving the river for an evening meal."

"Do they have any enemies other than man?" I asked.

"Sometimes crocodiles attack them, but hippos can take care of crocs. The crocodiles have to worry about huge lizards, Nile monitors, attacking their nests and young."

Back at our camp, Sandy had a dinner of shrimp and pasta ready for us. She served Tiwai Island's special banana pancakes with pepper sauce for dessert. I ate three.

After all the pancakes were gone, Terence did the list and told us to get some sleep. "Be ready for an early breakfast. We have only one full day and a morning left to bird this island, so we want to get an early start tomorrow. Sandy will send us off with a hot breakfast. We'll try for six thirty."

Iris grabbed my hand. "Let's go for that walk."

We took our flashlights and headed into the clear grassy space in front of the buildings. I handed her the poem she had requested and asked her to read it as I held a flashlight on the paper where I had written the poem:

Her voice made my poetry sound beautiful. "No scudding clouds slipping across the moon climb higher than our soaring love, yet I am alone. I feel despair as loneliness prompts me to dream memories of your kiss," Iris read. "It's beautiful. It says just what I feel when we're apart."

I turned the flashlight off. We kissed and clasped tightly, gazing at each other in the starlight. Then I searched the sky until I found the Big Dipper. I pointed it out to Iris.

"I'll dream of you tonight. I swear on the Big Dipper," I said. I slipped my hand under her bra and fondled her breast.

"And I of you."

"I expect an erotic vision."

"It had better be about me," Iris said, nuzzling me.

"Imagine yourself in all the positions of the *Kama Sutra*."

"It sounds delightful." Laughing, she ran her fingers through my hair. "I'll want you to show me those, when it's suitable."

We walked to her dormitory and kissed goodnight.

"May both of us have sweet dreams," Iris said.

CHAPTER 33

Next morning Sandy produced a hot breakfast of eggs, bacon, and toast, plus cold papaya slices from a platter, and the usual tea and coffee. After breakfast, we headed down the woodland trail. As soon as we entered the woods, Sean called our attention to a bird the size of a starling moving in a tree ahead of us.

"Try to focus your binoculars on that bird. It's a spotted honeyguide, very difficult to find," he said. When everyone had had a good view of this undistinguished brown bird with a brown-striped dirty-white breast, we continued down the trail.

Just then I saw something white moving parallel to us behind tall grass.

"What's that bird walking away from us, Sean?"

He looked where I pointed. He became excited, "That's a white-breasted guineafowl. Try to get a view of that red head and big white collar and black body. It's a very rare bird."

About half our group caught sight of the guineafowl. Jimmy Russo wasn't one of them, but Gabe Goforth was.

Jimmy spit out his chewing gum. "Damn. I didn't see anything but tall grass moving."

Gabe laughed. "I'm one closer. Count and weep."

Jimmy glowered. "I'm still ahead, pissant."

There was considerable flack resulting from this sighting during much of the morning. I was already high on Jimmy's blacklist. Now I went even higher, although I failed to see why he should blame me for his being too slow to see the bird.

"You're one lucky devil, Burnside," Jimmy said. "But be careful. Your luck may run out." He raised a fist in my direction.

To deflect his antagonism, I joked. "Even a blind pig finds a truffle now and then." Aware he was belligerent and mangling my name because of Jane's interest in me, I turned away to avoid further confrontation.

Giving me a sad look, Jane took Russo aside.

Alice admonished Gabe. "Don't rub your luck in, honey. You know he has a short fuse."

"Jack, you just stay calm and ignore him," Cameron said. "He's trying to rile you enough to fight. Don't give him the pleasure."

"I'm doing the best I can. He's difficult to ignore."

"Just go on to the next bird. There're plenty to look at. Let him stew in his own list."

"That's good advice I'm trying hard to follow. He's a lot heavier than me. He'd probably beat me to a pulp."

The trail we were on led to the river, where we saw kingfishers actually hunting fish instead of insects in woodlands like those kingfishers we had seen above Freetown. In bushes at the water's edge, we found a shining blue kingfisher—small, blue-backed, and red-breasted with a huge beak for a bird of its size, specializing in small minnows. Out in the river, a beautiful black and white pied kingfisher sat on an old piling and made sorties to hover and dive for bigger fish.

"I really like kingfishers," Iris said. "They are such good photo subjects. Good-looking, active, and fairly tolerant of photographers who keep their distance."

I added a caveat. "Kingfishers in the States are more wary than here. Fishermen there shoot them, thinking to get rid of the competition."

Iris sighed. "How shortsighted and greedy."

"These kingfishers don't seem to interest Jimmy," Cameron said. "I guess he was up before breakfast and saw them all on his own."

Some white-faced whistling ducks flushed off the river whistling, and a little ringed plover flew from the sandy beach, the plover's plaintive call drowned by the ducks' whistling.

Then we had our best spotting of the morning. In marsh grass near the river, we heard something calling a rapid *ti-ti-ti-ti-ti-ti*.

Sean and Terence raised their hands, signaling us to stop and be very quiet by putting their fingers to their lips, then motioning us with flat palms to sit near each other on grass a couple of yards from the marsh. When we were settled, they played a tape of a rapid *poo-poo-poo-poo-poo* call.

We waited. In the silence a small rail poked out its orange-red head, followed by a shining black body with large white spots, a stunning little six-inch bird.

The rail didn't linger long. After it disappeared, Terence and Sean high-fived. "A white-spotted flufftail," they said in unison.

"What was that call you played?" I asked.

"It was the territorial call of the species. The male came out to look for the interloper," Sean said.

"A great way to end the morning walk, a white-spotted flufftail seen by all," Terence said. "You should appreciate how lucky you are. Flufftails are very secretive. I guess that's a life bird for you and Gabe, Jimmy,"

Both nodded yes. Now Jimmy was in a better humor than he had been after missing the guineafowl. He even joked.

"That's the best tail I've had lately," he said, provoking laughter from the more uncouth among us, including Cameron and me.

I noticed that Jane gave Jimmy a sour look. She wasn't laughing, and Alice was glaring at Jimmy.

"Evidently he does have a sense of humor, even though it's of questionable taste and doesn't extend to you," Cameron said.

After another lunch of soup and sandwiches, Terence recommended a siesta before our afternoon hike.

"Let's take a walk by ourselves," Iris said. "It's not very hot, and the woods should be pleasant."

I noticed that Jane was watching us as we headed down the trail into the woods, but I put that out of my mind. As soon as we were out of sight of the camp, Iris turned and kissed me. The thrill of her touch and her taste made me long for something more intimate. I slipped my hand under her blouse and bra and caressed her breast while I kissed her again.

I couldn't help expressing my frustration. "It's been too long between kisses. This is a difficult honeymoon—too many people around."

"Sandy says we'll be camping out at Gola in tents. If we have our own tents, maybe we can find a way to be alone there. Be careful. I don't want to be indiscreet and provoke an unpleasant incident that might attract attention. I've seen the way Jane is eying us."

The afternoon group walk produced fewer birds than our morning hike, but it revealed some colorful finds—a golden black-winged oriole, an aptly named blue-bellied roller, a white-crested hornbill, and some black crakes—a fairly common, small, all-black rail—all in addition to views of many of the birds we had seen in the morning.

For supper, Sandy produced a bouillabaisse of shellfish and fish fresh from the Moa River. There wasn't enough left for everyone to have a third helping.

"Sandy, that was delicious," Cameron said as he finished the last of it. "I haven't had any better in Texas."

"It's hard to imagine that," Jimmy said, visibly sneering. "That's high praise. I can't believe Texas doesn't have the best seafood dishes in the world. After all, everything's better in Texas, according to you. You're a braying jackass ad for Texas."

I spit. Iris rolled her eyes. Jerry flashed a discreet middle finger in Jimmy's direction. As Jane hung her head, Alice put her finger over Gabe's lips. Cameron just rolled his eyes upward.

After the ritual of the list was done, Terence told us to get some sleep.

"We have an early morning boat ride back to the mainland and our bus tomorrow. Those who want can go with Sean on a short walk before breakfast as soon as it's daylight. Sandy will give us a continental breakfast when the hikers return and it's full daylight. Then the boats will arrive."

I walked Iris to her building. After a long kiss and many caresses, I trudged back to the men's building. As I got into bed, I noticed Algernon Wheatley talking to Jerry Buck. Algernon seemed worried about something. I yawned. It didn't take me long to fall asleep.

Sometime afterward, I was awake again, drawn out of sleep by loud noise. Sitting up, I saw Jimmy Russo exchanging punches with Jerry Buck. They seemed about evenly matched at first. They were hurling words as well as fists.

"You pissant bastard," Jimmy yelled, "you keep your fucking nose out of my business." He threw a punch that Jerry ducked, landing a counterpunch to Jimmy's chest and another to his midriff.

Though appearing out of breath, Jimmy threw another punch that Jerry ducked.

"I think you ought to know I was on the boxing team at UVA," Jerry said.

"So what, blowhard," Jimmy said, as he landed a glancing blow to Jerry's face.

"You're nothing but trouble, Russo. You've gone out of your way to insult Maude. You're obnoxious. All I did was offer to check some things for Algernon." Jerry ducked another blow from Jimmy and answered with counterpunches of his own that landed hard blows to Jimmy's face and a combination to his midsection.

Jimmy grunted, slumped to his knees, and collapsed on the floor.

Just then, Goforth woke and sat up. "What's all the fuss? We need to get some sleep."

"Tell this bully to let me alone then," Jerry said, wiping the blood from his nose.

"It looks to me like he's getting the worst of it, but I imagine he started it. Jimmy's forever starting fights. He comes close with me sometimes," Gabe said.

"Shut up." Jimmy growled as he made an effort to stand. "You just mind your own damn business from now on, Buck."

"You're not my boss. I'll do as I please. You stay away from Maude and me. You'll be sorry if you don't. I don't like to fight, but I can take care of myself."

"Cool it, you two. Let's all get to sleep now. Morning will come early," Gabe said. He set an example by pulling up a sheet.

Glad that I had escaped Jimmy's ire, and more convinced than ever that avoiding his wrath was a wise course, I followed Gabe's example and was soon asleep again, dreaming of a life of love with Iris—and more life birds.

*   *   *

After breakfast and our boat ride back to the mainland, we climbed aboard our familiar Toyota bus and relaxed while we rode to our next stop, the wetlands at Kanema. Bee-eaters, rollers, and a variety of other birds perched on the roadside power lines and dead snags occupied those of us who stayed awake.

Iris spied the effects of the fistfight the night before. She leaned over and spoke in a low voice. "Jimmy and Jerry look the worse for wear this morning. Jimmy apparently had the worst of it. I don't remember his having those bruises at our meal last night. What happened?"

I whispered. "There was a fight after I left you. Jimmy got the worst of it, although he gave Jerry a bloody nose. Jimmy picked on a collegiate middleweight champion."

"What was the fight about?"

"Apparently Jerry was doing a favor for Algernon—something about stock."

The miles dragged on despite the snarling of Jimmy Russo, who kept muttering about a "damned busybody" despite Jane's efforts to quiet him. During the ride, I saw many of the soaring hawks we had seen before—hawk eagles, the bateleur, darting bird hawks like the shikra, and long-crested eagles—perching on power lines. I stayed busy updating my list.

We made a stop for lunch at an old grove of kapok trees shading a large area next to the road. We were close to a furniture shop, where beds and bureaus of native wood sat in the yard in finished and unfinished splendor under the trees. I marveled at the workmanship and the beauty of the wood used by the makers. We relaxed in the cool while Sandy fixed sandwiches to go with tea and coffee and soft drinks.

While we waited, Sean and Terence found a pearl-spotted owlet and imitated its rapid, monotonous hoo-hoo-hoo-hoo-hoo call. A flock of small birds came in to mob the owl, avenging the predator's nighttime attacks on them.

I had fun identifying the daytime attackers, primarily sunbirds and drab old world warblers like the chiff-chaff in Africa for the northern winter. There was a little green woodpecker tapping the trees, and a shikra flew in to take a sparrow for lunch. Scarce white-winged blue swallows and other birds, more common swallows and swifts, flew over us while we ate.

When our bus finally reached Kanema in the early evening, I asked about the wetlands on the edge of the village.

"These marshy fields belong to the local Christian mission school where we'll spend the night," Sean said. "Many of the higher parts of its fields are being prepared for rice."

Until twilight descended, and we left for a late dinner, some of us occupied ourselves sorting out the shorebirds in the moist ploughed fields below the school. It was slow going over the wet sods. I and the other members of our group who dared to bird the cultivated fields discovered them damp and slippery but full of shorebirds and waders, such as little egrets and gray herons, hunting rodents and insects dislodged by agricultural activity.

Among our finds were a drab wood sandpiper, a colorful greater painted snipe, and, best of all, a rare Forbes's plover, a handsome brown and white bird with a black and white face mask, new for everyone's list, including the lists of our leaders, who were called to judge the accuracy of our identification.

"That Forbes's is almost as good-looking as the painted snipe," Gabe Goforth said. "He compares well to our Egyptian plover on the Moa—a bold refutation of people who claim shorebirds are drab."

"You enjoy the beauty. I'll enjoy adding a bird to my life list," Jimmy Russo said.

Cameron shrugged. "I don't see why you can't do both."

I laughed. "Beautiful birds make a beauteous list."

Iris pointed her camera and took some shots. "And stunning photographs."

At our quarters on the edge of the town, we found many species of doves and pigeons, including rock pigeons and a few handsome speckled pigeons, whose red tints shone in the lingering sunlight. We had excellent views of numerous light tan laughing doves. In trees on the edge of the wetlands, we located a pastel blue and pink vinaceous dove, another new bird for our lists. The members of our group who had been unwilling to venture into the boggy fields and had seen the shorebirds only at a great distance through a scope especially enjoyed these closer birds.

Our night at the mission school required another dormitory setting, separate sleeping arrangements for men and women. Iris and I exchanged sad looks and hugged while nobody was around.

"We'll have to dream our love again tonight," Iris said. She made a wry face.

"I hope my dream tonight is as pleasant as last night's. You were really great," I said, grinning.

"You weren't so bad yourself, in *my* dream, but I could suggest a few improvements," Iris whispered, as she nibbled my ear.

We ate at a restaurant in the village to give Sandy a break and time to restock in preparation for our camping at Gola. We did our list at the restaurant.

After our listing ritual, Terence spoke about the next day. "We'll board the bus early and have a leisurely continental breakfast along the way. In late morning, we should reach the village where we leave the bus. We have to meet the chief and get permission to go onto tribal land. There's no need to worry. This is just ceremonial. Kenneth completed the arrangements well in advance."

"We'll be tenting while searching for the Gola malimbe," Sean said. "We've arranged for single people to have their own tents. Each couple will share a larger tent. Sandy will cook over an open campfire. Don't worry. She'll have great food for us."

As we were preparing to go to our dormitory accommodations, I slipped Iris a piece of paper with another poem: "A few short yards seem miles separating our bodies tonight—in my mind I fly to you uttering a curlew's mournful cry, protesting forced loneliness— hoarding memories under a shining moon."

Iris sighed. "We'll have to make do with memories."

CHAPTER 34

Next morning, as we boarded the bus, Sandy passed out our breakfast of yogurt, hard-boiled eggs, and juice. About ten o'clock, we turned off the main road onto a dirt track that became rougher as we progressed.

Cameron shook his head. "This is a real test for our Toyota bus."

The first time we disembarked to take weight off the bus, I held up crossed fingers. "I guess Kenneth thinks the bus can make it to the village. He's had everything under control so far. Have faith."

Jimmy Russo overheard. "Burnside, are you a religious nut like Maude Buck?"

Cameron gave Russo advice. "Jimmy, you could profit from minding your own business."

Russo replied as he walked off. "Another pissant sector has reported."

The way to the village where we would receive permission to camp in the Gola reserve soon became a rocky route more accustomed to hand-pushed carts, wheelbarrows, and horse-drawn wagons than motor vehicles. Despite the uneven roadway, our bus smoothed out the rugged spots.

"I have trouble believing our bus can survive this so-called road," Iris said.

The rocky, rutted track tested the skill of Kenneth and the toughness of our bus more each mile. I became a little worried when Terence stood again.

"Everybody off the bus," he said. "We need to lighten the load temporarily."

Outside, we saw that the bus needed to cross a low saddle in the roadway.

"Some of us may need to push," said Sean. "Maybe not."

In a very low gear, the bus slowly entered the dip and made its way up the other side. Then it slipped a little.

"Okay, blokes, let's push," Sean said. "Be careful. Don't get caught under the bus."

As we pushed, the bus came through without serious slippage. Several more times the passengers had to lighten the load by exiting the bus and walking behind it. Only one other time did we have to push the bus a few feet.

Jimmy complained. "This bus-pushing is a pain."

"You don't know what bus-pushing is," I said. "In Gabon with Sean, our group had to push a bus bigger than this that was stuck halfway up the wheel rim. We were caked with dirt after getting it out of the mudhole."

Jimmy howled with laughter. "I wish I could have seen you as a mud-caked pissant jackass. I'd have given money to look at that. You must've been pretty."

Jerry, who'd done the most pushing, looked over at Jimmy. "Fat chance you'd get muddy pushing a bus."

"Nobody asked your opinion," Russo said, giving Buck the finger bird.

Jerry grinned. "I believe you'd like a rematch. Let me know when you're ready to try."

I silently applauded Jerry. With great effort, I kept my mouth shut and got back on the bus. In retrospect, I could see the amusing aspects of my mud-covered figure.

It took only an hour and a quarter more of slow moving for Kenneth to get to the village, a collection of long rectangular mud buildings with thatched roofs. They were arranged in four parallel rows with a wide area between rows and a smaller space between buildings in each row.

"I'll load up on Toyota stock if this bus makes it back out when we're through camping," Iris said. "I believe it's as good as the company claims. I know now why we see so many in Africa."

It took another twenty minutes or so to get the chief and his council of elders together for the formal ceremony to approve our entry into tribal territory. While we waited, Iris took some photographs of the village, all the time making sure that she appeared to be photographing our group so that no locals objected.

A minor problem arose from Jimmy's photography. He took pictures of people without their permission. Several objected and an ugly incident threatened our mission. Sean saw what was happening and intervened, apologizing and making Jimmy pay the aggrieved victims a small amount to assuage their dismay.

When a dozen venerable, gray-headed village elders with aquiline features had assembled in clean white robes, the ceremony began. As Terence had promised, it went smoothly. Little was required of us. All the men in our group had to shake hands with the chief as a sign of our agreement with the terms of our stay.

"We greet you in friendship, Chief. We thank you for allowing us to enjoy the beauty of your land," Terence said.

"You are most welcome. May your search for our birdlife be rewarded."

"We will try to find the Gola malimbe," Terence said.

"Good," said the chief, and all the elders nodded agreement, as did we. "May good luck greet your search."

Then our band moved out. We had to hike to the camp. Runners went ahead, carrying part of our equipment. Kenneth, Sandy, and a crew had gone ahead to set up tents at our campsite near where Kenneth had located Gola malimbes. The journey turned out to be more strenuous than we expected, but we didn't begrudge the effort we were to expend to find the rare Gola malimbe, found nowhere else in the world.

"We're in for a stiff hike to get to our tents," Terence told us. "We'll bird along the way, so don't carry much. Binoculars and one camera are all that I recommend. Take advantage of the men Kenneth has paid to carry some of your loads. Use these helpers so that you can give full attention to the birds."

Iris pulled my arm. "Look at Maude and Jerry. Maude's loading Jerry with equipment."

Instead of using bearers to full advantage, Maude was making Jerry a bearer again. She wanted to have her toys handy.

I whistled. "I wonder if Jerry can carry all that?"

Iris laughed. "We'll see."

Cameron, Iris, and I set out together. Iris was no slouch at hiking. Her pace amazed me. Cameron and I were quite willing to stop and look at birds along the trail. "Iris, you're more athletic than I expected," I said.

"I played tennis in high school and college. I was pretty good. I still play, and I hike a lot."

Despite our friendly reception at the village, I sensed something ominous in the air as we began our hike to the campsite. I remembered the fight between Jerry and Jimmy at Tiwai. They were still scowling at each other, but Gabe and Jimmy soon left us, their wives, and the Bucks behind. Maude was not a happy hiker. Neither was Jerry, weighed down by the equipment Maude had refused to trust to the bearers. They soon fell behind even Alice and Jane.

As I remembered what Terence had recommended, my skepticism grew. It was not too far, just a few miles, he had told us. Bearers went ahead to take our equipment. There must be a reason Terence so strongly encouraged us to use them.

Those who followed our leader's advice were glad we had when the few miles stretched into twelve. The walking *was* easy. The first miles were pleasant and filled with numerous birds, including a Finsch's flycatcher thrush, a handsome reddish-orange bird lurking in the understory. Around noon we all sat down along the trail for lunch brought to us from the village—-juice, bread, fried chicken, and hard-boiled eggs.

We birded while we ate. "Look," I said, "there's the bird I chose for you, Iris, the African paradise flycatcher."

"It really is beautiful and graceful. I'm glad you associate me with paradise. I think of you as my fire-bellied woodpecker, like the one we saw back on the trail."

"Why did you pick a woodpecker?"

"Woodpeckers are steady, reliable birds, and this one is really stunning. Its white checkered sides contrast with a red belly and a tan back—colorful yet understated."

"Do you have a soft spot for woodpeckers?"

"Sure do."

As we prepared to resume our hike, I looked around at the second-growth forest surrounding us. "I'm surprised we see so few large trees."

"I haven't seen any old trees, even though there's forest all around us," Iris said.

"Have you noticed the slightly acrid but minty odor of the forest?" I asked. "It's pleasant, fresh, despite the humidity."

"I smell some flower that reminds me of magnolias. Its aroma is delightful."

"It's enticing, but I prefer lilacs."

She smiled. "You're biased."

Cameron chuckled. "As an unbiased observer, I agree with Jack."

As the day wore on, we began to worry about getting to the campsite in time for the evening meal, so we picked up the pace and paid little attention to any birds that weren't new. Now the Bucks were having even greater trouble keeping up.

"I'm feeling really tired," Maude complained after we had maintained the new pace for a quarter of an hour.

"*You* are? I'm carrying most of your gear. How do you think I'm doing?" Jerry said, slumping heavily to a large rock.

"Could we have some help?" Maude called to us who were ahead.

Cameron and I went back, and each took a few pieces of equipment from Jerry and put them in our backpacks. Cameron decided to walk with them. So Iris and I moved ahead together.

Jerry felt better with the lighter load, and he expressed his gratitude profusely. "Thanks, guys. Thanks very much. We'll give more stuff to bearers on the return trip, I promise you."

* * *

Four miles later, we smelled a campfire. After crossing a stream, we reached the campsite. Dark green tents matching our forest surroundings were already up. Sandy was getting her fire and utensils ready to fix our evening meal.

Iris and I separated to find our tents. I located mine and stowed my gear. As promised, each of us single people had his or her own tent neatly marked with our names. The larger tents for the couples were marked too. The Russos' tent was next to mine. When I went out to look around, I located Iris's tent on the other edge of the camp. In my exploration, I saw two beautiful old friends, a fire-crested alethe and a diderik cuckoo. I discovered our campsite was in a large opening in the forest near a bluff with a large grassy field about a hundred feet below.

Kenneth's men had completed a rustic shower stall and a latrine, both with marked male and female sections. After investigating more and finding another fire-bellied woodpecker, I stopped by the campfire, picked up a cup and herbal teabag and poured hot water. The tea tasted delicious. I sat and savored its aroma. It revived me— just what I needed after the long hike. We were camping in style.

Going back to my tent, I lifted the flap to go in. An odor of lavender struck my nostrils. It filled my tent. To my surprise and chagrin, I found my sleeping bag already occupied. Jane was sitting there. Damn, things had been going so well.

"Hello, Jack."

"How did you get here so fast? You and Alice were behind most of us."

"We just got in. My tent is next to yours. Jimmy is already out birding. I thought it would be neighborly to visit. After all, it's been a long time since we were alone together."

"Not long enough. Don't you ever give up? I don't think your being here is a good idea. Jimmy might be back at any time. Aren't you tired from that hike?"

"He'll be out for at least one or two more hours, so don't use that excuse. You've been neglecting me."

"On purpose, I'm sure you know. I've made commitments to Iris. I intend to keep them."

"Well, you talked about marriage to me in Argentina. You led me to believe you found me very attractive."

"I did. I do, but there's no future for us. You don't want to leave Jimmy, and I've fallen in love with Iris."

"That's too bad. You're still attracted to me. I can tell. Just the scent of me arouses you. Admit it."

"Dammit, you're right. But sex is not love. I admit my body hasn't caught up with my mind."

"If you don't want Iris to find out I'm here, you'd better ease my longing for you. I could make a scene, and tell her you invited me in. I'm not leaving until you show me a little attention."

"Just what kind of attention?"

Jane felt my pants, laughing. "It's hard to hide your desire for me. Now let's put this to use."

"Jane, I don't want to have sex with you."

"Your body says you're lying."

She had a point, and I feared her threat to tell Iris I had invited her into my tent. What a fool I'd been back in the Abedarres. I hesitated, unsure what to do. Caught off guard, I succumbed to Jane's blackmail. "Will you promise to be quiet? You made a lot of noise at the Abedarres."

"It'll be difficult, if you do well, but I'll try to be very quiet. I'll whisper."

She pulled off her shorts and panties and then freed me from my clothing. Soon she had what she wanted. My body responded as if my lust for her was without constraint. Lines from Graves's poem ran through my mind: "Poor bombard-captain, sworn to reach / The ravelin and effect a breach ..." My mind filled with guilt for breaking my vow to Iris but could not deter my body from responding to Jane's active desire.

"Remember those olive baboons at Samburu?" she said. "Let's try that. I think you're a sexy primate."

Fifteen minutes and several positions later, Jane moaned softly and bathed me in her climax.

"Please go back to your tent now." I said, falling back on my sleeping bag, exhausted both physically and mentally.

"Not just yet. I haven't used up that erection."

Damn. My body kept betraying me. She lowered herself onto me, gyrating slowly. "Doesn't that feel good? I'm going to keep this up until you respond the way I want. Maybe we'll climax together."

I couldn't help biting my lip. "Haven't I already satisfied you?"

"Yes, it was good, but I want more, something reciprocal."

I wiped the sweat off my brow. "Can't you understand I love Iris?"

"Your body says it still wants me. Let your boy have his way. I'll do other things to please him." Putting words into action, she took me into her mouth until my will collapsed and my body gushed. Jane smiled triumphantly. "Now, that's reciprocity."

"Call it what you want, but please go to your tent. Just get the hell out of here."

Jane dressed and leaned to kiss me goodbye. I turned my head so she had to kiss me on the cheek. "Look to see if anyone's around," she said.

Dragging myself up, I stuck my head out of the tent and gazed both ways.

"I don't see anyone. Go ahead."

Luckily, Jane made it to her tent without being discovered.

A wave of anxiety washed over my mind. I realized too late I had made the wrong decision. I was left alone, depressed, considering my guilt for having broken my oath to Iris. I wished I could turn the clock back and rebuff Jane's advances at the Abedarres. My guilty mind told me I had little choice now. Jane was resorting to sexual blackmail. My body had betrayed me. It consented to the attack. It responded to the lavender odor that had become noxious to my mind.

Above all, I didn't want to lose Iris, even if keeping her demanded the oxymoron of being unfaithful to her. What a mess. My dream of life with Iris seemed in great danger of being dashed despite our growing love. I had to find a way to end Jane's hold over me.

I needed rest to recover from my labors. I was physically and emotionally spent. My guilt kept gnawing. A traitor to my vow, I couldn't deny my body's refusal to follow the signals my mind was sending.

I was beginning to doubt the notion that sexual desire is primarily dependent on mental activity. I no longer believed that the frontal lobes dictate sexual arousal. Jane's lavender scent must be something similar to what produces drug addicts.

In my stupor, I imagined myself walking aimlessly in a dark labyrinth from which I could not escape. At my every step a harpy, flying about my head, attacked.

*   *   *

After I had showered and changed clothes, I dashed on a lot of deodorant. Then I went over to inspect what Sandy was preparing.

"Sandy, is that steak I smell?" I said.

"Yes, steak, potatoes, baked beans, with bread pudding for dessert," Sandy said.

"It's really great to get a hot meal out here in the bush."

"That's Kenneth for you. He believes a good meal keeps tourists happy."

"I agree with him," I said, "especially after that long hike."

As I was speaking with Sandy, I saw Cameron, Jerry, Maude, and Algernon arrive. Except for Cameron, all of them appeared dejected, Jerry most of all.

Having scouted our meal, I went to the Bucks' tent and returned the equipment I had carried for Jerry. Then I headed for Iris's tent at the opposite side of the camp. I was hoping the deodorant and the smoke from the campfire would cover any lingering hint of lavender. I forced myself to go to Iris and pretend nothing had happened. I struggled against confessing to ease my guilty mind. I hoped my tryst with Jane would not affect my lovemaking with Iris.

"Knock, knock," I said.

"Come in, Jack."

So I got down on my hands and knees and entered the tent. The scent of lilacs revived me. I kissed her.

"It's quite cozy in here," I said, leaning forward to give her a deeper kiss. "We're having steak and potatoes and baked beans for dinner."

"As the saying goes, I could eat a bear," Iris said, running her hand through my hair. "That was a longer hike than I expected. I built up a big appetite. Did Maude and Jerry get here?"

"They and Cameron and Algernon dragged in about thirty minutes after Alice and Jane. I don't think Jerry could have made it without the help. I guess that fight took more out of him than I realized. But he packs a mean punch. Jimmy was lucky Gabe broke up the fight at Tiwai."

Iris leaned over and kissed me. "I'm hungry for you as well as food. Do we have to wait?"

I kissed her, running my tongue deeply in her mouth while caressing her breasts. "That's a promissory note."

Iris laughed as she grasped my fly. "I expect to be paid with interest."

CHAPTER 35

Everybody expressed enjoyment of the hot meal as they ate Sandy's feast. Most of us went back for seconds. The free cold beer that Kenneth supplied helped make the celebration a great success. Before we broke up for the night, Terence told us we'd do two lists the next night.

"It's been a long day with little time for birding as a group. We will be located here for a few days."

"We've come through a lot of forest, but it seems to be all second growth. I've seen only a handful of large trees. What's the reason?" I asked.

Terence answered. "We're in part of the Upper Guinea Rainforest, home to chimpanzees, pygmy hippos, forest elephants, and at least ten species of endangered birds."

Gabe broke in. "How large an area does that cover?"

"A large part of West Africa—it extends from Guinea to Togo. It's considered an International Biodiversity Hotspot. Where we are is, for now, West Gola Forest Reserve. It's to be part of Sierra Leone's Gola Rainforest National Park."

"That still doesn't explain the lack of big timber," I said.

"Many acres of this area, including where we're camped, were logged intensively in the 1980s and 1990s. Now the forest is recovering under protection. It's a combined effort of the national government and a number of international environmental groups, including the Royal Society for the Protection of Birds."

I couldn't help noticing that Jane was eying me with a self-satisfied smirk. Wracked with guilt, I avoided her eyes as much as possible.

"It's good to know this forest will be protected," Gabe said. "It's recovering quickly. A sustainable logging operation could give the local people an income and enlist their support to protect the wildlife."

Jimmy snickered. "After I see my Gola malimbe, they can do what they want with the forest."

A murmur of disapproval ran through the group.

Iris expressed the feelings of the group. "That's a horrible thing to say. If everyone took that attitude, you wouldn't have any birds to list."

Sean changed the subject. "Tonight, listen for the spotted eagle owl Kenneth says his people have been hearing. It gives a long, drawn out *hoooui, hoooui*. Tomorrow we begin our search for the rare Gola malimbe. Don't worry, this forest has plenty of birds."

Iris caught my hand and leaned to me, whispering in my ear. "Come to my tent when everything quiets down, and we'll listen for the owl together." I squeezed her hand yes.

When the group broke up. I decided to take another shower before anyone else could get to the water. Soon my body felt clean, but my mind was still filled with self-loathing. I considered myself the Benedict Arnold of love.

Back at my tent, I changed clothes again, straightened my bedding, and brushed my teeth while I waited for the camp to settle down. I put on some more deodorant to cover up in case I had picked up any lingering hint of lavender from my tent. After half an hour by the fire to take advantage of the smoke to cover any remaining lavender odor, I made my way to Iris using my small flashlight. When I was near, I cut it off. My eyes had trouble adjusting to the dark.

"I'm here," I said, bending down to enter the tent. "Where are you?"

"Right in front of you. Sit down beside me."

She took my arm and pulled me down.

"I haven't heard the owl, have you?" I asked.

"No, but we can make love without much noise and listen too, don't you think?"

I hoped my encounter with Jane would not interfere with my response to Iris. "I'll try. It'll be a new owling experience for me."

"Me too, the girl who-who-who loves you," Iris said, giggling softly.

We slowly undressed each other and lay facing, enjoying our closeness.

After a few quiet minutes, I kissed her, burying my guilt in her flavorful taste. I felt I had truly found the kind of love I'd been searching for. I silently cursed Jane's continued pursuit—-it threatened to become a major obstacle to my Iris worship. I hoped my body did not fail me during the night.

Though I was afraid of losing Iris, the more I thought of losing her, the more I longed for her. Thinking of returning to a life without her depressed me. I eased my guilt between her breasts, nibbling and kissing them while my hands roamed lower. I whispered in her ear as I held her close:

"Imagine we are free as birds soaring in a paradise of air, displaying in acrobatic pirouettes like swift falcons in courtship, able to speak better than human beings, merely by thought composing poetry of love."

"I'll fly with you, my love." Caressing me, Iris whispered her desire and guided me into her.

I kissed her deeply as she drew me to her.

"There are no fetters tying us to earth. Our fresh molted feathers meld to create a lover indivisible, a beautiful creature of one."

"Oh, I long to fly higher."

"Imagine us soaring high above the jungle, moving effortlessly over countless miles, reaching the paradise of ultimate desire."

Subtly she shifted us, moving above me. She bent down and whispered in my ear, "I wish we could soar like this forever. I am your honey glove. You must wear me always in your mind and heart."

"I will. You'll always be with me ..."

*   *   *

Awake, Iris shook me. It was still dark. "We heard the eagle owl tonight, lover."

I laughed. "I heard a nightingale sing too."

"Remember your promise. You will always wear me in your mind."

"I will."

"I want you to put me on again in body as well as mind." Astride me, she caressed me and kissed me until I responded to her satisfaction. "Fly with me again. I want to soar as high as the mountains of the moon."

I pulled her down to me to kiss her breasts and neck. She expressed her delight by tightening her grip on me. I suckled her breasts more as she bent down. She kissed me, running her tongue into my ears and over my neck. We moved together until she collapsed upon me, moaning her pleasure, begging me to join her. I moved above her. Soon we were lying exhausted together.

Resting with Iris in my arms, I again acknowledged to myself the difference between my love for Iris and what I had experienced with Jane. Remembering my last encounter with Jane, I became anxious, and my chest tightened. I did not want to leave Iris, but she insisted.

"Go back to your tent while it's still dark, Sweetheart. I still want us to keep our engagement secret."

I kissed her goodbye. Anxiety swept over me, but I kept silent and slipped out of Iris's tent. I went to my own—reluctant, dragging, but obeying Iris's wish for secrecy despite my fear.

I was back well before the rest of the camp would wake to the smell of Sandy's bacon and sausage in our community of tents. Sandy was still asleep. Smoke from the smoldering campfire was pungent on the morning air. Our tents were in a relatively flat clearing, which made moving from one tent to another easy. A good breakfast would be a fitting prelude for the Gola malimbe hunt.

I lifted the flap of my tent and crawled in. I noticed a strong odor of lavender still remained. To my chagrin, someone was lying there. The figure moved and grabbed me and pulled me down. Soon I was in a wrestling match with a half-naked Jane Russo, who was stripping my pants from me and pulling me as she pressed me to her nakedness.

Shit, not again. I felt my stomach churning. "Jane, what in hell are you doing? Jimmy'll go crazy if he catches us together. It's almost morning."

"Oh shut up and screw me. It's still dark. Jimmy's been out hunting birds all night. If he comes in early, I'll tell him I went to the latrine. I don't ask for much. Just give me some quick sex before the camp wakes up. If you don't, I'll yell, and your precious Iris will discover us."

I became even more anxious, aware I needed to end her abuse but still at a loss of how to thwart her. "You must be quiet." Her lavender odor was arousing me against my will.

"I was quiet last time. I'll be silence itself, even if I have another orgasm."

"I'm exhausted. I don't think I can oblige you."

Jane laughed quietly, grasping me and encouraging a response with both her hands and her lips. It was not long before she had accomplished her goal.

Heartbeat pounding, propelled by anger at my continued physical attraction to Jane, I proceeded to fulfill her desire before the sun came up. My body still did not seem to agree with my mind. It functioned with no difficulty. After what was about fifteen minutes, but seemed like an eternity, she shivered, squeezed my erection, and moaned her satisfaction.

Moments later, she hurled an accusation at me. "Wasn't I good enough?"

Now what. "Didn't I give you what you wanted?"

"Yes, but I want to feel I satisfied you."

"Your going back to your tent *now* would satisfy me."

I felt a need to spit. Damn, she must really be horny. She rubbed her breasts over me as she pressed herself against me. She began kissing me expertly. My tired body eventually acted as her willing accomplice.

As she put her clothes back on, Jane looked at me intently. "If Jimmy were to disappear, you wouldn't have him as an excuse not to have sex with me."

What was she thinking of? I felt a need to shower. "That's right, but I'm in love with Iris." Was Jane thinking of ways to rid herself of Jimmy?

I didn't want her to suppose she could have me if she did. "Sex is not love. I don't love you, although I once thought I might."

"Oh, shut up. See if it's clear outside."

I mustered what energy I had left to peer outside to see if she could safely exit. I was relieved when Jane was back in her tent.

I cursed the situation. As I calmed down, drained of energy, I considered my plight. I could not confess to Iris or Cameron what had happened. I was thankful the tour would end soon. My stomach was churning.

I did not enjoy my success in creating Jane's pleasure. I felt used, angry at not being in control of my own sexual activity. Though my situation might seem laughable to many people, I felt I'd been subjected to a kind of mental as well as physical rape. Or as Graves says, beauty is wayward "but requires/More delicacy from her squires."

Obviously my body had its own agenda in conflict with what my mind deemed the proper way to show love for Iris. My body did not share the guilt my mind felt. I collapsed on my sleeping bag and closed my eyes.

* * *

Walking alone through the jungle, I felt a huge snake drop upon me from the trees overarching the trail. It wrapped itself around my waist and began constricting me. I struggled to pull free, but the coils kept exerting more and more pressure while exuding a lavender odor. I was about to give up the fight when the head of the constrictor appeared. It was red. It reminded me of Jane as it sought to devour me. As it continued to squeeze and suck the life from me, I managed to pull my knife from its sheath and cut the constrictor's throat. Slashing its coils, I escaped.

* * *

I woke half an hour later, a sour taste in my mouth, got into my field clothes, put on a heavy dose of deodorant, and headed to breakfast. My mouth watered at the smell of bacon frying. Again I hoped the aromas of the cooking would help cover up any lingering lavender odor.

Eggs, bacon, sausage, toast, and pineapple—I filled my plate, got a cup of tea and sat down beside Iris, resisting a desire to hide. I couldn't shake the notion that I'd been raped, although I was sure that idea would have provoked derision had I told anyone.

"Sandy can really cook great food over a campfire," Iris said.

Despite my worry, I proceeded to indulge a great appetite. "I'm surprised how hungry I am after that big meal last night."

"You expended a great deal of energy after dinner, if I remember correctly." She laughed when I stuck my tongue out at her.

Iris didn't know just how much energy I had expended. I hoped it stayed that way. I didn't want to lose her. I countered my guilt with food.

A half hour later, Terence told us to get our gear together.

"Let's go find the fabled Gola malimbe," Sean said.

Jimmy snarled. "About time. We pamper our stomachs too much."

* * *

A bevy of birds rewarded us for our efforts in our malimbe pursuit. We found red-vented malimbes right away, beautiful sparrow-sized black and red birds, but not the malimbe we most desired. Hornbills of several species—red-billed and African pied hornbill—and a pastel bronze-naped pigeon added to our trophy list.

Despite the thrill of seeing more beautiful life birds, I had to fight off nausea every time I remembered my problem.

Luck was with us as we traced a forest robin to its singing perch. Everybody had a great view of this elusive small bird with a haunting song and brilliant red breast. Iris, Maude, and a few others even got photos. A blue-headed crested flycatcher rounded out the morning's good birds, but we had not had even a hint of a Gola malimbe.

"Do you think we're going to find a Gola malimbe?" Maude asked. She looked tired and despondent, her camera hanging unused.

"Yes, I believe we'll find them this afternoon," Sean said. I sensed confidence in his voice.

Tired and hungry, we straggled up the trail toward the camp for lunch. Sandy passed out egg sandwiches, hard-boiled eggs, and yogurt. I washed them down with hot tea.

"I truly feel we'll find our target bird this afternoon," Sean said. "We may not have gone down the trail far enough since we were seeing so many other good birds. We'll just go farther down the trail to begin with this afternoon, closer to the stream. Kenneth says we're more likely to find Gola malimbes there. We must have a positive attitude— no negative vibes, you blokes."

"You better find that damn bird. That's one that I need," Jimmy said. "You told us Kenneth guaranteed it was here."

Sean frowned. "He's seen it every time he's been here. He says he found it down that trail. They like to feed along streams. We can't list Kenneth's sightings. We should be able to find them too. Don't leave it all to me. It's up to *us*."

CHAPTER 36

We were much farther down the trail than we had been in the morning. It was late afternoon. We had just found a beautiful Narina's trogon male with electric green back and deep red breast peering at us from its perch. Just then Gabe yelled.

"Hey, there goes a malimbe. I think it showed some yellow." He was pointing to his left. Sean began running in that direction. We all followed him through the woods.

"Keep your eyes open," Sean said, as he stopped for a moment, and turned, out of breath. "We're heading toward a stream. That's the likeliest place to find this bird. We're looking for a sparrow-sized black bird with a yellow breast or, if it's a male, a yellow breast and a yellow nape." He turned and made his way downhill through the forest toward the stream.

We all followed as fast as we could, but he stayed some distance ahead. Near the stream, he called to us. "It's a small flock. Hurry up. It's a Gola malimbe flock of five or six birds."

Scattered, we all eventually caught up. The gold and black Gola malimbes were catching insects in the trees next to the stream and didn't pay much attention to us.

Surprising me, Russo held up his arms in a V. "Another damn life bird." He smiled as he spoke.

Jubilant, we raised our binoculars and feasted on the images of bright yellow and black birds brightening our optics. Gabe embraced Alice. I hugged Iris. Jerry hugged Maude. Even Russo forgot himself and hugged Jane. Finally, everybody claimed to have had a good look. Then the cameras began clicking.

After more than half an hour, everyone had seen the Gola malimbe, and all who wanted photos had them. A raucous crowd headed up the trail to camp without trying hard to identify more birds. Many of the group did stop for a few species new to our trip list, including a great blue turaco. I couldn't help enjoying this gray, blue, and yellow rainbow with its huge crest.

I insisted Iris photograph it. "What a beauty."

She laughed and began photographing.

I couldn't resist eagerness to see her work. "Have you got some good photos?"

"Yes, I've taken some great shots of it."

"It's fairly common—not rare like the Gola malimbe," I said. "I'm surprised we didn't see this marvel earlier."

"Can you believe how beautiful Gola malimbes are?" Iris asked. "They're svelte, and so elegant."

"I wouldn't think a black bird could be so pretty. I'm sure your pictures do them justice. I'd like to see them after supper."

Hope for a hot supper became uppermost in my mind, and, from the pace at which we were hiking, everyone else seemed to have the same idea. The group moved like an army on attack.

Sandy did not disappoint us. She had prepared spaghetti with a fabulous meat sauce and garlic bread. For dessert she had made another bread pudding. To top off the celebration, the leaders broke out free beer.

Sitting down beside Iris, I asked, "How did your pictures of the Gola malimbe turn out?"

"Great. I'm pleased with them. Somebody should pay for one or more. Take a look." She held up her camera's viewing screen for me to see and showed me five great shots.

"You have sharp pictures. A toast. To the Gola malimbe, good birds, and true love," I said, raising my beer.

"I'll drink to that," said Cameron. "And I wish you two lovers well. To your happiness."

Iris leaned against me. "I like that toast too."

I raised my can again and proposed a further toast. "May we lovers be like those in John Donne's 'Ecstasy,' so together we'll form one perfect soul with our bodies as its book."

Iris put her arm around me. "That's another great toast."

Later, in Iris's tent, she told me my toast moved her more than she wanted to reveal in front of Cameron. "I think it's a beautiful way to express our love," she said. "That's the way I feel about us."

"It's not original with me. John Donne expresses what you and I feel. I'm bound to you in spirit and body. Our spirits are inseparable—though our bodies spend time apart."

"Kiss me. It's time for our bodies to convey our soul's desire."

I covered her body with kisses as she caressed me.

Raising herself above me, she kissed me intimately. "Your honey glove is ready. Lie back." I lay back as she placed her glove around me.

That night I became even more aware of the difference between mere sexual activity and intimacy prompted by love. We did not sleep for many hours.

*   *   *

I awoke in a state of euphoria while the moon was still shedding its light on the darkened camp. I stole back to my tent with trepidation, my leg muscles tightening, fearing a repeat of what had occurred the night before. I felt intense regret that Iris required me to keep our engagement private. I knew I must deal with Jane.

When I entered my tent, I found my fears were justified. I felt pain in my head and mind. Jane was waiting for me.

"Jimmy is out after night birds again, so I thought it would be lovely to have an encore of your magnificent performance last morning," she said.

I couldn't stand much more of this. I had to end it. "You're out of luck. My apparatus can't function any more now."

"We'll see about that, lover boy. I know you can't resist me," Jane said, as she unzipped my pants, took my sadly depleted penis and began to apply fellatio. Her kiss was magical—her lavender scent effective, seductive to my body, though now abhorrent to my mind. In spite of my reluctance, she was having her way.

These ambushes had to end. I had to take a stand. In anger, I threw my hat across the tent. "If I don't tell Jimmy what you've been doing, will you promise to let me alone from now on?" I said.

"What if Jimmy isn't in the picture anymore?"

I pounded my sleeping bag. "That won't matter. I love Iris. I intend to marry her. You're forcing me to be unfaithful to her. If you push me any further, I'll tell Jimmy and deal with the consequences." I began to choke her. "Dammit, you can't keep using me!"

She struggled to push my hands from her throat, gasping. She looked frightened. I kept choking, but she pulled a hand away. "All right ... all right ... I ... promise.

I let go for a little, but threatened to choke her again. "Be sure you keep that promise." I choked her again but then let go. She gazed at me with a face I thought contorted in terror. I took my hands away, and gradually she calmed.

"I'll miss you, lover," Jane said as she prepared to leave. "I think I may have made the wrong decision in Argentina."

"Get over it. That's history." I wouldn't miss her.

I felt another wave of guilt sweeping over me. What if I lost Iris? I doubted that I could trust Jane, but I felt I had no alternative except killing her or confronting Jimmy. If she didn't keep her promise, I'd go through with my threat. I wasn't going to be victimized any more.

"If you know what's good for you, you'll keep your promise."

After Jane left, I collapsed on my sleeping bag—worried, guilty, exhausted—and fell asleep.

CHAPTER 37

When Iris and I returned to the camp from viewing Jimmy's body, Sandy offered us the breakfast that we'd missed. Somehow she'd kept food warm without burning it. I ate some bacon and eggs and drank a couple of cups of tea while Iris and I sat in front of her tent and discussed what had happened.

Iris frowned. "I wonder if we should worry about a murderer among us?"

"I don't think so. Whoever killed Jimmy must have reached a boiling point."

Breakfast finished, I fought to stifle a yawn. "I'm tired. I've got to take a nap."

Iris stroked my cheek. "Sweet dreams. I may nap a bit too. We'll feel better after some rest. We spent a lot of energy last night. This murder is unsettling, even though Jimmy wasn't our favorite person."

I rested in my tent the remainder of the morning, napping off and on, too tired to attempt looking for birds, or any other activity. The camp was eerily quiet.

Having reviewed in my mind the events leading up to this unpleasant day, I remembered Cameron. He should have some lunch and some company in protecting Jimmy's body. I roused myself to find Iris.

I found her at the campfire finishing a sandwich and sipping tea. "I think we need to take Cameron some food," I said.

"You're right. I'll get Jane and Alice."

"Just find Alice. I'll have Sandy fix some food."

Despite my reluctance to include Jane, Iris enlisted both women. I tried to be positive. With Jane along, at least I would know whether she said the wrong thing to Iris.

Cameron was sitting comfortably in shade. He was entertaining an inquisitive ground squirrel by tossing it bits of peanuts. A faint breeze was stirring the leaves of the trees behind him.

"We came to join you. We thought you might like some food, so we brought along some lunch."

"Jimmy didn't find that new bird he was after, I guess," Alice said as she and Iris spread the food for Cameron on a tarp I had brought. "I guess I'm being callous, but after the way he abused Jane, I think he deserved a horrible death."

"Probably he didn't see another life bird after the bat hawk," Cameron said. "We'll never know. At least he got to see the Gola malimbe."

Remembering Jimmy's outbursts, I couldn't summon any sympathy. "I doubt that he died happy."

Cameron ignored my unkindness. "Jane, if Alice or Jack hasn't told you, we're dealing with a murder."

"Jimmy murdered? Are you sure? You're not making a bad joke, I hope."

"No. He definitely was murdered."

"Alice told me Jimmy had fallen to his death. She didn't say he had help."

Tears began to trickle down Jane's cheeks. She tried to hide them by turning away from us. Maybe she was mourning Jimmy more than she wished us to see. Or maybe it was guilt, and she was torn between grief and elation at her release from her tormentor.

"I thought it would be better coming from you, Cameron," Alice said.

Cameron nodded. "Jane, I'm sorry. Somebody hit him hard on the head before he fell. We're all murder suspects."

"I'm scared of being around a murderer. I hope the police won't accuse Gabe," Alice said. "He went out early hunting birds for a few minutes, but he spent most of the night with me in our tent, not hunting birds with Jimmy. I know he didn't kill Jimmy, and neither did I."

Jane turned back to us. "I don't want to go home now. I'd like to do the rest of the trip."

I thought I heard a faint sob. Her cheeks were still wet. She certainly appeared to be a grieving widow, but her grief appeared to me to be mixed with relief.

Jane groaned. "Jimmy irritated everyone, including me, but murder seems a little extreme. It's unsettling to think about life without Jimmy ordering me about, even though he got pretty rough sometimes. And what if his killer doesn't stop?"

What a hypocrite. I remembered our recent conversations. She'd evidently been contemplating life without Jimmy for some time. But guilt might be prompting feelings of remorse, or possibly fear that she might be next on the killer's list.

"I agreed to stay with the body until Terence comes back with the police," Cameron said. "I can't allow Jimmy's body to be moved now, even if you want to get it back to camp for transfer to the States."

Jane looked up at the vultures that had begun to light in the trees. "I brought a blanket to cover Jimmy. I don't want him out here uncovered for all the flies to swarm around. This heat is likely to draw animals. Look at those vultures." Jane said, staring at the black figures gathering in the trees. Her head drooped. "What will I do without him? He ran my whole life."

Alice helped Jane spread the blanket. "Honey, you need to go back to your tent and think things over—what to do now. You don't need to hang around here. Cameron will take good care of Jimmy."

Cameron tried to comfort Jane. "That's a good idea. We're lucky it's not a hotter day."

The vultures weren't circling yet. "You must ship the body back to the States for burial. Are you leaving the tour to take Jimmy home?" I asked.

"I don't want to leave. No. I'm thinking of continuing the tour. We don't have many days left. After the tour's over, I'll take Jimmy home."

Alice put her arm around Jane. "Honey, you don't have to make any hasty decisions."

Iris looked at me and winked. I knew she was thinking Jane saw her field clear to continue her hunt, now for a new husband, not just an amorous adventure. Other than me, there was no near object for her hunt except Algernon Wheatley. Our guides were both married men.

"I'm here to rescue you," Iris whispered. I was glad she didn't know I no longer needed rescue.

Cameron appeared surprised that Jane wanted to continue the tour. I knew he was aware that Jimmy had not treated Jane well, had physically and mentally abused her, and that she had sought to fill the lonely time by having an affair with me. He looked at Iris, then Jane. "You may find continuing the safari less interesting now, Jane. I'd recommend going home with Jimmy as soon as the police allow."

Jane put a hand on her head. "I have to learn to live without Jimmy."

Alice patted her on the back. "You can. Let's go back to camp now."

"Thanks. I guess I should go to my tent and rest."

Taking Jane's hand, Alice led her back up the trail to the tents.

While the three of us waited for the police, Iris and I chatted with Cameron about who might have killed Jimmy.

"I doubt that it was a premeditated murder," Cameron said. "It looks more like someone got into an argument with Jimmy and killed him in a sudden fit of rage."

"I can understand how someone could get that angry talking to Jimmy," I said.

"I wonder if the killer plans another murder?" Iris asked. "I know it wasn't you, Jack. You were busy with me almost all night," Iris said. "Come to think of it, that gives me an alibi too."

"I think I heard the argument that led to Jimmy's death," Cameron said. "It must have been after midnight. My tent is close to the campfire. I heard two people arguing near there. Two men; I think one of them was Jimmy. I couldn't make out what they were saying. Both of them seemed very angry. I heard a scuffle. Then the sounds moved off. Looking at Jimmy's hands, I saw evidence he hit somebody hard enough to draw blood."

Cameron's analysis made sense. "You think maybe whoever did it could argue self-defense? I wouldn't be surprised if Jimmy started something. He was trying to rile me enough to get me to fight. Remember, he got into a fistfight with Jerry Buck at Tiwai Island," I said.

"This morning I didn't see anybody who had been in a bruising fight," Iris said. "I feel sorry for Jimmy, even though he was violent."

"That's right. But not everybody was here this morning," Cameron said, as he tossed the ground squirrel another bit of peanut.

"Who was missing?" I thought back, but the morning had become a blur in my mind, though I had a vivid memory of the hornbill I'd seen.

Iris wrinkled her brow. "If my recollection is correct, Algernon Wheatley wasn't in our group when we discovered the body."

"That's what I remember too," Cameron said. "We need to find Secretary Bird as soon as possible and examine him for bruises, cuts, and blood."

"What could the motive be? Algernon seemed to get along better with Jimmy than the rest of us," I said.

"My guess would be that Jimmy talked Algernon into some unwise investments," Iris said. "But I remember somebody else who wasn't there. I don't remember seeing Jerry Buck. Jane wasn't there either."

"I doubt that Jane could inflict the blow that killed Jimmy, but Jerry certainly is strong enough," Cameron said.

"I remember seeing Algernon talking to Jimmy our last night at Tiwai Island. Wheatley seemed upset. Later that night, Jimmy and Jerry were fighting," I said. "Jerry might have done real damage if Gabe hadn't calmed things down."

"I'm going back to camp now. Are you coming, Jack?" Iris asked.

"I'll stay and keep Cameron company."

Cameron waved for me to leave. "Go ahead. I don't want you to miss all of the excitement."

"If you don't mind, then, I'll go with Iris. It might not be safe for her to be alone."

She waved her hand in derision. "You stay. I don't think the killer will try again, and I can run fast enough to get away if he does."

Cameron waved me off. "Go ahead. I'm okay. I don't think Jimmy will rise from the dead and smite me, and I don't think the killer will return. I think whoever did this didn't plan it."

"Are you sure? I'll stay with you until the police come. Will you be okay, Iris?

She waved her hand to brush my doubt aside. "I'll go right to Sandy's campfire and get some coffee. I'll be okay. I'll sip my drink and enjoy the forest fragrance. It reminds me of the magnolias in our yard in South Carolina."

So Iris left without me. I knew not to say I could give Jane an alibi for early this morning. I wondered how guilty she felt at attempting to achieve sexual joy while Jimmy met his death, or was already dead. I didn't feel a thing about Jimmy. I felt so guilty about breaking my vow to Iris I had no room for Jimmy. Would Jane keep to our bargain? That was my main concern.

CHAPTER 38

Iris had not been gone more than an hour when Terence Stavens returned from the native village. He brought the local constable and four helpers with him to view the body.

"Dr. Cameron MacDonald, this is Constable Carter Oshabi, a kinsman of Kenneth Oshabi. Please tell him your findings. You're the closest thing we have to a coroner," Terence said.

"Pleased to meet you, Dr. MacDonald," the constable said, extending his hand to Cameron. This Oshabi was as tall as, but not as dark as, Kenneth. For this reason and because he was wearing a uniform, he seemed different. Otherwise, they might have passed for twins.

"Likewise, Constable Oshabi." They shook hands.

Cameron related what he had found, including the fact that Russo's bruised and bloody hands indicated a violent encounter with another person. "I heard two people engaged in loud quarreling near the campfire last night."

Oshabi nodded. "That fits with your examination."

"None of the people in the group at my examination of the body this morning showed signs of a violent struggle, but three of our group weren't present. My advice is to find the three who weren't with us when I examined the body. Question them. Whoever gives evidence of combat, he's probably your man, although he can likely plead self-defense."

"Do you have an idea of anybody in particular I should look for?"

"It's either Algernon Wheatley or Jerry Buck, I think. Jane Russo was absent too, so she might be considered, but I don't think she has the strength to inflict the wounds I have found on her husband. Besides, I've seen her since this morning. She shows no signs of having been in a violent struggle."

"Thank you, Dr. MacDonald. You may have made my job easy. Would you please continue to watch the body while I arrange for its transfer? My men will carry the body up to the camp."

"Of course, Constable."

"Though you don't show signs of a bloody struggle, you'd better come along with us, Jack," Terence said.

"Okay, I'll go," I said. "I feel bad leaving you here, Cameron."

"Go ahead. The constable's men will be with me. I don't want you to miss any of the excitement. I'm sure you'll find Iris and the inquisition more gripping than watching me accompany Jimmy's dead body."

*   *   *

Constable Oshabi asked Terence and Sean to assemble our whole group while we waited for Cameron and Oshabi's men to bring Jimmy's body to the camp. After all of the tents were emptied and the group assembled, Oshabi proceeded.

"Will Mr. Jerry Buck and Mr. Algernon Wheatley please to step forward?" the constable asked. Jerry responded immediately, but Algernon came forward only after Oshabi made another request, and then moved slowly. Oshabi began to examine the two, asking them to stand facing the group, show their hands, and remove their shirts.

Jerry showed his hands and took off his shirt without saying anything.

"This is crazy. Jerry's been with me—all night and almost all morning," Maude said.

Jerry interrupted. "Be quiet. I don't have anything to hide."

Showing bruised hands, Algernon protested. "I object to having to go through an examination. I don't wish to undress—in front of a crowd." His tall body was quivering.

Oshabi shook his head. "I assure you, I have the authority to insist on this, and can force you to do so, if you resist."

After more hesitation, Algernon did as Constable Oshabi ordered. He took off his shirt and slouched over like an exhausted player on a losing team, bending and taking deep breaths. A murmur arose. With Wheatley's shirt off, we could see a large bruise and two cuts on his stomach and a cut on his lower neck that had been concealed by the collar of his shirt. After having Algernon turn and show his back, Constable Oshabi pointed out some other cuts and bruises.

Iris, next to me, grabbed my arm. "One of those wounds is more than superficial. It must have been quite a fight."

I agreed. "Algernon changed his clothes. The ones he has on don't show much blood. He's lucky he's not a *bleeder.* A hemophiliac would have died of those cuts. Algernon must have a great medicine kit."

"Mr. Wheatley, it is apparent you were in a rather violent fight not too long ago. I'm afraid I must place you under arrest for the murder of James Russo. Do you have anything to say to account for your wounds other than a struggle with Mr. Russo?"

Shaking, Algernon wrestled with his emotions in order to speak. Rage, hate, and despair took turns on his face. Finally, he uttered disjointed words which were almost sobs, but became less broken as he proceeded to tell his tale.

"I can only say ... ah ... I ... acted ... ah ... in self-defense. Russo tempted me ... uh ... to invest ... with him ... uh ... in what he claimed to be a safe investment ... despite its offering ... a very good return ... I just discovered ... days ago ... with Jerry's help ... my investment has declined ... by 40 percent. When I challenged Mr. Russo last night, he began pummeling me ... I fended off the blows ... he pulled a knife ... began slashing ... I picked up a large piece of firewood ... I swung as hard as I could ... You ask anyone here. Russo was always looking for a fight."

Jerry spoke up then, pointing to himself. "I can vouch for the truth of that, Constable. Jimmy assaulted me at Tiwai Island, because I checked on Algernon's investment."

"That's right, Constable. I saw the fight," I said.

"If this is correct, I'll take statements from all of you before we leave." He turned to Algernon. "You must go back with me, Mr. Wheatley, but you can make a believable plea of self-defense, if what you say is true."

"I would like to go to my tent and get my notebook and other items before we go," Algernon said. "I think you need to have my true name. It's not Algernon Wheatley. It's Egerton Watson. I used my *nom de plume* when registering with Fantastic Flights because I was gathering information for another tour group."

Iris nudged me. "You were right about his spying, but I still like him."

Oshabi replied without hesitation. "Go ahead and get what you want to carry, but don't think about getting away. You wouldn't get very far. Mr. Stavens will go with you."

Oshabi turned to address Jane. "It will take time for me to get depositions. My men will carry Mr. Russo to the village, I'll send for help to move the body back to Freetown, Mrs. Russo. I'm afraid it will be some time before the body will be released to you. I recommend that you continue with the tour.

"Mr. Wheatley, or Watson, before you collect your belongings, I want you to show my men where Mr. Russo last attacked you with the knife. If we find the knife, that will certainly work in your favor."

The men with Constable Oshabi made the search he ordered. Before going to his tent, Algernon showed them the point on the bluff where Jimmy fell. After about ten minutes of searching, one of them raised a hand high with Jimmy's still bloody knife.

He shouted, "Here! Here!" and brought the murder weapon to Oshabi.

While Terence went with Wheatley to his tent, Oshabi's four men and Cameron worked with the body. They made a litter to carry Jimmy's body by slashing some small trees to make poles and crosspieces they tied together with long grasses and vines. We marveled at their quickness and handiwork as they lifted the body up to take it to the village.

Cameron admired what they had constructed. "It seems sturdy. I'm amazed how fast they've worked. No doubt the vultures watching from the trees have been equally amazed—and very chagrined. By the way, my vigil added to my life list. I was glad to identify an African white-backed vulture to my satisfaction."

"Congratulations. You were right, Cameron. You and Iris came up with both method and motive," I said.

Cameron was relieved to be through with his watch. "I'm glad Algernon had a plausible defense. He should get off without too much trouble, even though he didn't alert the camp. He must have realized he hit Jimmy hard enough to kill him."

By the time the constable finished taking depositions and discussing arrangements with Jane Russo, it was past time for our evening meal. Sandy gave Constable Oshabi and his men food to carry with them. Then she prepared to serve us.

"Do you have anything hot for us tonight, Sandy?" I asked.

"How does fried chicken sound?"

"Pretty good to me. How about you, Cameron?" I asked.

"I'll happily eat Sandy's fried chicken. I guess we can ask Kenneth to pull out some beer and call it a wake for Jimmy Russo. I hope people will try not to appear too happy. I myself am prepared to shed crocodile tears."

I laughed. "I must admit I'll have a hard time shedding any tears at all, but I'll try to be solemn."

"You'd make a very poor crocodile. I'd have to pinch you a bit, I expect," Iris said.

I tried to smile, but I was too concerned about what Jane might tell Iris. She had remained silent during Algernon's confession, apparently dumfounded that he was Jimmy's killer. She had absented herself from the group that gathered to see the culprit led off and wish him well. I found it difficult to read her actions now. Was she mourning or feeling relief, or a combination of the two? Would she keep her word? I resolved to keep a close eye on her.

CHAPTER 39

The food and beer helped to relax me. I was a little surprised that Jane took part in the festivities, but Alice persuaded her friend to come out of her tent and join the group.

Iris asked Jane the question I had in my mind. "Have you decided to finish the tour?"

"Yes. Constable Oshabi told me I couldn't expect the release of Jimmy's body for at least three or four days. He took me aside and told me I'd be better off with the group than waiting in a hotel room or wandering about alone in Freetown. It may seem callous of me to say it, but I have felt a burden lifted from me."

Though I was not pleased with her decision, I was relieved that I no longer reacted to a lavender scent when Jane was nearby.

During our pseudowake with beer around the campfire in honor of Jimmy, almost all the campers slipped off to their tents early. Iris and I sat around the fire after everyone else had left.

Iris sighed. "I feel sorry for Algernon, or Egerton, or whatever his name is."

I nodded my head. "It's ironic. Cameron and I suspected him of chicanery, yet he's arrested for defending himself from someone who sold him risky stock."

"I hope he'll get off with a plea of self-defense, but I'm going to change the subject. We should sit by the fire for a while longer and do some serious planning. I don't want you to give up your college position. I know you've been at a small school and haven't published much. It would be difficult for you to move."

She looked at me intently, waiting for my answer. I didn't know how to respond. I was still worried that Jane would not keep her promise.

"Isn't that true?"

I was a little embarrassed to admit my lack of professional achievement. "Yeah, I'm a full professor, but I haven't published enough to be able to move to a comparable position at another school."

"What about your poetry?"

"The academic world doesn't have much use for poetry. Only poets who've died, or at least established themselves as public figures, are of interest in academe. It's the exceptional poet who's admired before he's dead."

Iris gave me a pat on my cheek. "On the other hand, I can do my job from just about anywhere that I have Internet available. I can access all the information I need to make my decisions about what to buy and sell. All else I need is an air connection."

I had to admit she was right. I admired her clear thinking. It occurred to me that I had read how successful women in their late twenties began to think about nest building.

Not hearing a demur from me, Iris continued. "There's a large airport near your college. I have to do a great deal of traveling in my work, so it makes sense for us to use your place as our base of operations."

No objection came to mind. I touched my fingers to my lips and then hers. I let out a large breath.

"What do you think?" Iris asked, breaking the silence and grasping my arm. She seemed very concerned to get my approval. I couldn't think of any reason to disagree with her acute analysis.

"You've worked out everything. Your plan's sensible. But it requires you to make all the changes."

"No, that outline does not cover everything. What about our engagement? I want a ring."

"Okay. I'm going to buy you a ring as soon as we're back in the States. It won't be huge, but I'll try to get one you won't be ashamed of." I knew just where I'd buy it. The jeweler was a good friend of mine.

"Where will we marry?" Iris asked.

"Anywhere that suits you will be all right with me. The sooner the better, I don't care where."

Iris nodded. "Okay, we'll have a wedding in South Carolina at my parents' church.

"Great, I'm eager to meet your folks."

"You'll like my dad. He's always loved the outdoors and wildlife. His love of nature rubbed off on me."

"I hope they'll approve of me."

"I'm sure they will. Mother will be happy to have a respectable son-in-law and will do whatever she needs to please you. Dad will view you as a birding buddy. But there are lots of other decisions to make."

"Honey, you make my head swim. Do we have to make all of these decisions at once? Given how I feel about you, I'll do almost anything you wish except commit murder. We've had enough killings." *I just hope Jane keeps her promise.*

Iris laughed her tinkling laugh, but she was determined. She pressed her lips together.

"I'm not going to make all the decisions alone. I don't want to find out later you're unhappy with them." She crossed her arms and waited.

After a brief silence, I found the words. "When we marry, I'll put my grandmother's wedding ring on you. A church wedding, a small one, suits me. It's the bride's decision, and your family will be paying for it. I'm not going to define small."

"My folks will be so happy I'm marrying they'll agree to whatever I want. What about children?"

"I'm not opposed to them. I have two already, a boy and a girl, who ask for my advice and money. They no longer think I'm the incompetent their mother taught them to see. They'll be on their own when they finish graduate school. My father sired me when he was fifty. How many kids would satisfy you?"

"Silly, when it comes to children, you accept what happens. I don't have any religious scruples about contraception, as you know. We'll plan a family. I could be satisfied with one child, but two would be better."

I felt myself responding to her gray eyes and lilac scent. I kissed her to enjoy her exquisite taste.

"Distractions won't help," she said. "What else should we settle? What about expenses?"

"No problem. I think my salary's enough for all of our household needs and more. Besides, I have other income. I inherited quite a bit of money from an uncle after my divorce. It wasn't part of the divorce settlement."

"That's great, but I'll want to do my share."

"What about birding trips? We must make at least one major birding trip a year as long as we're able. Love of nature is part of what brought us together."

"Of course. I'll finance those. How else would I continue to photograph the wildlife of our planet? Besides, each trip would be another honeymoon. I'll have plenty of money for extras."

I agreed. "Then we've solved all of the major problems except how often we have sex," I said, grinning.

"Every day we have available, Sweetheart. I don't think that will be a problem unless you have to start using store-bought stimulants." I detected a smirk.

"All I have to do is look at you, taste you. I don't need any other stimulant. Repeat performances take longer."

She gave me a playful slap. "From what I've experienced so far, we won't need more than a few repeat performances at any one time," she said, laughing before she kissed me. "Your tent or mine?"

"Yours; we can hear the owl better there." I didn't add I feared she might detect a lavender odor in my tent.

*   *   *

Sitting at the entrance to Iris's tent, we snuggled together and watched the stars while we listened for the eagle owl. We could smell the campfire as it began to burn down and smolder.

I was curious about how we had met. "Why did you decide to take this tour?" I asked."

"I suppose it was the idea of seeing so much of Africa."

"That was what decided it for me too."

Then I heard the owl. "Do you hear that *hooooi, hooooi, hooooi?*"

"It sends shivers up my spine. It sounds so mournful. Hold me tighter."

"I feel it's mournful too, yet I feel happy just being here beside you, man to man, bird man to Fogelman."

Iris laughed softly at my joke. "I do explain the meaning of my name a lot. But I'm happy. I can't feel bad when I'm near you. My heart beats faster when we touch."

"If I could sing like a great opera performer, I'd offer you a Puccini or Verdi aria proclaiming my love for you. As you and Cameron pointed out, I'm no Caruso, just a poor poet inebriated with your charms, so this poetry will have to do: 'Warm summer hills rippling in a soft breeze are my love's legs glistening in deep twilight before the red wine of her thighs, and I would dream upon the hills.'"

Iris tweaked my ear. "Let's see if we can persuade the nightingale to sing on my hills for a few hours." She kissed me and rubbed her breasts across my chest. Soon I was drinking her wine and dreaming.

When I slipped back to my tent in the morning, I was relieved to find it empty. I could detect Jane's lavender scent only with great effort. So far Jane was keeping her promise. Maybe the shock of Jimmy's death had made a difference. She didn't need to stir his jealousy anymore. Maybe she felt guilty about her adultery. Or perhaps she was a little afraid of me now. I mulled the situation over in my still uneasy mind.

The murder was solved, but I still had to worry about whether Jane would out me to Iris. Or, if she were really angry, she might make a scene. If that ever happened, I would simply have to attribute it to

Jane's wishful thinking. That was partially true. After I fell in love with Iris, my mind never agreed to how my body performed with Jane.

I often considered I was not worthy of Iris's love but resolved to become as blameless as possible. I hoped I was right that Jane didn't feel a need for me anymore. Maybe she did still have feelings for Jimmy. I liked to think so. I didn't want to believe I had been so attracted to a heartless, shallow person. After all, I had once contemplated marrying her if Jimmy was out of her life. I tried not to worry, but I did. I took an antacid. The thought of losing Iris caused me to feel heartburn.

CHAPTER 40

Only a few stops remained on the trip after our successful hunt for the Gola malimbe. Terence said we would make our way back to Freetown at a leisurely pace—now minus two of our original group. Hour by hour, day by day, I became less fearful that Jane would break her promise, but I couldn't shake my distrust of her.

Our first major birding venue after leaving the Gola camp and hiking to our bus was an extensive area of dense woodland at another spot in the Gola reserve.

"Here's where we will make our second try for *Picathartes*," Terence said.

A hike of several hours through forest brought our chatty, laughing group to a hillside facing a huge boulder with a rock face similar to the one where we had seen the rock fowl near Freetown. Again two quarter-moon mud nests were affixed to the stone about twenty feet above the ground. Terence asked for quiet and told us to arrange ourselves on the hillside, and to sit in silence like statues.

"Watch the nests on the rock face. We'll hope some birds visit them," Terence said in a low voice.

I wasn't worried about listing the rock fowl any more, but I wanted us to see it well enough for Iris to photograph it. I wouldn't mind seeing it a second time, though. I never have understood people who have no interest in seeing birds again after they list them. The panorama of the natural world never ceases to fascinate me.

Nature study had given me a reason to continue living after my world fell apart in divorce. Like Wordsworth, I feel my heart leaping up when I encounter the beauty of a cloud, a forest, or a new bird. Like a good poem, the beauties of nature thrill me with an emotional reaction known as a poetic pang, for me a prickly feeling down my neck and upper back.

Iris crossed her arms. "I hope we don't wait too long," she whispered. "I'm eager to take a photo of this elusive bird."

We had not been sitting more than half an hour when a head appeared at the top of the rock. Then a bird, moving like an ill-jointed toy, jumped out and visited a nest. Everyone had an excellent view before the bird flew off.

"Is there anyone left who hasn't had a great view of a rock fowl?" Sean asked. Nobody answered.

"All right, photographers, you can use your cameras if another bird shows itself," Terence said.

We waited twenty minutes before another rock fowl appeared. As it visited the nest on the left, cameras went into action.

After several minutes, I was startled by a voice to my right. It wasn't Maude. It was Jane. "I got it. I got it. I got a sharp photo of the whole bird."

Alice patted her on the back. "Way to go, girl."

At the sound of their voices, the cooperative bird disappeared. The group didn't have another clear view, although I glimpsed parts of several birds lurking behind the boulder holding the nests.

Iris showed me some excellent photos revealing the comical tan body, long neck, and round yellow head of the bird as it inspected the nest. I had a few more brief views of the birds skulking around in the brush behind the rock before Terence told us our time was up. I was glad to ease my aching buttocks.

"Now everyone has a rock fowl on his or her life list," Terence said. "All of you should have had another excellent look. And you photographers should be happy too."

"I am. I've got splendid pictures of the rock fowl, praise the Lord," Maude said.

Iris and I lifted our arms and high-fived. "Me too," she said. "I hope to fund my next birding trip with these pictures."

Catching her hand, I laughed. "I hope you mean a trip for two."

Iris pulled my ear. "I guess we'll limit our trips to your vacations."

Jane showed her pictures to Iris and anyone else who'd look at them, including me. No hint of lavender diluted Iris's lilac scent. Jane was obviously very proud of her accomplishment as she listened to Iris's critique.

We had only one more night before returning to Freetown. We would spend it in Bunbuna, just a drive of a couple of hours away.

"At Bunbuna we'll stay in a brand-new motel," Terence said. "Good quarters, we'll be the first large group to stay at this place. This afternoon and some of tomorrow we'll bird. Then we'll head to Freetown and spend the last night at our hotel there."

New rooms and a return to roommates would probably make any further pursuit of me too difficult for Jane, even if she hadn't given up her chase. I felt a great weight beginning to lift from my chest, but I still retained skepticism about her promise. She still might tell Iris in a fit of pique what had happened between us at the tent camp.

We enjoyed another of Sandy's roadside lunches. While we waited for her to fix chicken salad sandwiches, I watched two shrikes hunting insects, a small brubru (a colorful melange of red, yellow, black, and white) and a somewhat larger but more subdued gray and tan black-crowned tchagra. The brubru made its soft *prrriiii* call twice, and the tchagra occasionally whistled and gave a cackling laugh like a crazy crone.

Together with doves flying by and hawks soaring above, the shrikes entertained us during lunch. Jane and Alice joined Maude and Iris in taking bird pictures after they ate.

There weren't any unpleasant altercations, although Jane's enthusiasm for her new hobby caused her to irritate Maude once.

"Look out where you go, Jane. You stepped in front of me just as I was videoing a calling brubru."

Unlike Jimmy, Jane responded politely. "I'm sorry, Maude. I guess I'm a little too new to this photography."

I shared a laugh with Cameron. "It certainly is quieter without Jimmy around," I said. "I'm going to miss your company when this trip is over. You've been a great roommate."

"You and Iris will have to come down to Texas to visit," Cameron said. "We have lots of good birds. Besides, Anne, my double-breasted roller, needs to be convinced I helped further true romance."

"I'll be glad to vouch for you. You can be my best man when Iris and I get married, if you're willing to come to rural South Carolina. Bring your double-breasted roller along."

Cameron promised to come. "I will. As Alice would say, it'll be pure pleasure."

"We can assume Gabe won his contest with Jimmy by default. I wonder if he'll continue chasing Phoebe Snetsinger's listing record? He seemed very depressed at losing his competitor—just when Gabe had taken a commanding lead," I said.

Iris shook her head. "I don't think he'll quit. I think Alice and Jane will keep him going. They've asked me several times for advice on photography. They're already planning more trips."

"That's hard to believe. Adjusting to Jane as an ardent photographer is difficult."

Iris chuckled. "So far she's doing well. I suspect Jane will be looking for another husband as well as birds and other things to photograph."

I felt uneasy. I hoped Jane wouldn't look in my direction in her searches.

"You've done a good deed getting those women to embrace a pleasant hobby," Cameron said.

No one was more pleased to see Jane occupied with a photographic hobby than I. So far she had kept her promise. I kept telling myself that if she finds other interests, she will forget about chasing me. I silently wished her great success with photography.

After Sandy's sandwiches disappeared, she conjured up apple cobblers. Nobody complained.

Bunbuna turned out to be a wonderful place for a final foray to list African birds. In the afternoon, we worked wetlands in the area and listed African jacana, Hartlaub's duck, spur-winged goose, a giant kingfisher, and the large brown heron called a hammerkop because of its strange head shape, as well as many other small birds, egrets, and ibises.

We found a flock of small green parrots with red heads. Sean identified them as red-headed lovebirds. Iris whispered in my ear, "I like the sound of that name, don't you, Jack?"

Our lodgings were new and clean as advertised. Kenneth supplied free beer to celebrate the second viewing of rock fowl. Sandy took the night off and joined us at dinner. The motel restaurant offered us an aromatic meal of fried chicken, rice, potatoes, and yams served with a groundnut stew and palaver sauce made of fish, beef, onions, pepper, taro leaves, and other vegetables—a popular local dish. Everyone palavering agreed it was tasty.

All of the lighting and plumbing worked in the room Cameron and I shared, but I spent almost all of the night with Iris, reveling in her lilac scent and delicious taste, running my fingers through her auburn hair, kissing her incessantly, and imagining her to be a box of delicious candy I was eating one piece at a time.

I did not want to waste the final hours of what we had come to see as our honeymoon even though our wedding was weeks or months away. Iris agreed. So we made love throughout the night, achieving as many delights as our bodies could discover, in varying ways conveying our single soul.

A full moon shone on us through a window. Gazing into her eyes, I offered Iris more poetry. "Your outstretched hand offers me a drink from your crystal goblet filled with the wine from your fountains of spice."

A nightjar called outside our window. "Drink deeply," Iris said. She kissed me for several minutes.

"Your voice on the night wind whispers my name. Only you can hear my dream, only I can hear you."

Iris whispered as she rose above me. "I'm so glad I found a poet who loves me. The number crunchers I associate with in my profession don't have much poetry in them."

Iris set her honey glove around me. "Our soul plays the orchestra of our flesh," she said.

Savoring her delights, I forgot words.

CHAPTER 41

The next day sunshine and clear skies bathed us in warmth as we birded brush and woodland and recorded a bevy of bee-eaters and other small and medium-sized birds. We saw pin-tailed whydah and Togo's paradise whydah males in their fantastic breeding plumage, the tail four or five times longer than the rest of the bird.

"It's hard to believe that these beautiful show-offs become just little nondescript creatures after breeding is done," Iris said.

Sean laughed. "It's true. In nonbreeding plumage, they're just small brown birds similar to the females."

I saw my kinship to these birds. "These guys rival male birds of paradise in showmanship. We males are show-offs."

Iris grinned. "But you're not as gaudy as they are."

"You have me there—a hit, a palpable hit."

In the same brushy habitat, we found the shiny black male Cameroon and Jambandu indigobirds. Because all the indigobird males look so much alike, just small glossy black birds with white bills, we separated them by their calls. They too are parasites and imitate their host species.

"All of these odd species are polygamous brood parasites whose females lay their eggs in other species' nests," Sean said.

"Then I've been able to photograph some spectacular brood parasites," Iris said. "It's a good thing my camera can record songs. Otherwise I wouldn't be able to tell which indigobird I photographed."

The colorful plumages of the whydahs were complemented by showy flowering plants covering the surrounding field. Their scents and colors pleased me and attracted several species of nectar-eating sunbirds.

I offered some philosophy. "These birds and I in my past life had something in common, though I'm not as showy, but I won't be linked to them in the future. I'm planning to stick to one nest."

Iris twisted my finger. "I'm pleased to hear that. I wouldn't advise your straying. I don't like to share, and I'm a good shot."

Though resolving to be faithful, I changed the subject. "It's hard to get used to how peaceful life is since Jimmy's demise. I'm still adjusting."

Iris laughed. "And Maude is a very quiet, polite, less competitive photographer now."

I was glad Iris did not know just how much competition she had had for my embraces. So far Jane had kept her word—and her distance on the bus and at the dinner table—but I was still uneasy about how long her word would hold. I loved Iris. I swore to myself now she'd have no competitors for my love—or my body.

The day grew warm as the sun continued to shine down. There was no end of beautiful birds. Several species of flycatchers and rare emerald starlings, naked-faced barbets, and black scimitar-bills were among the many other species we spotted.

"Those emerald starlings glittered in the sunshine," Iris said as we returned to the van. "I hope my photos do justice to their brilliance."

I agreed they are beautiful. "I find it difficult to adjust to all of the colorful starlings in Africa. But our dull starlings back in North America are pretty in new spring plumage."

Jane and Alice walked over from across the field. "I took some more pictures with Jimmy's camera. I think they turned out okay," Jane said. "Would you take a look at them, Iris? Alice thinks they're pretty good."

Iris nodded. "Let me see them during lunch."

I wondered about the life-list competition. "Alice, what's Gabe's list up to now?"

"He's at 120 over seven thousand, not counting this morning's birds," Alice said. "His listing enthusiasm is returning, but it's not the same without Jimmy's egging him on."

"What about the prizes?" I asked.

"By default, he's won the twenty thousand dollar prize they were competing for. There isn't anyone else in the competition with a list nearly as high as Gabe's. He's going to divide the quarter-million conservation prize between a project in Africa and one in the States."

While we were eating, Jane showed her pictures to Iris. "What's your opinion?" she asked.

"These are sharp and well-organized," Iris said. "I think you're doing quite well. That camera and lens you're using make a good outfit."

"Thanks," Jane said. "It was Jimmy's. Alice likes it. She's planning to get one, or something similar." She smiled as we viewed her pictures. I was relieved she seemed to be oblivious to my presence.

"Photography's a way to capture the beauty of the world, the essence of our existence," Iris said. "You've made a good start."

As Jane left to join the other people eating lunch, I snapped a picture of Iris. "I've just caught the beauty of my existence," I said, grinning, as we rose to join the hungry crowd.

After sandwiches and yogurt with tea and coffee, we boarded the bus and took the road to Freetown. Along the way, we made one more stop, where a field full of tall brush and cane happened to be afire, possibly set to clear land for agriculture. The acrid odor of burning brush assaulted me.

Sean stopped the bus. "Here's a great place to do our final birding. We'll have great looks at some hawks, bee-eaters, and other birds. So get out and look."

Listening to the crackling flames licking at the cane and smelling the acrid smoke, we watched grasshopper buzzards, red-necked buzzards, and long-crested eagles snatching large insects and small mammals fleeing the flames. We turned our binoculars and cameras on the hawks and feasted our eyes on flycatchers, shrikes, and other small birds as they dined.

I put my arm around Iris as we watched. I felt we were privileged spectators viewing nature red in tooth and claw—beings challenged to make some sense of nature's fierce splendor. As ecotourists, we were doing our part to help these creatures survive.

"Our ecotourism provides jobs for local people," I said.

Iris agreed. "Our money helps preserve wildlife habitat. Animals depend on local folks' saving nature. Our money gives them a reason to save it."

We reached Freetown in time for another mouthwatering seafood dinner at our hotel. It was a very peaceful celebratory meal without sour notes except for the sadness of Jane Russo. Whether it was for Jimmy's death, or for my forthcoming marriage, I couldn't tell when I searched the dark shadows on her face.

I was a bit concerned when Jane and Alice sat down beside Iris, Cameron, and me at dinner. At least Jane was on the other side of the table.

I felt a thud in my stomach when Jane made eye contact with me. Her first words surprised me. "I hope you two will be very happy." *She must be giving up her chase of me.*

"I'm so glad you encouraged me to try photography, Iris. I sorta think I'm going to enjoy it. Immensely. And Alice is enthusiastic too. I can hardly wait for her to get a better camera."

"I hope photography proves a lifelong pleasure for both of you," Iris said. "Consider trying to sell some of your better shots. If nothing else, they'll make your trips tax deductible. I've found that very helpful."

"I've already found it gives Gabe and me a new way to appreciate his birding," Alice said. "I'm liking this photography."

My enjoyment of the local beer I was sipping increased. I savored its full body. I was elated and relieved. Jane was not rubbing my leg. Iris had found a great way to occupy Jane's attention. I felt positive, satisfied that I was no longer the quarry Jane was pursuing. I lifted my mug in a toast. "Good luck with photography, you two."

Jane smiled. "Thanks. It's really fun."

"You're lucky to have found such a satisfying hobby," Cameron said.

Iris not only made money from her photographs but created a tax deduction at the same time. I was impressed once again with her financial acuity as well as her ability to make friends of rivals. I felt she must be equally acute in her decisions with her stock fund. I remained in awe of her abilities wrapped in such a winsome mind and enticing body. How lucky I was such a wonderful woman loved me. She had erased the wounds from my divorce.

As Terence and Sean conducted the ritual of the list a final time, I ordered another round of beers for Cameron and me, and wine for Iris, Alice, and Jane. After the lists and dinners were dispatched, our leaders wished us a safe journey home.

"We'll e-mail the annotated official trip list to you within a month," Terence said. "I hope some of you photographers will send us a few of your best shots for our brochures. I think you'll agree with Sean and me that we've had a very successful tour, despite our sad experience with Jimmy's death."

I was happy with the many birds I had added to my life list, but the listing of new species had become less important to me than adding Iris to my love list.

"Just what is happening to Algernon?" Iris asked. "I feel sorry for him. I believe he was just defending himself."

"Apparently the murder has been judged self-defense," Terence said, "an unintended consequence. Algernon probably will escape with a fine and possibly a very brief jail time that might be made even shorter or nonexistent with some pleas and money in the right places. Kenneth will help with that. Algernon, or Egerton, has his notebook and bird guide with him to help pass the time."

"I'm glad he's not going to suffer much more hardship," Jane said. "His investment has lost even more money. I had Jerry check for me."

Jerry nodded. "It's lost another 10 percent."

"I hope you blokes agree we covered an extraordinary amount of territory and saw an amazing number of birds," Sean said. "I'll only add that we've had lots of fun and have seen tons of birds despite the sadness at the end of our trip."

Terence told us what to expect in the morning. "Kenneth Oshabi and his crew will be on hand tomorrow. Sean and I will be there to see you safely to your bus. It will carry you from the hotel to your final conveyance to the airport. It's my understanding that your return to the airport will be by helicopter. Kenneth's men will be with you all the way to your plane. Do what they tell you, and you'll be okay. Please join us on future tours."

I shook hands with them, thanking them and slipping each a fifty-dollar bill for their excellent work.

We were all going out on the same flight, so we saved our goodbyes until the next day.

Turning to Cameron, I said, "I'm walking Iris to her room."

Cameron laughed. "What a surprise. I'll see you in the morning."

"I'll want a shower and change of clothes. Don't use all the hot water," I called back as we walked away.

"We'll be separated when we reach London," Iris said. "We'll be on different flights back to the States, so this may be the last we see each other alone for some time."

I gave her a small nod and grimaced.

She had a few suggestions. "You have my phone number. I have yours. We'll be making frequent calls. You should try to get one of the Internet services that transmits voice and picture too. That way we could see each other when we talk."

I felt gloomy at the idea of a long separation. "I hope it won't take you too long to settle things at your job. It's going to be lonely without you."

Iris patted me intimately. "Just make sure you stay lonely until I get to Virginia. Tell all the ladies you're spoken for."

"I will. I'll announce it at a faculty meeting. I'm committed to you, no one else."

"I expect there may be some disappointed women at that faculty meeting." She pulled my ear playfully.

"I'll wait for you to choose a place for us to live other than my apartment. It's not too bad. I think it might do for a while, but if children arrive, it'll be way too small."

"It shouldn't take long for me to make arrangements, unless something unexpected comes up. I'll have a lot of work to do even after I reach Virginia."

"I hope you won't spend all of your time working."

"Don't be silly; of course not, but I think we've already had our honeymoon. I won't be able to spare more time off at first, other than a long weekend for our marriage. And I still want to marry at my parents' home in South Carolina."

"We need to make the most of this last night." I pulled her to me and kissed her, savoring her sweetness. "Something memorable. Something to celebrate our soul of one with all the feeling our bodies can offer."

She turned off the room lights, but moonlight through the window cast a soft aura over us. "You're right. There are some more ways to make love that I still want to put on my love-life list." Iris grinned as she unbuttoned my shirt. "Remember—you used the *Kama Sutra* in your dreams. I expect you to put your dreams into practice. Let's take a shower together."

"I'd love to. Lead the way."

She petted my forehead. "I'd like to hear the nightingale sing all night long in all the tunes of your book of delights. I want it to sing as long as it can hold a tune."

"We can do better than the *Kama Sutra*." The moonlight cast a romantic glow over us as we stepped into the shower. I admired her moonlit body as we soaped each other and entwined while we washed. Afterward, we lay together on the bed, kissing and petting, preparing to be one.

I gazed into her eyes. "Your gray eyes mesmerize me. They confirm your inner beauty. I can already hear our greater soul creating a symphony of love."

"I hear it too, sweetheart. I'm so glad to have you on my life list of love."

"And I'm glad to have you on mine. My love list's complete."

She whispered in my ear, "It better be."

"I think a love like ours, one without impediments, combined with the thrill of enjoying nature and our place in it, may be as close as we can get to heaven on earth ..."

Iris interrupted, placing her finger over my lips. "To quote your favorite poet, John Donne, 'For God's sake hold your tongue and let me love.'"

The End

ABOUT THE AUTHOR

R. H. Peake is a lifetime amateur ornithologist and a former president of the Virginia Society of Ornithology. A professor emeritus of the University of Virginia's College at Wise, he taught at the college level for over forty years. He has published four volumes of poetry and two novels. A father and grandfather, he now teaches bird identification and Shakespeare at the Osher Lifelong Learning Institute in Galveston, Texas.

Printed in the United States
By Bookmasters